GENERATION NEXT

Oli White

www.YouTube.com/OliWhiteTV
www.Twitter.com/OliWhiteTV
www.Instagram.com/OliWhiteTV

Terry Ronald

www.terryronald.com
www.Twitter.com/TerryRonald

GENERATION NEXT

OLI WHITE

With Terry Ronald

HODDER &
STOUGHTON

First published in Great Britain in 2016 by Hodder & Stoughton
An Hachette UK company

1

Copyright © Oli White 2016

The right of Oli White to be identified as the
Author of the Work has been asserted by him in accordance
with the Copyright, Designs and Patents Act 1988.

A CIP catalogue record for this title is available from the British Library

Hardback ISBN 978 1 473 63437 4
Trade Paperback ISBN 978 1 473 63438 1
eBook ISBN 978 1 473 63439 8

Typeset in Sabon MT by Palimpsest Book Production Ltd, Falkirk, Stirlingshire

Illustrations by Austen Claire Clements

Printed and bound in Great Britain by Clays Ltd, St Ives plc

Hodder & Stoughton policy is to use papers that are natural,
renewable and recyclable products and made from wood grown in
sustainable forests. The logging and manufacturing processes are expected
to conform to the environmental regulations of the country of origin.

Hodder & Stoughton Ltd
Carmelite House
50 Victoria Embankment
London EC4Y 0DZ

www.hodder.co.uk

ELLA JACK AUSTIN AVA SAI

THE INTERVIEW

Beverly Hills, California, August

It's just after 11.30 a.m. by the time the limo drops us off outside the Four Seasons Hotel. I feel tired – kind of – but somehow wide awake at the same time. It's like there's a weird buzzing in my head, but I'm trying my best to ignore it and stay calm, just so I can retain a tiny sliver of cool in what feels like a totally mad situation. It's not easy, you know? I bet you couldn't do it. In fact, I bet most seventeen-year-olds in my shoes right now would be all over the place, just like I am. But then again, how are you supposed to behave when you're only a couple of hours away from the most important moment of your life and everything is falling apart? How are you meant to stay calm when the stakes are so high? What do you even tell yourself at a time like this? Just keep it simple, I guess. My name is Jack Penman, and I've just arrived at The Four Seasons Hotel in Los Angeles, California. It's as easy as that. The rest can wait.

We follow a talkative porter through the impressive hotel

lobby towards the reception desk, where our manager, AJ, checks us in before suggesting we head upstairs while he finalises a few last-minute details in preparation for this morning's event. Once we're inside the room, my travelling companion, who's been unusually quiet during the taxi ride to the hotel, finally speaks. Actually, he shouts.

'Oh what? This hotel room is insane. It's mental. Can you seriously believe all this is for us, J? I mean, just look at it, it's awesome.'

I get the feeling that Austin is pleased with the room, although technically it's not a room. It's a suite of rooms, about the square footage of a football pitch, I'd say at a guess. Not that I play much football, but that would be about right. I let my eyes sweep across the floor and up the walls, scanning every corner. Taking in the L-shaped black sofa opposite the sixty-five-inch curved-screen ultra-high-def TV; the three steps leading up to the bed, which is twice the size of my entire bedroom back home, and the smooth dark wood and grey metal of the industrial-style dining table in the far corner. Yeah, of course there's a dining table and eight chairs in my hotel room – why wouldn't there be? I nod my approval but I don't speak because I'm not sure I'm quite ready yet. Right now I'm trying to process the events that led me to be standing here in this football pitch of a hotel suite. I'm trying to compress those events into a single thought, but it's impossible. It's just . . .

'J! Oi, Jack! Are you listening to me?'

Austin is my best friend and business partner. Yeah, that second part still sounds weird, but that's what we are these days. I guess that was the plan all along only we didn't expect it to happen quite this fast and for things to be this . . . full on. Austin likes to talk. A lot. He's usually not a fan of peace and quiet, and of course I can hear him, but I'm not sure how to answer because . . . well, to be honest, I'm just as blown away by all this as he is. I'm just trying to keep my excitement on a low one.

'So here we are, then,' I offer eventually.

'Yeah, I definitely think we've arrived,' Austin says.

'One hundred per cent.'

I drop my bag on the carpet by my feet, which is so thick there's barely a soft thud when the bag hits it. Austin cocks his head to one side and glances through the big white double doors on the far side of the room.

'There's another massive bedroom through there. I think that one must be mine 'cause, you know, the TV's bigger.'

We look at one another, our grins widening in unison until we both fall about laughing. We laugh until our sides hurt, until our faces ache. And why not? It's pretty hilarious, all this – funny and stupid and terrifying all at once – and to be honest, if I don't laugh right now, I'm probably going to lose it, and now is definitely not a good time for that to happen.

Once we stop laughing, Austin strides over to the big glass coffee table in front of the sofa and picks up one of about six white boxes.

'What's all that?' I ask, falling backwards on to a ridiculously soft bed.

He pulls a pair of blue and white Converse All Stars from the box. Then he pulls a pair of grey and white ones out of a second box.

'Nice,' he says.

'What size are they?' I ask.

'Austin and Jack size.' He smiles.

He picks up the little white card that is sitting on the table next to the boxes and starts waving it around like an idiot, talking in a silly posh voice as he reads it. '"Gents, we believe these are to your taste. We'd be very happy if you'd like to wear a pair each at the interview tonight. Good luck and all the best from Andy Smart, head of press and promotions, Converse US."' He drops the card back down on the table. 'Mate, people are giving us flippin' shoes. Why are people giving us shoes? And six pairs; I've only got two feet.'

'They want us to wear their trainers tonight because the interview is going to be watched online by, like, millions of people or something,' I tell him. 'So the idea is that other kids watching will say, "Yeah, I want to wear All Stars just like Austin Slade and Jack Penman."'

'Why?'

'Because they'll want to be like us is why.'

I watch Austin trying to process this information, his eyes narrowing, his floppy blond hair hiding a scrunched-up forehead. 'Yeah, I get that,' he finally says, 'but will they even be able to see our feet?'

This makes me crack up all over again. Austin has got a point. A stupid point but a point nonetheless.

Twelve p.m. I'm showered and dressed now but I'm feeling even more tense. The old tummy's doing a few gymnastics under my T-shirt and the dry throat is creeping upwards until my tongue sticks to the roof of my mouth. AJ is sitting at the dining table, poking at his phone and sending

4

emails. He doesn't look all that relaxed either, but when I glance over in his direction, he smiles. 'Everything's cool,' he says.

He's a man of few words is AJ, but he's a good manager: smart and very competent, even though he doesn't look much older than us most days. He's overseen this sort of event before and he knows the drill. I just nod back at him and chew my lip nervously. Meanwhile, I can hear Austin on the phone to his new girlfriend, Jess, in the next room; I recognise that lovey-dovey tone he adopts when he talks to her. Suddenly I feel quite envious; it just kind of sweeps over me. It would be nice to have a girl-friend to wish me luck right now, wouldn't it? Someone other than my mum and dad to reassure me and say, 'Don't worry, Jack, you're going to smash this interview.' I feel like I need that today.

When the knock on the door comes, I don't feel ready. AJ jumps up and darts across the room to answer it. Austin looks over at me. 'Are you all right, J? You look a bit pale, man.'

I notice he's wearing the blue and white Converse. 'Yeah, I'm all good.'

'Here we go,' he says.

'Here we go.'

A plaid-shirted hipster greets us as the door swings open. He has an excessive amount of facial hair but I can just about tell that he's grinning under the bushy red of his beard.

'Hey, Jack, Austin, AJ. Duke Hamilton. I'm one of the producers of tonight's event. How y'all doing?'

Surely his name can't be Duke. That's a dog's name, isn't it?

5

'Are you ready for your big moment, guys? The world's waiting.'

'Is it?'

'It sure is, Jack. OK, guys, I'm going to take you down to the room where it's all happening and we'll get you a drink, say a few hellos, then set you up with mics and give you a little sound and camera check. We go live at one. We'll do a quick warm-up chat with you guys first, just in case there's anyone out there who still doesn't know who you are and what you do, and then we'll get to the main event. Exciting, huh? Does that sound OK?'

'Sounds good,' I tell him, but I'm bricking it.

'Don't worry, boys. I'll be with you every step of the way,' AJ assures us. 'Just chill and enjoy it.'

Austin puts his hand on my shoulder, giving me a gentle shove towards the door, but I feel like I'm in a kind of semi-daze; like I'm about to be jolted awake at any moment and I'll find myself sitting in my bedroom back in Hertfordshire in my boxers and a T-shirt and not in some stupidly swanky hotel in Beverly Hills at all.

Halfway down the hall, my phone rings and makes me jump.

'Guys, you should turn off your phones before we go live to the universe,' Duke says.

Instinctively I pull my iPhone out of my side pocket, slide my thumb across the screen and answer it, even though the caller's number is blocked. I wish I hadn't. The sound of the voice on the other end hits me like a train. I feel like all the blood has run out of my face and I'm numb. Crap. Not this, not now. I listen to the voice for a while, and then I speak.

'Yes, I hear you. Yes, I understand.'

I've stopped walking now, halfway down the hall leading to the elevator. I can feel the sweat on my neck, my dry mouth returning with a vengeance. 'Look, I can't do this now, man. You couldn't have picked a worse . . .'

Austin and AJ are walking back down the hall towards me now, both wide-eyed. Duke is standing by the elevator, beckoning impatiently. 'Let's go, guys!'

'I need to hang up,' I say. 'Don't threaten me . . . Look, I don't even believe you have what you say you have, so back off, all right?'

Shaken, I shove my phone back into my pocket and look up at Austin, who is now facing me. 'Is everything cool, J?'

'Yeah, mate, everything's totally cool,' I say, lying through my teeth.

'What was all that about?' AJ asks.

'Nothing,' I say. 'Let's go.'

I follow Austin and AJ further along the hall to the elevator and we head downstairs. We cross the shiny lobby towards a noisy room packed with people: some drinking low-fat decaf soya lattes, or whatever they drink in LA, and others gulping down mini-burgers, all standing under a stupidly large chandelier. Just outside the room is a big unoccupied sofa. It looks inviting, so I sit down.

Poor Duke looks flustered. 'What's happening, Jack? Why are you sitting down? There's no sitting down now.'

'I just need a minute,' I tell him.

'But . . .'

'Take Austin through,' AJ tells Duke. 'We'll follow you in a minute.'

'No. All of you go in,' I snap back. 'I just need to be on my own.'

Austin looks concerned. He leans over me, studying my face for a telltale sign of what the hell might be going on.

'Are you positive everything is all right, J? Who was that on the phone?'

'It's all good, mate. One hundred per cent.'

The corner of Austin's mouth is doing the involuntary twitching thing. It's something that happens when he's nervous or he knows something isn't right. He's had it since the day I met him.

'Go and get us a drink. I just want to get my head straight, that's all.' I try to sound as calm as I can. 'This is a massive thing we're doing; I need to gather my thoughts. I told you, I just need a minute.'

Once they've gone, my mind races. How can this be happening, right at this particular moment? And how can I do anything about it when we're about to do something so important? I sit back, enjoying the softness of the sofa, and I suddenly feel shot; so tired. If only I could just shut my eyes and sleep. Just for . . .

'Jack, we need to move. Now, please.'

AJ is standing over me. He's holding a glass of what looks like champagne, even though it's only noon, with Austin hovering behind him. 'Have this, Jack. Dutch courage.'

'He's not Dutch,' Austin says, grinning, but I can tell now that he's as scared as I am.

Maybe not quite as scared.

I decline the champagne – the last thing I need is for my thoughts to feel any more scrambled than they already are.

I virtually catapult myself off the sofa and move into the crowded room, smiling and nodding at people I don't know but who clearly seem to know me. A young woman jumps in front of me, walking backwards while trying to pin a mic on me as I move through the crowd. There's a lot of noise, a massive buzz, and I know what it's all for but it sort of doesn't compute, and as I get closer to the small stage that has been set up at the far end of the room, I feel like the whole scene is going a bit fuzzy around me and the sound of the chattering crowd is getting louder and louder.

Before I can catch my breath, my phone beeps again and I grab it because I really need to turn it off now, but there's a text from the same blocked number – someone has sent a video. My heart sinks like a stone, but I know I have to look, just to be sure. I turn my back on the stage and hit play and . . . there it is. It does exist, and I'm screwed. We're all screwed.

Before I know what's happening, I'm ushered on to the stage and find myself sitting on a stool next to Austin, looking into a huge camera lens. A guy in a denim shirt comes over and shakes our hands in turn and then sits on the third stool, on the other side of Austin. Duke jumps on to the stage and hushes the crowd before glancing at his watch. Have I missed something? Has somebody been talking to me while I've been walking and I've not been listening, because I can't really remember a single thing since . . . since the phone call.

'Ladies and gentlemen, Jack Penman and Austin Slade of GenNext!'

The voice comes from nowhere, and now there's rowdy

applause in the room, but this bunch are the least of my
worries; there could be millions of people watching this all
over the world. No pressure then. Duke gives the thumbs-up
and a red light goes on above the camera, then the young
dude in the denim shirt leans forward and shakes our hands
all over again. I look at Austin, who is smiling, so I smile
too. Then the denim shirt dude speaks.

'So, guys, welcome, so glad you could be here with us.'

'Thanks, we're excited to be here,' Austin says.

After a bit of small talk about the flight over and what
we think about LA so far, all of which Austin deals with,
the guy addresses me and I gear myself up to speak. Pull
yourself together, you idiot. This is it; it's happening now.
You can't screw this up.

'So, Jack, let's hear from you first on this. How did you
guys come up with the idea for GenNext, something that
has become so amazingly successful so fast?'

I stare into the guy's face for a moment and then I look
at Austin. All I can think about is the video, which sends
hundreds of scenarios shooting through my mind at once,
none of them good. I look down at my new Converse shoes,
resting on the bottom bar of the stool, and I hear Austin
speak.

'Sorry, he's still a bit jet-lagged. Jack? Jack!'

'My shoelace is undone.'

I imagine this is just a private thought, but apparently
not. Some of the audience are sniggering.

'Your shoelace? Jack, what's wrong with you?'

I look up at Austin and his mouth is twitching again. And
then everything just . . . stops.

Can you imagine it for a moment? The eyes of the world are on you – quite literally – and you can't speak or even move. It's funny, I'm struggling to remember how it came to this; how I even got here. When was it? Has it really only been a matter of months since I walked into that classroom at St Joseph's with all eyes on me? It might as well have been a lifetime ago. I was just the new boy with something to prove back then, but so much has changed in these short months. So much . . .

THE BEGINNING

Hertfordshire, England, five months earlier

I was twenty minutes late when I walked into Mr Allen's advanced media production class, and, on top of that, soaking wet. I mean, completely and utterly drenched – torrential downpour just as I jumped off the bus, so unavoidable really, but not ideal. Not when you're talking first impressions – you know what I mean, right? Your strategy is to walk into a roomful of people you don't know looking fresh and unruffled, like it's absolutely nada starting a brand-new school with brand-new students and brand-new teachers at the ripe old age of seventeen. Your strategy is not to fall through the door looking like you've just crawled out of a duck pond wearing a jacket that smells like a dishcloth. That wasn't how things had played out in my head while I was lying in bed that morning, anyway.

Mr Allen looked up from his desk as he heard the door click shut.

'Are you Penman?'

'That's me, sir.'

'OK, well you're late,' he said, like I didn't already know. 'Just find an empty seat and someone will fill you in on what you've missed. Class, this is Penman, he's just transferred.'

'Where from, the aquarium?'

There's always one smart-ass in the class, and this one was a guy with slicked-back dark hair, grinning and balancing on two legs of his chair with his feet on the table at the back of the room. There was a bit of sniggering from a few of the other students as I navigated my way across the floor, looking for an empty space in the already packed classroom. When I eventually spotted one and pulled the chair out from under the two-seater desk, the dark-haired guy piped up again from two rows behind me.

'Not there!'

This time I turned around and met his stare, which was clearly designed to intimidate. Then I smiled sweetly, turned my back on him, slowly continued dragging the chair out and sat down. That's the way, Jack, I told myself, pulling my textbook out of my bag, start as you mean to go on. *This* time at *this* school was going to be different – I'd promised myself that. No trouble, no being pushed around, no compromising or trying to fit in just to be accepted. And no getting your head kicked in. Definitely no getting your head kicked in.

The classroom itself was smart and modern. Much more so than the rooms at my other school, which seemed antiquated compared to this one. I clocked a couple of very nice Canon cameras on tripods in one corner, and a row of spanking-new MacBooks lined up on the workbench along the far wall. The students seemed interested in what they were doing, too, which was a good sign. In my last media studies class no one listened to a word the teacher said and three of the cameras were stolen on the first week of term, so all in all this class seemed like it might be an excellent one to take, and with my AS levels coming up, I needed as many good classes as I could get.

Once I'd settled down at the desk, I turned to say a quick hi to the person I was sharing it with. You see, that was the other thing I'd promised myself – to make more friends at St Joseph's and not be the reclusive geek I'd been at Charlton Academy. Anyway, that was when I saw her: blonde hair, piercing blue eyes, the most kissable mouth turned up in a half-smile. Literally the most stunning girl I'd ever set eyes on.

'Oh wow! Er, hello.'

At first glance, she seemed to have an air of effortless cool about her: the long-sleeved black and white striped T-shirt under a denim dress that kind of looked like dungarees but with a skirt instead of trousers, the funky silver rings shimmering on both hands, the bright red Converse. It all looked so right.

It was clear that I hadn't been expecting anyone like her when I'd turned around; in fact it showed big time.

'I'm, er . . . hi. I'm Jack . . . Jack . . . Jack . . .'

What was my name again?

'Jack Penman is who I am, and that's my name.'

The girl looked through me like I was a total weirdo.

'You're dripping,' she said.

'I'm sorry, what?'

'You're dripping on my *Gatsby*.'

Slightly puzzled by this declaration, I looked down at the desk and noticed the small pool of water gathering on a well-thumbed paperback copy of *The Great Gatsby*. It fast became clear that the water in question was actually dripping off my hair, running down my nose and . . . well, you can guess the rest.

'Oh damn, I'm really sorry,' I said. 'I got caught in the rain.'

'Never,' she said sarcastically, but then her half-smile blossomed into a full one and I was properly in love.

Like an idiot I picked up her wet book and shook it, sending the rainwater flying everywhere.

'Now I'm as wet as you, thanks,' she said.

'Sorry.'

It suddenly dawned on me that my relationship with this heavenly creature, whoever she was, had probably begun and ended all in those few short seconds, but my suffering was short-lived as Mr Allen stood up and addressed the class. He wasn't badly dressed for a teacher, and actually didn't look that much older than most of his students.

'All right, everyone, listen up. For this term's main project I'm going to need you to work in pairs. So this morning you're going to have to find yourselves a study partner, and I'd like you to do it quickly and quietly.'

I turned slowly to meet the eyes of the girl next to me again.

'Don't even think about it, Jack Penman,' she said sternly. Oh well, at least she remembered my name. Then her expression cracked and she started to giggle, putting her hand out for me to shake.

'I'm Ella,' she said. 'Ella Foster.'

'Hi there, Ella Foster.'

'So do you want to partner up for this project then, new boy?' she said.

'That would be . . . yeah, cool.'

You never want to sound too eager in that kind of scenario, do you?

'OK, brill. Let's do it,' she said.

So my initial instincts had been right. This was definitely going to be an excellent class to take.

Austin Slade had been in Mr Allen's media production class that morning, but I didn't notice him till later in the day. It was lunchtime and I was making my big entrance into the sixth-form common room, which was clearly the hub of the entire school; totally different to the dry atmosphere of the communal areas of my previous school. In contrast, the St Joe's common room was busy and bright, with a coffee machine *and* a snack machine, plus there was a huge amount of chat and noise, loads going on, and it was all happening to a soundtrack of Radio 1's *Live Lounge* playing merrily away in the background. Nice, you know? All in all it seemed like a pretty cool place, but at the same time maybe a bit intimidating, especially when you're the new kid. Ah, but hang on a minute. I stopped that thought in its tracks and had a little word with myself. No, Jack, there isn't going to be any of that crap. No intimidation this time, remember? Just walk into the room like it's yours; like you own the place. Start as you mean to go on, mate.

There were various cliques of kids dotted around the common room and I amused myself for a while trying to decipher which clique was which and, more crucially, what the pecking order might be. The 'populars' were a mix of boys and girls, and mostly Year 13, I'd say at a guess. Their general demeanour was cool, calm and collected and they were easy to spot by the whiteness of their teeth and their immaculately ironed, expensive-looking clothes. The boys in this group all seemed to have that hair that looks effortlessly swept forward and messy but they've actually spent four and a half hours fiddling about with it in the mirror, applying just the right amount of fresh-out-of-bed-look surfer-dude hair fudge. The girls were mostly of the hot variety and looked as though they'd just jumped out of a make-up artist's chair and were about to step in front of a camera. If, as a new student, you could get in with any one clique, this lot would be the prize. Just by looking at them you could tell that not only did they know where it was happening, they were mostly the people that *made* it happen.

Close to them – but not too close – were what I'd call the fringe group. This was a smaller group of kids who clearly lived in the shadow of the popular group and basically followed the same principles but weren't really all that popular and their teeth weren't as white. This was a noisier, more attention-grabbing crowd, the girls generally showing a bit more flesh and yakking a lot louder about what they'd been doing the previous night, and the boys swearing every other word so they looked hard. Then there were the usual scattered cells of athletes, geeks, hipster kids and loners. Standard, really.

As I stood at the door, I pondered on which of these random groups might spot me and invite me over to join them. Maybe none of them would. Maybe it would be a repeat performance of Charlton Academy, where I spent ninety per cent of the time with only a laptop for company. I was lost in thought, reminding myself of my pledge to make more of an effort to be social, when I heard someone shouting at me.

'Penman! Oi, Penman! Come over here, man.'

I scanned the room to see which of the cliques the yelling might be coming from. I knew it wasn't going to be the popular kids – they were much too cool to shout across the room at anyone – and it obviously wasn't the sporty lads in their Adidas tracksuits, or the small nest of vampires dressed in black in the far corner, or even the . . .

'Penman! Over here!'

Of course. It had to be . . . the geeks.

'Over here, man.'

To be fair, the kid shouting at me didn't look all that geeky, but the rest of his associates were the quintessential school boffins. I made my way towards them.

'Austin is the name,' the kid said, sticking out his hand.

As I went to shake it, he pulled it away quick and pushed it through his floppy hair.

'Funny,' I said, not really laughing.

'I saw you in media production earlier,' Austin said, grinning. 'Are you into all that stuff? Filming, editing, videos and all that?'

He nodded towards his small group of pals, who were lounging over a small sofa and a couple of leather armchairs.

'We are. Plus games, of course. Anything techy, really.'

'Yeah, that's my thing too, a hundred per cent,' I said.

'Cool beans, Penman. Well, you looked a bit lost standing in that doorway just now, so I thought you could do with a few introductions.'

I nodded. 'Sweet, thanks.'

Austin playfully slapped the head of a boy sitting in front of him.

'This here is my man Sai,' he said. 'He's from Sri Lanka.'

'Wow. That must take a while on the bus, mate,' I said.

I noticed the pretty girl in a beanie hat sitting next to him start sniggering.

'No, I live in Hemel Hempstead,' Sai said, dead serious, causing much laughter within the small group.

Austin continued, unfazed.

'Anyway, Penman, I noticed you were sitting next to *the* most smokin' babe in the class earlier.'

I scowled back at him. Smokin' babe? Seriously? Mind you, his remark, however cringeworthy, did stir a flickering reminder of the girl in question. Ella Foster. And what a nice flickering reminder it was.

'Yeah, she's OK,' I said, as if I'd hardly noticed.

'She's more than OK,' Sai muttered under his breath.

Austin turned his attention to the girl next to Sai, who was still sniggering.

'And this is—'

'Ava,' she said, jumping up and sticking out her hand. 'I'm Ava, and you're Jack, right?'

19

I noticed that underneath the beanie hat, her hair was a washed-out pastel lilac colour, and she was wearing black fingerless woollen gloves – indoors, and it wasn't even cold. I ignored this quirk and shook her hand anyway.

'That's right, I'm Jack. I just transferred from—'

'Why?' she barked.

'Why what?'

'Why did you transfer? Did you do something terrible in your last school? Were you forced to leave?'

'Er, I . . .'

'My cousin Dermot laced the fruit punch at his school prom with vodka,' she said, 'and after five glasses of it, he tried to snog his chemistry teacher outside the gym, but she tripped over some bunting and fell backwards down the stairs and broke her tibia. Was it that sort of thing, the reason you were forced out?'

'I . . . I wasn't forced out.' I laughed nervously.

'Well it must have been something,' she said, 'or why change schools in Year Twelve? That seems quite unintelligent to me.'

'It *was* something,' I said firmly, 'but not that.'

'Yeah, sorry, this is our Ava,' Austin interjected. 'She's pretty much a genius but sometimes a little outspoken, you get me?'

Ava made a sudden move closer to me and looked me dead in the eye.

'You can tell me anything you want, Jack Penman,' she said. 'My sister's got a minor eating disorder, so nothing fazes me.'

'Right,' I said, backing away a tad.

'And just in case it matters to you,' she went on, 'we are *not* the cool group around here.'

I looked at her, Austin and Sai, one by one.

'You think?' I said.

After I'd said hi to a couple of the less alternative members of Austin's tribe of misfits, he filled me in on a few of the key players in the school hierarchy – the big hitters – as well as some of the eternal losers, plus who was cool and who was best avoided.

'You know Hunter?' Austin said.

'Who?'

'The guy who shouted out to you in the class earlier.'

I nodded.

'Well he's definitely one to be wary of. Total knob-head. Lots of kids look up to him 'cause he's stinking rich, but he's massively arrogant and never misses a chance to tell everyone how amazing he is. Prone to violence on occasion, too, so watch yourself around him.'

'Noted,' I said. 'Thanks, mate.'

As we were leaving the common room, Austin invited me to one of the group's computer game nights, which they took turns in hosting. Deep joy. The next one was at his place, and, he assured me, it would be the coolest one because his parents had made their cellar into a den for him and his younger brother and they had a massive fifty-inch flat-screen TV with surround sound down there. The whole thing sounded unfeasibly lame to me, but I had promised myself I'd make an effort, so I nodded and smiled agreeably.

'Sure, why not?'

I could have actually come up with about thirty reasons

why not off the top of my head, but sometimes you just have to take the plunge in a new situation, you know? That was one of the reasons I agreed to go along, the other being the fact that nobody else in any of the other cliques had spoken to me, so I thought I might as well give this lot the benefit of the doubt, right? If I'm totally honest, they seemed like they might be an OK bunch. Little did I know then how momentous that decision was going to turn out to be.

THE PAST

'So how was it, then? How were the other students? Did you meet anyone nice, make any friends?'

So many questions and I'd only been in the house for three minutes. While I poured myself an orange juice, Mum hovered around me in the kitchen, halfway through making what she called her world-famous lasagne. The fact that nobody outside our family had ever tried it cast some shadow of doubt over the 'world-famous' handle, but we all thought it was pretty good anyway.

'Yeah, it was fine, Mum. Really cool.'

'That's good, Jack,' she said. 'Because this time your dad and I really want . . . I mean, we don't want—'

She stopped, suddenly, as if she might be about to say the wrong thing. I sat down at the breakfast bar and looked across at her standing over the sink with her back to me, her best chopping knife suspended in mid-air as she thought carefully about what to say next.

'You and Dad don't want what?' I asked her.

I knew what she was thinking; what all her conversations

with Dad must have been about for the last two weeks. Is Jack going to fit in at this school? Is he going to make friends? Will there be any more . . . bullying. Yes, that was the word she couldn't bring herself to say. That was the elephant in the room. Her only son had been bullied at his last school and then had to leave. Boom! Of course they'd been amazingly supportive at the time, but sometimes I wondered if they might be a little bit ashamed of me for not sticking up for myself more. Probably nowhere near as ashamed as I had been of myself when it all went down. Still, I'd left that in the past where it belonged. It wasn't going to happen again; things were different this time. *I* was different, wasn't I? Anyway, I decided to put her mind at rest.

'Actually I met quite a decent guy today, Austin. He's invited me round to his place with a few of his mates, gaming night or something. They're all a bit geeky, but they seem nice, y'know?'

Just as I finished the sentence, my dad walked in from work, throwing his briefcase down on the stool next to me.

'Well that sounds positive,' he said, joining in the conversation. 'Fresh start.'

'Doesn't it, Paul?' Mum agreed, a beaming smile on her face as she hacked into an iceberg lettuce.

I recognised that tone in both their voices – a mixture of concern and hope – and I was seconds away from yelling at them, telling them to back off and stop making such a fuss, but then I stopped myself. After all, why wouldn't they be concerned? Seeing their son bloodied and bruised the way I was on that very, very bad day back in January, of course they were going to worry.

'They're into the stuff I'm into, this crowd,' I said instead. 'Making videos, tech stuff. They all seem pretty intelligent, even though a couple of them are a bit weird. There's this one girl, Ava—'

'A girl already, eh?' Dad chimed in. 'You don't waste much time, do you, son?'

'Well he's a nice-looking boy, Paul, of course he's going to have girls flocking round him,' Mum said.

She's always been my biggest fan.

'No, I was about to say that this girl, Ava . . . she was a bit wacky, but yeah, very pretty. Then there was this other girl . . .'

I stopped mid-sentence, as I was about to veer into TMI territory. They didn't need to know that I'd already developed a crush on my very first day at St Joe's, did they? That would just give them more to talk about, and sometimes with my mum and dad, much as I loved them, less was most definitely more, you know?

Up in my room, I began to think about my time at Charlton Academy. That place had been a total nightmare. In fact I couldn't fathom how I'd survived it for five whole years. An all boys comprehensive, it was well known all over Hertfordshire as being a tough school, but for the first few years I kept my head down and held my own pretty well. Most of the students in my form seemed happiest when they were coming up with new ways to disrupt a class, and the only time half of them concentrated was when they were on the football field or during rugby practice. Look, it's not like I'm trying to big myself up – I wasn't bloody Einstein or anything, but I wanted to learn, and in that environment it was next to impossible. Feeling like I was ahead of the pack in English, maths and history was one thing, but in the technical classes – computer science and graphics, which were important to me – I felt like I was in a different post-code to everyone else, including a couple of the teachers. You see, ever since my seventh birthday, the day I got my first proper computer from my mum and dad, technology and how it works had been my utter passion. It started off with games – and yes, like most kids, I loved playing them – but as time went on it went deeper than that. I wanted to know what made those babies tick: how they worked and how it was possible to make all those amazing things happen at the mere touch of a button or the flick of a lever.

Originally I'd gone to Charlton because of their so-called excellent technical departments, but that turned out to be a joke. By the time I was fourteen, I was writing code, making programs and inserting virtual weapons, tools and all manner of other stuff into games: things that didn't even exist in the game until I put them there. Eventually I became known as 'GODLYM0DZ' in gaming circles online – M0DZ being slang for modifications. It was like being a bit of a celebrity, with people writing about me on forums, desperately trying to find out my real identity like some crazy internet version of Batman. You know what, it felt good . . . for a time. Meanwhile, in my computer science class we were still covering the basics.

I guess that was when the trouble started. The other boys could see I was bored; they watched me rolling my eyes and slumping forward on my desk while the poor bloke teaching the class tried to explain the rudiments of something I'd known how to do since I was ten. Yeah, I know what you're thinking: I was probably too big-headed, a know-it-all who deserved to be taken down a peg or two. Maybe that was true. I mean, it's all very well being GODLYM0DZ when you're sitting in the safety of your bedroom, fighting your enemies with a fast flick of your wrist, but out on the streets, things weren't quite as neatly tied up as that. In real life I was seen as an outsider by the other boys in my class, and maybe they were right – I certainly felt like a bit of a freak, being one of the few kids who seemed eager to learn something and to get somewhere in life. OK, so I'm not exactly what you'd call a straight-A student, but I sometimes felt like I was the only one in the class knuckling down to study for exams.

Some of the boys in my form even took the piss out of me because I had a paper round in the week, and before my revision schedule started to get really heavy, I worked in a local clothes shop on a Saturday and Sunday. To be honest, I didn't really care what they thought; I wanted to earn my own money so I could have a bit of independence and buy my own things. It wasn't like my mum and dad were super rich, so anything new I wanted I worked for and bought myself.

During break times and lunchtimes I sat in the computer room trying out new stuff, discovering something great and then trying to work out how to do it myself. I withdrew more and more from the other kids until it seemed like nobody ever saw me outside during school hours because I was always shut in a classroom in front of a screen. I ignored the name-calling when it was just some idiot shouting 'Freak!' at me in the playground, but when it came into the classroom, that was a different matter. There's nothing worse than being insulted and belittled in front of a roomful of your peers, especially when you're trapped and there's nowhere to run.

There were two kids, Dillon and David, or Dim and Dimmer, as I like to remember them, who did this kind of thing on a regular basis. After months of making my life a misery, I eventually got my revenge by hacking into their Facebook accounts and locking them out so they couldn't post anything, use Messenger, or even look at their own pages. It drove them nuts, and for a while they didn't have a clue it was me. After a few weeks, however, there was more and more online speculation about who this GODLYM0DZ character might be. I was pretty horrified to see my name come up on a few of the forums, and even more horrified when Dim and Dimmer turned up at school one day begging me to stop attacking their accounts. So was my secret out at last? I wasn't certain, but I wasn't taking any chances, so I told them both to . . . Well, you can guess what I told them both to do.

It's funny, all the rest of that day I felt like I had a little bit of power, and I thought maybe some of the other kids might even have some respect for me after they found out what I was capable of. Maybe things would turn around and get better at Charlton. That feeling didn't last long. On the bus home from school that night, Dim and Dimmer plus a load of their mates cornered me. I was sitting upstairs on the back seat, nose in a magazine, and before I knew it they'd all bombed up the stairs and gathered around me. I was pretty much trapped. I tried to look past them to see if there might be anyone else on the top deck who could help me, but there were just a couple of other kids and an old lady who disappeared as soon as she realised there was going to be trouble.

'Think you're funny, messing with my Facebook page?' Dillon said through gritted teeth. 'You're lucky I haven't got a blade on me.'

Before he'd even finished the sentence, I felt a punch to the side of my head, then my face hitting the window, and then pain shooting up my legs as they put the boot in. After the fourth or fifth punch I sort of went numb. I could still feel it, but it didn't really hurt any more, you know? In the end it just became a blur of fists and kicks, cussing and name-calling, and then finally there was a ringing in my ears and I think I must have blacked out. The driver stopped the bus in the end and came up the stairs, but they'd all legged it. He found me sort of half crushed between the back seat and the seat in front of it.

'You got a lot of blood on you, man,' was all he said.

I remember Mum's face when she arrived at the hospital where they were patching me up; she was utterly horrified.

'It's not too serious, Mrs Penman,' the nurse assured her. 'Just surface mess and a few bruises. Nothing's broken; he'll be fine.'

Mum looked relieved there was no permanent damage, but she still cried a bit. I did too.

'I'm not going back there,' I told her, barely able to open my mouth. 'I'm not a coward but I'm not going back. There's nothing for me there.'

She just nodded and hugged me, causing me to wince with the pain. Then I felt her tears fall on my shoulder, so I told her not to worry, and promised her I'd be OK and that things would be different from now on.

'Jack, your lasagne's ready!'

It was her voice that shook me out of the unhappy memories of that day two months earlier, and as I jumped up off my bed, my heart thumping in my chest, I told myself that I would never, *ever* let anything like that happen again.

THE TEAM

My first week at the new school went by in a blur. I spent most of it trying to learn the ropes, getting to grips with some of the study projects I was going to have to tackle and listening to the teachers banging on about revision and AS exams. Apart from the odd 'How are you getting on, new boy?' and a few short bursts of small talk with people whose names I never really got to know, I drifted through the corridors like a ghost for most of that week. It was only when I bumped into Austin or one of his mates that I got into any serious conversation.

The one bright spot in the week was seeing the incredible Ella Foster in the media production class on Monday. The downside of that was that Mr Allen forced us to sit through several cringingly arty film clips to give us ideas for our upcoming project, which, he kept reminding us, was worth a massive chunk of credit for the AS level. So apart from a quick chat at the start of the class, Ella and I didn't get to talk much. To be honest, I didn't see half of what was happening on the screen anyway, as I spent most of the lesson just looking across at her, sort of mesmerised. I know, it sounds a bit lame, but as I watched the light from the screen flickering across her beautiful face, I wondered . . . well, mainly I wondered if a girl like that could be interested in somebody like me. And no, it wasn't just the way she looked, either. Ella seemed to have a kind of self-assurance about her that I could only dream of having, and in the brief moments when we did speak that morning, she looked me in the face and I felt like she meant every word she said. OK, so it was only small talk about the weekend and the mountains of homework we both had, but there was an honesty about her that fascinated me. She most definitely wasn't a girl who just spouted words for the sake of it, and I liked that. As the week went on, I spotted her around a few times, just hanging out between lessons or at lunch, and I wasn't surprised to discover that most of her friends seemed to be of the popular variety. Still, she always waved or smiled and said, 'Hey, Jack Penman,' whenever she saw me, and that was good enough for now.

Later that week I panicked slightly when Ella didn't turn up for Thursday's media production lesson and I was left without a study partner for the start of the filming project we'd been assigned. When I heard one of the popular girls say that she was home in bed with mild tonsillitis, I reassured myself that since it was unlikely you could still die from mild tonsillitis in this day and age, she would eventually be back in class and I could continue getting to know her better. Then I spent ten minutes googling and reading about tonsillitis, just to make sure that you *couldn't* die from it.

*

Before I knew it, Austin's gaming night was on, and with no better offers for that Friday evening, I went along, hoping it might be at least a little more exciting than I'd imagined. Look, don't get me wrong, it wasn't as if I was unhappy about making friends – jeez, I needed to after the disaster of my last school – but a bunch of nerdy tech kids playing computer games wasn't exactly out of my comfort zone, you know? And the evening that lay ahead certainly couldn't be put into the category of trying something new.

As it turned out, Austin and his mates weren't what I was expecting at all, and I was pleasantly surprised when I walked into his house and his chatty, smiling mum directed me downstairs to where they were all hanging out in a converted cellar. Ducking my head under the low ceiling above the steps, I could hear laughter and music, and once inside I was greeted by three faces who all looked happy to see me.

'You came.' Austin sounded more than a little surprised. 'Come in and get comfy, man.'

Over by a large TV at one end of the room, Austin's fourteen-year-old brother Miles was engaged in an intense *World of Warcraft* battle, while Sai and Ava were hunched in a corner over a MacBook, messing about with what looked like a serious graphics program.

'So what skulduggery goes on down here?' I asked, looking around at Austin's neat set-up.

The whole room was white, including the concrete floor, which had been smoothed over and painted, and there were LED spotlights on the ceiling as well as two or three lava lamps dotted around and a mini-fridge stocked with Diet Cokes, bottled water and cartons of juice. The room was also kitted out with a Sonos speaker system, currently playing Justin Bieber, and there was a desktop with a thirty-two-inch monitor sitting on a table plus several laptops of varying brands and a couple of iPads lying about. This was a pretty sweet den and I was slightly envious that I'd never had a headquarters as cool as this to work and play in.

'What do you want to do?' Austin said. 'These nights were just gaming get-togethers at one stage, a laugh, but now we mostly hang out and work on stuff.'

'What stuff?' I asked, heading over to see exactly what kind of program Sai and Ava were working with.

'Well, er . . . if we've got school projects to do, we get together and help one another out, and we, er . . . we've been trying to come up with ideas for our own project, too.'

'What kind of project?' I asked.

'That's the problem, man,' Sai said, turning around. 'We haven't decided yet.'

'We promised ourselves last term that we'd come up with something serious,' Ava explained. 'It might be a game or a website or even an app, but it has to be something that makes use of all our individual talents.'

'Are you lot nuts?' I laughed. 'Haven't you got enough going on revising for exams?' They all glared back at me as if I were the crazy person in the room. 'Of course,' I said, 'you guys are all such geeks, you probably don't even need to revise. Anyway, what exactly are your individual talents?'

'Well, Ava is brilliant at anything film- and video-related: shooting, editing, sound editing – all that kind of stuff,' Austin said.

'Sounds good. I'm pretty handy with a camera, too,' I said.

Austin went on, getting more animated as he spoke. 'Sai is a master at graphics, web design, layouts and anything arty, and I'm pretty fearsome when it comes to coding and technical jargon.'

'And what about him?' I said, nodding towards Miles.

'My little brother comes in handy for running errands sometimes, but mostly he just hangs out playing *World of Warcraft*,' Austin laughed.

'Look, we've got all the bases covered,' Sai said. 'Trouble is, we spend most of our time together looking at the brilliant stuff other people are doing and not doing anything ourselves because . . . Well, because we haven't had any good ideas of our own yet, I suppose.'

Sai looked at me hopefully, as if he thought I might say some magic word to make something amazing happen right then and there. His stare was intense, as if he was trying to figure out my entire character just by looking at me. Then Ava stood up and headed towards me, her forehead knotted in a frown.

'And what about you, Penman? What are you good at?'

I pondered the question for a moment; what exactly *was* I good at? Then, as if a cartoon light bulb had flashed above my head, it dawned on me that I might be just what they were looking for.

'Actually,' I said, 'I'm a bit of an ideas man. I s'pose that's what I'm really good at. Ideas.'

'So have you got any?' Ava said, laughing. ''Cause I can only spend so many weeks locked in a small space wasting time with these two idiots before I go psycho with Austin's mum's bread knife.'

'Er . . . could you at least let me have a minute or two? I've only just walked in the door. You need to give me a few clues about what sort of thing you want to do,' I said.

'That's the problem, man, we haven't got any direction,' Sai said, shaking his head.

Out of the blue, Miles looked up from his game and shouted over his shoulder from the sofa.

'Yeah, man, you're GODLYM0DZ, you can help us.'

'What did he say? GODLYM0DZ? How the hell . . .?'

My blood ran cold and I looked at my new mates one by one, all staring at me as if I was about to sprout horns or wings or something. Then my heart sank as the penny dropped. Austin looked guilty. They all looked guilty.

'Miles has been online gaming since he was nine,' Austin mumbled. 'He reads all the forums.'

'So is that why I'm here? Is that the only reason you called me over and befriended me the other day, because you knew who I was and you thought . . . ?'

I didn't know whether to feel angry or flattered or . . . No, what I actually felt was hurt. I'd stupidly thought this smart, quirky little group had reached out and invited me into their inner sanctum because they thought I was a decent bloke; that I was worth befriending. Turns out it was because of some stupid online persona I'd shaken off ages ago. Turns out they wanted something.

'How?' I asked. 'How did you know it was me?'

'I wasn't sure at first, but a bit of fishing around on some online forums and it seemed pretty clear that GODLYM0DZ was Jack Penman,' Austin said.

'So you targeted me when I arrived at St Joe's just so I could help you out with your non-starter of a project,' I said.

'No, it wasn't like that, Jack. Not targeted, just—'

'Do you know how much crap that stupid name got me into? Do you know how much I've tried to move on and forget it?'

'You sound really angry,' Ava said.

'Too right I'm angry. You could have been upfront about it. You've had all week. You could have . . . Oh, you know what, I'm out of here.'

After I slammed Austin's front door behind me, I stood there for a good three or four minutes before I walked up the path into the night. Just as I got near to the front gate, a massive shudder shot down my spine. What the hell had just happened? OK, so when I thought about it rationally, I knew Austin and his crew weren't trying to be devious or nasty, scoping me out like that, but they couldn't possibly understand how much I wanted to get away from the way my life was before. Even the thought of it made me feel sick.

As I swung open the gate, a soft, calm voice spoke from behind me.

'Jack! Hey, Jack! Why don't you come back in? The pizza's arrived and as usual I've ordered far too much.'

I turned around to face Austin's smiley mum, Tina.

'Yeah, I'm not sure I want to,' I said.

'Oh, come on, I've got my best china out,' she laughed.

'Look, Austin just filled me in on what happened. I know he can be a bit of a dozy sod at times, but he's all right really.'

'Is he?'

'Well I know I'm biased, being his mother,' she said, 'but why don't you at least come in and give him a chance?'

I thought for a moment, then took a few deep breaths and followed Tina inside. I know, I'm a soft touch, but what would you have done? If I'd walked away then, where would I have been? I was over being a loner, you know? I was over being lonely.

As we reached the kitchen, where everyone was gathered, Austin stood up.

'Jack, look, what it is, right—'

I put my hand up and shook my head.

'Can we just forget it for now, Austin? It's cool, honestly, mate. Let's just leave it for the time being.'

'All you need to know is that we think you're a really good bloke and we'd like you as a mate whatever,' Ava said.

'Good enough for me,' I answered.

It's funny, in the short trip from the front door to the kitchen, I'd come to the conclusion that I didn't really want any explanations or even to talk about it that night. I just needed to digest the situation for a while and think about it all later. At that moment it was all about pepperoni pizza, which was bloody delicious, as it goes.

Austin's kitchen was vast and white and there was a flat-screen TV on the wall opposite the table, which was also enormous. As we all grabbed a second slice of Papa John's finest, Austin flicked through the music channels, landing on a video featuring a girl singer backed by two guys – a keyboard player and a guitarist.

Ava jumped out of her seat.

'Oh, I love this band! Turn it up, Austin,' she said, spraying bits of pepperoni all over the table. 'They're called The Gloves – they're a bit wacky but so good. Have you seen them?'

None of us had, but I thought they had a pretty good sound: electronic beats with funky, scratchy guitars, and the singer had a voice like nothing I'd ever heard.

'They're American,' Ava said. 'Kind of old-school punky disco but with a contemporary edge. The girl's called Wren. Isn't that an amazing name, Wren?'

Sai laughed, waving his pizza at her.

'You're obsessed with her, and I've never even heard of them.'

'I am not obsessed, I'm just interested in great music that isn't forced down our throats via a TV talent show,' Ava said.

'Sad fangirl,' Austin said, laughing and running a greasy hand down her face.

'There's nothing sad about it,' Ava said, ducking his hand. 'She's a cool young woman who doesn't feel like she has to conform to that whole Taylor Swift pretty-girl vibe.'

'Oh here we go,' Sai said, rolling his eyes. 'Well I like Taylor Swift.'

'Me too,' Ava said. 'But some girls are not into that sort of music and don't want to be. And I totally get where Wren is coming from with the whole understated-look thing. I love her style. Anyway, shut up, I'm listening.'

I have to say, even after everything that had happened that evening, I was still quite intrigued by the dynamic within this group of misfits. They all seemed very smart, had a sense of humour, and took the piss out of one another mercilessly, but there was clearly a lot of love and respect between them as well, which appealed to me. I wondered if they'd been drawn to one another because none of them gelled with any of the other cliques in the school. All that week, during lessons and in the common room, I'd been hearing kids planning the stuff they were going to be doing at the weekend, whether it was hanging out at a skate park or the shopping mall or going to one of the three or four parties or get-togethers I'd heard talk of. Maybe Austin, Sai and Ava were the kids who never got invited to parties; maybe that was why they found themselves hanging out. It dawned on me that I'd been one of those kids for most of my life, I just hadn't been lucky enough to find others of the same species . . . until now.

Ava suddenly grabbed the remote and cranked up the volume.

'Oh listen to this! The interview section of this show is terminally lame.'

I tore off a large slice of pizza and looked up at the screen. The band were now sitting on chairs that looked like mini-thrones in a posh hotel lobby. The surroundings were properly fancy but the band members, with their torn jeans, vintage tees and air of understated cool, looked ridiculously out of place amongst the oil paintings and swirly antique furniture surrounding them. The girl-and-guy duo who were doing the interviewing looked like they'd dressed especially to appeal to the band, not to mention their teenage viewers, but you sort of got the feeling that they weren't wearing their real clothes and that they were maybe a little bit too old for the kind of banter and street slang they were chatting. Mind you, their masks slipped quite tragically with some of the questions they asked the three members of The Gloves, who by this point looked like they were about ready for a suicide pact.

'So do you have a glam-squad of make-up artists, hairdressers and stylists when you're on tour?' the female host asked the singer.

Wren was wearing ripped leggings with more rip than legging and a Mickey Mouse T-shirt. Her bleached hair with black roots was dragged back in a scruffy ponytail, and I'm no expert, but as far as I could tell she wasn't wearing any make-up at all. In fact, she didn't look like she even had the email address of a stylist, let alone had ever employed one.

'What do you think?' she answered, looking at the interviewer like she'd escaped from a high-security institution.

The male interviewer followed this up with equally rubbish questions to the guys in the band.

'So, fellas, what's your routine when you work in the studio? Do you start nice and early or are you night owls? What's the first thing you do when you get in there?'

'Crack open a beer,' one of the guys answered.

The interviewing duo wriggled in their chairs uncomfortably and we all rolled about laughing, the awkwardness of earlier evaporating fast.

'You are so right, Ava, this is the worst,' I said.

'Isn't it? It's meant to be aimed at us, this show. Youth!'

41

'Yeah, they don't look as if they're having much fun, the poor suckers,' Austin said.

I watched, fascinated, as questions, texts and tweets from the show's viewers shot across the bottom of the TV screen.

@LaURa5555
@TheGloves Where do you get your songwriting inspiration from?

@TweetyPieLovesYou
Watching @TheGloves interview right now. OMG Wren is my bae LOVE HER!!

@SamRedm0nd2
@TheGloves do you guys ever fall out on tour? Haha

@LucyReadsBooks
@TheGloves which of your songs means the most 2 you and why?

The messages were all totally ignored by the presenters, and it was at that very moment, as I was ripping into a lump of garlic bread, that the idea happened. That tiny acorn that was destined to get bigger and bigger until it exploded and took me to where I am now. Of course! Why not? It was bloody perfect!

THE IDEA

So what *was* my brilliant idea? I hear you ask. Well, it was all pretty simple really, and after studying a few more music shows with dead-awkward interviews and a couple of TV chat shows where the hosts literally fell over themselves to be as sickly and likeable as possible to all their celebrity guests, I was sure I was on to something. I mean, who wants to hear their favourite band answering the same boring questions over and over again in every music mag and on every website and TV music show? Those questions every interviewer is expected to ask and all the talent is bound to answer in the same way, because they've been primed by a press agent or manager. I'd seen it a hundred times and now I wanted something different. OK, so I wasn't sure exactly what that was yet, but it would certainly include more involvement from the people actually buying or streaming the music – the fans.

It was the same with concert and record reviews and blogs. Sure, they had their place, but wouldn't it be great to hear reviews and comments from people who'd just walked out the door of a gig, rather than a journalist who went to the show because she was given free tickets but knew she wasn't going to like it before she even went? And yeah, some of the entertainment channels were OK if all you were interested in was true-or-false dating rumours or the latest Kardashian family feud.

When I thought about that horribly bad interview with The Gloves, I realised that it was all those ticker-tape comments across the bottom of the screen that we somehow needed to focus on. The names without faces who wanted to know stuff and ask stuff. Was it a channel? Was it a website? I wasn't sure yet. And yes, I know what you're thinking. How were a bunch of teenagers from Hertfordshire going to get access to celebrities, bands and sports personalities? Good question. Well, we'd have to start small, of course: local bands doing shows in the area, and some of the older kids at our school who were training with local teams – that would be a good start, wouldn't it? Then, once we were up and running, I could concentrate on how we might land some bigger and better scoops. At that stage, however, I had no fricking idea whatsoever.

Anyway, I didn't say a word about my brilliant scheme that night at Austin's or over the weekend. I needed to let it take shape and mature in my own head before I put it into words, and besides, I had to decide whether Austin, Sai and Ava were worthy of my input, especially after what had happened. I guess I kind of forgave them pretty quickly because I knew there was no malice in what they'd done and, at the end of the day, they couldn't have known how much havoc the

GODLYM0DZ tag had brought down on me back at my old school. One day I would tell them, but for now it was still too raw. So when I wandered in through the school gates the following Monday – still half asleep – I made the decision that I was going to keep the idea to myself for a while. Well, a few hours at least.

At the sound of the first period bell, two hundred students swarmed into the corridors like ants, talking over one another, shouting at their friends and slamming doors as they disappeared into their lessons. Now you won't be surprised to hear this, but the sight of Ella Foster in the media production class, not dead from mild tonsillitis and looking more radiant than ever, very much lifted my spirits on that grey Monday morning. She was wearing a floaty white summer dress that stopped just above her knees, with a cut-off denim jacket, plus a tiny silver nose ring, which looked really amazing on her. When she beckoned me over, patting the seat next to her and inviting me to sit down, there was a moment when I thought my head might just explode. You see, up till then I hadn't exactly been very confident where girls were concerned. To tell the truth I'd never really given myself the chance, and I certainly never gave anyone else the opportunity to get close. In the not-too-distant past when a girl started a conversation with me, my default reaction was to play it cool and stand-offish – probably a little *too* stand-offish if I'm honest, as most of them assumed I wasn't interested. Of course I was bloody interested; what teenager isn't?

So I'd decided it was going to be different this time. The new me was still going to be cool, of course, but I was ditching the stand-offish stuff. That part had to go, you know?

'So what's up, Jack Penman?' Ella said as I sat down, throwing my textbook on the table.

'Not much. Are you better now?'

'Yeah, I'm fine,' she said. 'Ready to get started on this project we're doing together – have you had any amazing ideas?'

The truth of the matter was that I'd been so chuffed at the prospect of having Ella as a study partner that I hadn't paid attention to the detail of the assignment. Sure, I'd glanced at it once, but it hadn't really sunk in.

'Er . . . nothing mind-blowing,' I said.

I quickly fumbled in my folder for the slip of paper Mr Allen had given us the previous Monday, speed-reading it so I wouldn't look too much of an idiot when Ella started spurting genius ideas. The crux of it was pretty simple: to devise, film and edit a video that we felt had something to say as well as being dynamic and well executed. There was no real restriction on topic, style or content; it just needed to be informative in some way.

'So what do you think?' I said. 'You've been in this class longer than me, you know what Mr Allen's looking for.'

'It's funny,' she said. 'I worked on a project with similar guidelines when I was living in Hong Kong . . .'

'You lived in Hong Kong?'

'Yeah, my dad was there with his business for ages so we all went. I went to the American international school there. My dad's in international banking, so we've been dragged all over the place.'

Well travelled as well as intelligent and beautiful; maybe that was what set her apart from the other girls. Ella Foster was becoming more intriguing by the second.

'Anyway, on this project, a couple of the students inter-viewed the teachers and lecturers about their take on the kids they taught,' she went on. 'It was, like, their real thoughts on the way the students behaved, good and bad. The students doing the project managed to get under the teachers' skin and drag some home truths out of them, so it was really interesting. It caused a bit of a stir actually, because a couple of the older teachers who didn't have much to lose really laid it on the line. Some of the stuff they said was pretty full-on.'

'So what happened?'

'I actually think it made a lot of the kids think about the way they behaved and how it affected other people,' she said, 'but only for about a week.'

When she laughed, her face lit up and I felt something strange happen in the pit of my stomach.

'So do you think we could do something like that, Jack Penman?' she said, hopefully.

I wasn't sure that interviewing teachers was totally my bag, and God knows what they might say about some of the kids in this school, but I figured I'd go along with it if Ella thought we could make a go of it. At least it would be something that none of the other kids in class would think of.

'Look, if we can come up with some questions, I can handle the interviews; I'm happy being on camera,' she said. 'But we only have a couple of weeks to finish it, so we'll have to spend quite a lot of time together, if that's all right with you.'

She flashed me that brilliant smile again, and I was about to tell her just how all right with me that was when I felt

47

something tap my shoulder from behind. Looking down at my feet, I discovered a screwed-up scrap of paper, and when I turned around to find out where it had come from, I came face to face with Hunter, his eyes burning into into me with some kind of warning look.

What the hell was this guy's problem? What was I doing to warrant this unwanted attention? I shook my head dismissively, turning back to Ella, who hadn't even noticed what was going on.

'You OK?' she said. 'You look a bit distracted.'

'Yeah, all good,' I said, deciding it was best to ignore Hunter altogether. 'Let's just get on with planning our project. I'm looking forward to this, Ella Foster.'

After class, I said goodbye to Ella and we parted ways and walked in opposite directions along the corridor. That was when I had my first real one-on-one encounter with Hunter, who stepped out in front of me as I headed towards my next class.

'So, new boy,' he said.

'So . . . what?'

I was trying to sound casual – bold even – trying to stave off the memories of Dim and Dimmer kicking the crap out of me on the bus home that afternoon. It wasn't easy. There was something slightly disturbing about this bloke. Even when he was smiling, you got the feeling it might be because he'd just pulled the wings off a moth. Yet for some strange reason he seemed to be quite a popular student within the school. I thought back to what Austin had said about him being loaded, and figured that must be the reason.

'Can I help you?' I said.

'Maybe,' he said tauntingly.

He was that weird, dangerous mix of what some people might call good-looking but with a touch of evil thrown in. Not to be trusted, you know?

'So what have you heard people saying about me, new boy?' he said. 'Anything much?'

'Some stuff,' I said. 'I really haven't taken much notice.'

I went to sidestep him and move on, but the douchebag anticipated my move and mirrored it, so we were face to face again.

'And do they say bad stuff or good stuff?' Hunter said. He looked amused. 'It's all right; I'm not going to hit you or anything.'

I shrugged like I didn't care either way, but I felt relief surge through my body – as the old saying goes, I'm a lover not a fighter. All the same, I was ready for him if he did come at me. I may not be violent by nature, but I certainly wasn't going to cower away from any more dumb thugs either.

'What about Ella? What does she say about me?'

The shock of hearing Hunter even speak her name made me go slightly cold. Why did he care what Ella said about him? Were they friends? Did he have some sort of crush on her? Was that what this was all about?

'She hasn't mentioned you, funnily enough,' I said. 'Now if you don't mind, I don't want to be late for my graphics tutorial.'

He grinned at me, and for a moment I thought about those poor little moths without wings.

'I haven't made up my mind about you yet,' he said, 'but I'll be keeping my eye on you, new boy. Jog on.'

He stepped aside and I moved forward along the corridor. Do me a favour, 'keeping my eye on you'? Who did he think he was, one of the Kray twins? I reminded myself of Austin's words of warning to me on my first day at St Joe's: that Hunter was one to watch out for, one to avoid.

Later that week, I got to hang out with Ella as much as I wanted – mostly through the medium of the camera lens – while we conducted our first interview, which happened to be with Mr Allen. I thought he might be a fairly tough nut to crack, as I hadn't seen him smile once since I met him, but Ella had the old goat laughing like a kid at the funfair within five minutes. I couldn't blame him. She had a way about her that was pretty irresistible, or at least it was to me. She was a natural as far as the filming went, too – the camera loved her, and she wasn't the least bit self-conscious. Question after question, she pushed and probed, trying to get the most controversial remarks she could out of Mr Allen, hitting him with a few curveballs along the way. The best moment was when she mentioned the fact that many of the older kids at St Joe's were driving better cars than most of the teachers. Funnily enough, that was a point in the proceedings where Mr Allen didn't laugh quite as much.

As the week progressed, we interviewed a few more teachers and a few Year 13 kids, too. Every free period and lunchtime we could grab, Ella and I darted up to the media room to watch our footage back and decide what to use, where to make cuts, and what we should ditch altogether. By the end of that first week we had a seriously amazing mix of talking heads, funny quotes, plus a few off-the-cuff statements from staff that we knew they were going to live to regret. I have to say we were pretty pleased with ourselves, and do you know what? I couldn't remember a time when I'd been as happy and content, especially at school. Whenever I was around Ella, I was somehow more confident and felt like anything was possible. I felt like I could shout out all my craziest ideas without being laughed at, because I knew she was interested in what I had to say. It was like this whole new world was evolving in front of my eyes. Amazing. The question was, when was I going to pluck up the courage to ask her out?

That Friday in Austin's cellar, or HQ as Sai had now christened it, my three newest pals were a little icy on my arrival, and I realised right off that my spending the week virtually living in Ella's pocket had probably hacked them off somewhat – although they all kept shtum about it. I certainly wasn't going to lose any sleep over it after what had happened the previous week. They owed me one and they all knew it. Things soon thawed out when I hit them with the idea I'd had after our last meet. I could see the three of them digesting it as I spoke, turning the information over in their minds.

'My idea is to have a multi-faceted platform with reviews of gigs, music, sport and stuff that interests people our age,' I said, while we all huddled around Ava's MacBook Pro. 'Plus we would feature the bands and artists that you don't get on all the big TV chat shows and aim it specifically at the fans, encouraging them to send questions and get involved right from the start.'

'So is it a website or a TV channel or what?' Sai asked.

'There's no reason why it can't be both,' I said.

'So we would be like curators as well as creators,' Ava said thoughtfully.

It was hard to take Ava seriously while she was wearing a grey beanie hat emblazoned with the slogan 'You Can't Sit With Us', but I did my best.

'Exactly. It would be like pulling together all the things we love about YouTube, Buzzfeed, Facebook, Twitter and Instagram, but mostly aimed at music with a bit of sport and some other stuff thrown in. Look, it's not going to be dead easy or anything, but I think we can do it. We're all smart enough, aren't we?'

I waited for a reaction while they looked back at me. You could feel the excitement in the air, but it was like nobody wanted to say anything in case the bubble burst. In the end, Sai was the first to speak.

'So could we have forums and chat pages for people to interact?'

'Yeah, maybe. And possibly some celebrity interviews further down the line if we're lucky, but on our terms and guided by what our viewers want,' I said.

'It sounds amazing,' Austin said, just as Ava got up and started pacing the room.

'I have a question,' she said, spinning on the heel of her boot to face me. 'You said celebrity interviews. How the hell does a bunch of school kids get to interview celebrities? Why would they be interested in us?'

'And what about getting the proper rights to play music and all that stuff? That's a whole other can of worms,' Austin said.

'Look, it's not fully formed yet,' I said, 'but we start small. Get in with some local bands and artists who need extra promo for their gigs, YouTubers, people we know who are doing cool or interesting things, you know? As for music rights, let's not run before we can walk, dudes.'

Ava started pacing again.

'I still don't see how we're going to win these people over and get them on side. I mean, what have we got to offer them? Sure, we're all smart, but none of us are exactly . . . I mean we're all . . .'

'What?' Austin snapped, standing up and following her around the room. 'Are you saying that none of us are confident enough to do it, is that it?'

Ava shrugged.

'Look, Austin, we're all very smart behind a screen, but as personalities in front of a camera, I don't know.'

Austin looked to me for back-up, and I knew it was the right time to reveal the ace up my sleeve.

'I think Ava might be right,' I said, with a nervous half-smile. 'Maybe none of us are confident enough to do the on-camera stuff, but I've got an idea, a secret weapon to combat that.'

'Oh really, and what's that?' Sai said.

By this time we were all standing in the middle of the room and you could have sliced through the atmosphere with a chopstick.

'Not what, *who*,' I said.

I watched as a look of confusion spread across their faces. Then I walked over to the door and up the cellar stairs, descending again after a few seconds.

'Friends, meet the face of our new venture. Ella Foster.'

Ella jumped down the last step and did a comedy curtsy.

'Hey, geeks!'

Ava was clearly unimpressed.

'You've got to be kidding me. What the hell do we need her for? No offence, Ella, I actually like you.'

'Cheers, Ava, I like you too.'

'No, I mean, even though you're sort of a popular, I think you're reasonably cool. It's just—'

'Hang on a minute, Ava,' I interrupted. 'Look, I've been working with Ella for the last week on our media project, and she is an utter natural in front of a camera, she really is.'

'Why thank you, kind sir.' Ella smiled. Then she turned to the group. 'Look guys, I can do this, I know I can.'

Austin pulled me over to the sofa, muttering something about having a word in private.

'Look, J. If we're all going to work on this, whatever *this* is, it's got to be serious and we've all got to be dedicated. Before we start discussing the pros and cons of inviting Ella into the team, I need to know. Are you bringing her in just because you want to . . .'

'Want to what?' I laughed.

'You know what I'm saying,' he said, grinning.

'Mate, we're a long way from anything like that. We're just friends, all right?'

'If you say so . . .'

I ignored Austin and walked back into the centre of the room, holding court once more.

'Look, guys, the reason you sought me out is because you thought I had something to offer the team, right?'

Everyone nodded.

'Well, if you want me to get involved, then this is what I think we should do. I think it could be really sweet, but I also think that Ella needs to be a part of it. Trust me.'

'We do trust you, don't we?' Sai piped up.

Austin and Ava eyed one another, still unsure.

'Well, there's one more thing that even Jack doesn't know about yet,' Ella said, looking mighty pleased with herself. 'And if it doesn't persuade you that I'll be an asset, then I'll get my coat.' She pulled a small piece of paper out of her pocket, like a magician with a hat and a rabbit – well, if the magician was stunningly beautiful and wearing skin-tight jeans.

'What's that?' I said, grabbing at the paper.

Ella whipped it away fast, waving it in the air under our noses.

'This is my little piece of insurance,' she said.

'I knew it, she's going to blackmail us,' Sai said, but Austin managed to snatch the paper out of Ella's hand.

'Look, if it's those pictures that my ex put on Facebook last summer of me in my underpants eating an ice cream, everyone's already seen them.'

'He's right, Ella,' Ava chipped in. 'The lingering memory of those tighty whiteys gave me the horrors for weeks.'

'It's just a phone number,' Austin said, glaring at the paper.

Ella snatched it back.

'It's not just any old phone number. It's the phone number of a man who may or may not be the manager of a certain musical act who may or may not be called The Gloves who may or may not have agreed to let me interview them while they're still in town.'

'I'm confused,' Sai said.

'Are you fricking kidding me?' I said. 'The Gloves have agreed to let you interview them?'

'My dad oversees their management company's bank accounts,' Ella said. 'He's even met them once or twice. All we have to do is organise a convenient time to shoot the piece. I just thought it might be a great way to start your little venture.'

'*Our* little venture,' Austin said, putting his arm around Ella. 'Welcome to the team!'

'Why thanks, Austin,' Ella said.

I was suddenly seized with the urge to grab and kiss her, but – you guessed it – my nerves got the better of me, so I turned my attention to the rest of the team instead.

'OK! So are we all agreed that this is what we intend to put our spare time and effort into from here on in: a multi-platform website incorporating its own TV channel, focusing mainly on music, but also sport and culture relevant to our generation, the next generation?'

There was a resounding 'YES!' from the group, and then a burst of ecstatic laughter.

'Right, we need to bloody well drink to this,' Austin said, grabbing five cans of Diet Coke from the mini-fridge and throwing them to us. He shook his can and yanked the ring off, sending the fizzy liquid inside shooting up like a fountain. We all followed suit, covering ourselves in froth like Grand Prix winners.

With foam dripping off the front of her beanie hat, Ava held her can up high in front of her.

'OK, people! Let's toast us, then. Here's to the next generation, right? Generation . . . Next!'

THE BIRTH OF GENNEXT

Over the next six weeks, I spent every moment when I wasn't either asleep or studying for my exams holed up in Austin's cellar – sorry HQ – along with Sai, Austin, Ava and Austin's little brother Miles, who was a gold mine of information and knew exactly where to find all the coolest and most influential sites out there. I'm not going to bore you with a load of overly technical jargon, nor am I going to wax lyrical about the weeks of programming, researching, designing and generally slogging our guts out over hot laptops, but about a month later, we were just about ready to unveil our brand-new website, which we'd unanimously agreed to christen . . . GenNext.

Actually, the time flew past for me, especially on the evenings when Ella was around. As I'd predicted, she worked brilliantly alongside the four of us, and it didn't take me long to realise that although she didn't have the programming and tech skills that the rest of us did, she certainly wasn't short of ideas, and was just as amazing behind a camera as she was in front of it.

Everyone rose to the occasion during that month: Sai's layouts and designs for how the site was going to look were spectacular, and then Austin would take over, finding ingenious ways to make it all work. In fact whatever ideas I threw at them, however tricky or convoluted, Austin and Sai seemed to be able to make them fly. Sai also came up with a brilliant logo for the site, which got a unanimous thumbs-up from the team.

Meanwhile, I tried to keep myself involved in every aspect of GenNext's development, stalking around HQ and piloting the proceedings, laughing, shouting and waving my arms around like some insane orchestra conductor.

When it came to filming and directing the content, that was where the girls shone. The night we all took a train to London and stood outside Wembley Park tube station in the pouring rain till midnight, Ella was a total star. As drunk, excited fans poured out of the much-talked-about Years and Years gig, we grabbed as many of them as we could for on-the-spot video reviews and comments, and although she was soaking wet and completely knackered, Ella knew exactly where to position herself, who to target, where to get the best shots and which questions to ask, and drenched or not, she looked utterly stunning doing it. Afterwards, Ava sat up all night reviewing the footage, editing the interviews and searching out the funniest and most mischievous comments, just so she could bring it into school the next day to show us the results. Then she fell asleep and snored loudly through her history class – now that's dedication.

I guess when you're living in people's pockets like that, you get to know them pretty well, and what I knew was that this was a bunch of good guys. Call them what you like: geeks, nerds, whatever. They'd all known one another for years, yet they'd accepted me into their group and that meant a lot. They were a great team; they were *my* team. They were my friends.

Some nights I'd watch Austin work while I crammed in extra revision – we often revised and worked on GenNext at the same time, swapping shifts. Austin'd be hammering away at his keyboard, excitement and enthusiasm burning away in his eyes, then he'd turn around and do this weird crooked smile he does, like he knew we were on to something amazing. Other nights I'd be so tired I'd end up dozing off, propped up on the sofa, and would wake to find Ava curled up next to me, fast asleep with her head on my lap, a massive history textbook lying open over her feet like a cushion. Sai was the one who kept the jokes coming while we worked. With his blunt, slightly twisted sense of humour, he kept everyone sane when things didn't work or went wrong, which to be fair was almost every day. And then there was Ella. What more can I say about her apart from the fact that the more time we spent together, the harder I fell for her. Even when we weren't hanging out, she made her presence felt, firing silly videos at me over Snapchat and drawing me into extended WhatsApp chats whenever she needed a bit of a break from revision, the other major thing zapping our brain power.

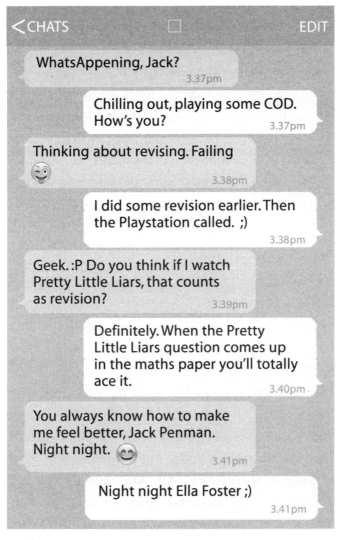

I guess it goes without saying that the five of us were very proud when the first version of GenNext was almost ready to go live, even though it was only the bare bones at first: lots of 'check back for this page next week' and 'coming soon' – you know the vibe. Still, we'd ultimately created a virtual space where people could watch videos and reviews of gigs, plus find recommendations for upcoming shows, music, clubs and so much more. Now we just had to pass the word around and sit tight until it went live.

Our ace in the hole was our video interview with The Gloves, which couldn't have gone better – actually, we killed it. The band were very cool and gave us a ton of time, despite the fact that we filmed them answering questions while they were climbing up, swinging from and jumping off various things in the local adventure playground. Yeah, I know, it sounds weird, but this was my bright idea as an alternative to all the dry, coma-inducing music interviews I'd had to sit through while I was researching the website. The thing is, the band loved it, and Ella did an amazing job of coming up with some genuinely funny, savvy questions, which they were happy to answer even while careering down a thirty-foot zip wire. Wren, the band's singer, who I'd never once seen smile in an interview, laughed the whole time.

After we'd finished filming, they invited us all to their gig at KoKo in London the following month, and, most import-antly, they promised that once GenNext went live and we put the interview up, they'd add a link to us on their YouTube channel and also tweet it out, hopefully sending a huge amount of traffic our way. Austin's gut feeling was that we shouldn't put the video up right away, but give it a couple of weeks until we started gathering a good amount of views and then hit them with it full throttle. In the meantime, I did a blindfolded football skills tutorial with Miles and a couple of boys who played for the Watford FC youth team, and appeared with some up-and-coming YouTubers whose subscribers were starting to go through the roof and who were happy to help us out.

The funniest thing we did in those first few weeks was have Ella follow one of the coolest new local bands around Asda while they went food shopping, interviewing them about what they were buying, and why, with a GoPro on her head while Ava replaced the junk food and ready meals in their trolley with healthier choices: music and nutrition all in one video – what's not to like? OK, OK, so our ideas were a little bit left-field, but that was the idea, wasn't it? That was what made us original and was going to make us stand out . . . I hoped. It was early days, yes, but I felt like GenNext was potentially off to an auspicious start.

There was only one thing bugging me during the final ten days leading up to the launch of the site, and that was a distinct lack of Ella. Although she'd worked her butt off with the rest of us for the previous few weeks, suddenly she always seemed to be busy doing something else – at least that was how it appeared to me. Even on the odd day she was around she seemed distracted and somehow . . . well, different, I suppose. Even the texts and WhatsApping action dwindled to almost nothing.

'I've just had a lot of family stuff on, and I've really got to step the revision up after all the time I've spent on GenNext,' she told me when I asked her – as casually as I possibly could, of course – what was going on. We were eating lunch in the school common room on a Monday, and I felt like it was the first time we'd sat down and talked in days.

'But you are still interested in being part of GenNext, right? You're not bailing on us already, are you?'

'Oh God, Jack, no way,' she said, pushing her prawn salad away and looking me in the eye. 'Please don't think that. It's just . . . well the thing is—'

At that moment we were rudely interrupted by Ava, who threw herself down on a chair and slumped across the table complaining for the next ten minutes about how tired she was. Eventually Ella grabbed her things and got up to leave, cutting our conversation annoyingly short.

'Look, we'll speak later, Jack,' she said. 'I'll be down at HQ tonight so we can catch up then.'

'Cool.' I watched her walk away, hoping I might finally get to the bottom of what was bugging her.

Only she didn't come down to Austin's that night, or the night after. And I felt lost.

It was all a bit weird, really. I mean, for quite a few weeks we'd been pretty much inseparable, working together on projects in and out of school, but now it suddenly felt like she had somewhere more important to be whenever I was with her. That was especially hard because it always felt so good being close to Ella. There was a connection between us that I'd never felt with any other human being, and I absolutely knew she felt it too. When I laughed, she laughed, and if we were working on something together and I had what I thought was a genius idea, it was like I could somehow telepathically convey it to her, because she'd be right there with me, having the same thought at the same time.

So you can just imagine how frustrating this new development was; even more so because deep down I felt like it was all my fault. Yes, we were the best of friends, but so far there was nothing more and that was down to me. I don't know why, but it was like there was some invisible force stopping me from taking that one step further and turning our friendship into a romance. Yeah, I hear you; maybe I was just a coward, but it was as if our friendship was something perfect that I was too scared to touch in case it shattered and broke.

Lying in bed some nights after we'd spent the day together, I'd mentally kick myself for being such a wuss about the whole thing, but then I'd see Ella the next day and it would be just the same. I'd sit there thinking about how well we got on, how smart and amazing she was. I'd read and inject hidden meanings into everything she said – come on, we've all done it, right? Like, if we were down in HQ and she made me a coffee while I was working on something on my laptop, setting it down next to me with a chocolate Hobnob and patting me on the shoulder, I'd be thinking, yes, she really cares about me. She didn't make a coffee for Sai or Austin or Ava. She didn't offer them a chocolate Hobnob, just me. When the truth of the matter was probably that she couldn't be bothered to make five coffees, or there weren't enough bloody biscuits left in the packet. Or the time she said something like 'I love working with you, Jack, I hope we can keep doing it.' Well, I sort of heard that as 'Will you marry me, Jack?' OK, OK, not literally, but you get my drift, right?

It wasn't easy, and although I'd put that vital sentence

together in my head a hundred times those past few weeks, the actual words 'Would you like to go out on a date with me, Ella?' or anything bearing any resemblance to that had not been forthcoming. Instead I spent hours checking her Instagram feed and wondering just how many times it was acceptable to text a person in a twenty-four-hour period. It was strange; I'd fancied girls before, of course I had, but I'd never felt anything like this crazy longing to be around someone. It was like going slightly insane but with the most beautiful kind of insanity I could imagine.

Now she'd been AWOL for an entire weekend and I was obsessing. In fact, it was pretty much all I could think about as Sai, Austin, Ava and I sat up on the roof of the block of flats where Sai lived. The rooftop was Sai's private little sanctuary, as hardly anyone else ever went up there; he loved it, and I could see why. It was so peaceful, and you felt like you were somehow disconnected from the rest of the world. It was getting dark by the time we'd headed up there that evening, and the lights of the town were waking up and starting to shimmer below us. Truth is, we were all a little bit burned out because we'd been working so hard on the website, as well as revising, so nobody was saying much. I broke the silence eventually, bringing up the subject of Ella, of course.

'Where do you think she's been hiding?'

Austin and Sai both groaned.

'You haven't even asked her out,' Austin said. 'We've been working together for weeks and you always seem like you're just treading water, waiting for the right moment, but it never seems to come. What's the matter with you?'

'Do you know what, Austin? I like Ella so much that the

66

thought of asking her out and then getting knocked back is doing my head in.'

'So you're basically bricking it,' Ava said.

'Pretty much.'

Sai was very quiet on the subject, but looked as though he was dying to say something.

'What do you think, Sai?' I asked. 'You look like you're a wise man where women are concerned.' Actually he didn't at all.

'It's just that . . . What I'm saying is, like . . .' Sai stopped in the middle of his garbled sentence.

'Spit it out if you have an opinion,' I said.

'Well I think you need to be careful around that situation,' he said, looking down at the floor.

'What situation?' Why did I think there was something he wasn't telling me?

'What Sai is trying to say is that if you have these feelings for Ella, you need to act now,' Ava said. 'Tell her the next opportunity you get.'

'Actually that wasn't what I was saying at all,' Sai argued.

'Look,' Ava said, taking control, 'if I was a girl – and I am – I would want a boy, or whoever, to tell me what was what and how they felt, right? So do it, man. Stop dithering or it'll be too late.'

'Maybe it's too late already,' Sai said.

'And there speaks the voice of doom,' Austin snorted, causing laughter amongst all of us.

After that, I felt like maybe everyone was a bit fed up with me banging on about my love life, or lack of it, so I decided to change the subject and get back to the thing that had brought the four of us together.

'Can you believe we actually roll out GenNext next week, guys? It's so amazing how it's all come together in less than two months. How are we going to celebrate? Shouldn't we have some kind of sick launch party?'

We were all slumped on a slightly damp abandoned sofa, heads back, looking into the evening sky.

'What, with just the five of us?' Ava said. 'How rubbish would that be?'

'We need to get the word around. We want people to check it out, at least the kids in our own school. How do we announce it if not by throwing some kind of event?'

'I've got an idea about that,' Sai said. 'There's a party on Friday where literally anyone who's anyone cool and important is going to be.'

Austin sat up, excited.

'And we've been invited?'

'No, not exactly,' Sai said. 'Well, not at all, actually. But I sort of have, and—'

'They said you could bring friends,' I said, also sitting up.

'Again, not exactly. But I could get us in, 'cause it's a kid in our year and I help him with his homework. Actually I end up doing most of his bloody homework, so he owes me a favour.'

That was when the penny dropped with Austin.

'Hunter? Hunter's having a party? What, at his mum and dad's ridiculous palace on Underwood Road?'

Sai nodded and I groaned.

'I heard it's gonna be sick,' Sai said. 'A pool party with

DJs, girls, drinks, everything. Bad things are gonna happen, I tell you.'

'Really, Sai?' Ava said. 'Bad things?'

Austin was taking it all in, staring into the night air like he'd been hypnotised.

'That's so amazing,' he said, temporarily lost in another world.

'But you don't even like Hunter,' I reminded him. 'You called him a knob-head.'

Austin leapt up, suddenly very animated and waving his arms around.

'No, it's perfect!' he yelled. 'We can make some flyers and pass them around.'

'Oh yeah, 'cause when I'm at a kick-ass party, there's nothing I like better than to sit down with a really good flyer,' Ava said.

'Or I could put together a business card design with some info included,' Sai said. 'Make it look like something cool and a little mysterious that people want to discover for themselves.'

'Better,' Ava said, nodding.

'Look, J, it doesn't matter whether we like Hunter or not – the main thing is that everyone else does,' Sai said. 'We need to be there, mate, and that's all there is to it.'

'But—'

'Ella's bound to be there – it's her crowd – and you did say you haven't seen enough of her the last couple of weeks.'

I hadn't thought of that, and yes, I know it was a bit shallow of me, but that's what love does to a man. That was when I caved. That was when I sold my soul. That was when I agreed to go to Hunter's party.

THE PARTY

Hunter was a kid who knew how to splash the cash around, despite the fact that he was only seventeen. Now obviously I wasn't exactly what you'd call close buddies with him – far from it after the unfriendly welcome during my first few weeks at St Joe's – but in the short time I'd been there I'd noticed he was constantly designer-labelled up to the eyeballs, with the most expensive boots, jackets and bags and the coolest gadgets money could buy. It was also apparent that about fifty per cent of the girls from Year 9 upwards wanted to be his girlfriend, and he seemed to have this strange, slightly dangerous kind of charm that attracted people to him. In fact it seemed to me that a fair few of the students at St Joe's actually wanted to *be* him, which I didn't get at all.

Word around school was that Hunter's dad was some kind of big kahuna on the property market and owned about a third of the county. Now, I'm pretty sure that was an exaggeration – but not a hundred per cent sure. Plus I'd heard all sorts of talk about how lavish his home life was: a butler

at the dinner table, au pairs who looked like Bond girls, two
– or was it three – Ferraris in his dad's garage, all of which
Hunter was allowed to drive, an indoor and an outdoor
pool. If you believed the school grapevine, Hunter's life was
a cross between *Downton Abbey* and *MTV Cribs*. Someone
even said that his dad had converted one of their bedrooms
into a dry ski slope, but as I said, this was all supposition
rather than cold hard fact, and when you questioned anyone
about who had actually seen evidence of this stuff, it all
went a bit quiet. Whatever the case, we were all eager to
find out just how sickeningly wealthy Hunter was, and exactly
what the house of someone that sickeningly wealthy might
look like, and at least he hadn't given me any trouble in the
last couple of weeks. Maybe it was going to be a bit of a
laugh after all.

'What's this shindig in aid of anyway?' I asked Austin,
who was sitting at the desk in my room, waiting for me to
get ready.

'I think it's his birthday,' Austin said. 'His mum and dad
are on safari in South Africa and he's taking over the entire
gaff. As far as I know, he's invited half the school.'

'All right for some,' I said. 'And we've definitely been
invited? You're sure about that?'

'Look, Sai does most of Hunter's homework, so we're in,'
Austin said.

'Remind me why he does that again?'

'For a small amount of money but mostly through fear
of violent reprisal,' Austin said, laughing. 'Whatever the
reason, Sai got invited, which sort of means I've been invited,
which sort of means you've been invited. Dude, this is the

social event of the year and we need to be there. We don't have to *like* the host, don't stress. We'll just walk in together like we're meant to be there, and while we're enjoying ourselves in a heated pool with hordes of hot girls, we'll be dishing out the new business cards and spreading the word about GenNext. It's a win-win.'

'Oh is it now?' I said.

Earlier in the week there had been a fairly heated debate regarding the pros and cons of the two of us turning up to Hunter's party together. One line of reasoning was that we should because neither of us had a girlfriend and rocking up on our own might look lame and a bit sad. On the other hand, Austin had a bee in his bonnet about people thinking we might be a couple. I pointed out to him that if I had even the slightest interest in dating somebody of my own sex, the person in question would be a lot better-looking than he was. Then he got all sulky and I had to assure him that he wasn't ugly and that he was sure to meet a hot girl at Hunter's party whether we walked in together or not. Jeez, the pitfalls, etiquette and dos and don'ts of teenage life could be very complicated at times. I swiped through my wardrobe, trying to make a decision about what to wear: a crisp white shirt, or was it better not to look too try-hard and just go for a T-shirt? After all, it was a mild night so a jacket wasn't required. Maybe a polo shirt was a good halfway house. Yeah, that was the way to go.

'Do you think some of those au pairs might be there?' Austin said, rubbing his hands together and staring at me, deadly serious.

'What? Serving us beers in bikinis?' I laughed. 'You wish, mate.'

'You never know, do you?' he said. 'Are you taking swim gear?'

'Of course, it's a pool party, isn't it?'

'And talking of beer,' Austin went on, 'we're all supposed to be taking our own alcohol. How are we going to swing that?'

'Well, I've had a few thoughts,' I said, grinning. 'My old man has got quite a nicely stocked liquor cabinet, so . . .'

'What's in it?'

'Wine, Bacardi . . . I dunno.'

'I don't like wine,' Austin said.

'What do you like?'

'I'm not entirely sure,' he said. 'Where is the drinks cabinet, anyway?'

'It's in the living room,' I told him.

'And where are your mum and dad now?'

'In the living room, watching *Game of Thrones*.'

'So unless you've developed the power of turning yourself invisible, how are we going to get hold of it?'

Austin had a point. This required a bit of fast thinking.

'Tell you what,' I said, after deciding on jeans and a light blue polo shirt, 'what about if you, like, pretend to fall all the way down the stairs and twist your ankle and then, like, scream out and then they'll rush out to help and I'll swoop in and put a bottle or two in my bag and . . .'

Austin looked at me like I'd come unhinged.

'Twist my ankle and scream out?' he said. 'Do I look like one of Dr Who's female companions?'

I shrugged, wondering if Austin might come up with an alternative plan. I mean, it wasn't exactly *Mission Impossible*, was it? We just had to get them out of the room and grab a bottle of something alcoholic.

'Or,' Austin said finally, 'we both go into the living room and then you say you need to talk to them in the kitchen privately and very urgently, with a proper serious look on your face. Then they get all worried and follow you out and I nick the bottle out of the cupboard.'

'Yeah, and what do I say once we're in the kitchen?' I asked.

'I don't know, do I? Tell them you feel a bit ill, or that you've got some really bad life-threatening illness.'

'Tell them I've got a life-threatening illness and then swan off to a party?' I said. 'Is that your idea?'

Austin nodded. 'It'll work, trust me,' he said.

And it was at that moment I realised why I liked Austin so much. He was both a clown and an optimist rolled into one, and as far as I was concerned that was a pretty good combination.

In the end I got them out of the room on the pretence of showing them a personal website I'd been putting together up in my room. Dad wasn't all that happy that I'd interrupted a particularly bloody battle scene, but they went for it anyway. While we were upstairs, I could hear the clanking of bottles as Austin rifled through the drinks cabinet, so I spoke to my parents in a stupidly loud voice to cover up the noise. Dad complained that I hadn't made any progress since the last time he'd seen the website so what was so urgent, and Mum asked me why I was shouting and assured me she wasn't deaf, but I think it did the trick because when we came back down the stairs Austin had a massive grin across his face and was standing by the front door, ready to go.

We left the house and headed off down the street armed with a small box of our new GenNext business cards and whatever alcohol Austin had managed to steal. I just hoped that neither of my parents fancied a glass of whatever it happened to be.

In the end, Hunter's house turned out to be a bit of a disappointment, at least from the outside. Sure, it was nice, and a fair size, but not really the rock-star mansion we'd all been imagining. It was just a smart house on the outskirts of town. My hopes of a dry ski slope in one of the back bedrooms was also dwindling. On the up side, we were greeted at the front door by a gorgeous young woman who Austin was convinced was one of the aforementioned au pairs, clearly ready to strip down to a bikini at the drop of a hat and cater to our every whim. Wrong again. Turned out it was Hunter's older sister, Fran, who had a degree in interior design and had just set up her own business.

The inside of the house was a bit more impressive than

the outside, with an awesome hallway that led to a huge staircase. Above our heads was one of the biggest chandeliers I'd ever seen, and there seemed to be doors everywhere – so many rooms. Fran led us to the back of the house and out to the pool, where it was all happening. As we stepped outside, I felt my eyes widen, and Austin and I gawped at one another, mutually awestruck. All around the sizeable pool and the smart patio area behind it there were people partying: some dressed up, others in swimming gear, and at first glance I didn't recognise a single one of them. Strands of lights decorated the walls, tables, trees and plants, and there were several flame-lit lanterns dotted around too. A guy in a chef's hat and Speedos was flipping burgers on a grill on the patio, and the pumping dance music was courtesy of a DJ who had set up on one side of the pool. Everyone seemed to have a drink in their hand and a smile on their face, and you could hardly hear yourself think, let alone speak.

'Oh mate, this is seriously amazing,' I said to Austin.

'You like it, do you? It's all my own work.' Fran smiled, shoving between us and gesturing across the magnificent scene.

'We do,' I said. 'We absolutely do.'

'Yeah, we need to get involved.' Austin nodded eagerly.

'Well enjoy yourselves, boys,' Fran said, putting a hand on each of our shoulders. 'Rules are, don't smash the joint up or pee anywhere that isn't the toilet, which is over there in the pool house. There's also a bar in the pool house but it's soft drinks only if you're under eighteen, I'm afraid – Dad's condition for letting Hunter have his birthday party at the house. Of course, Dad's not here and I'm in charge, so I might turn a blind eye if you've brought something of your own and you slip me a tenner.'

Fran was very beautiful in a punky sort of way, with deep red lipstick and heavy dark eyeliner. She wore a tight-fitting black T-shirt that almost reached her thighs, but no shoes, and she was smoking a cigarette, which mostly I don't like but on her it was somehow cool. She must have noticed me noticing her because she smiled knowingly when my eyes met hers.

'I was only joking about the money,' she said. 'I'm sure you're both very sensible boys.'

'We are,' I said.

She took a drag of her cigarette and moved closer to me.

'Not *too* sensible, I hope,' she said, winking.

I gulped like I was swallowing an ice cube and Fran laughed.

'Very cute,' she said, just as Hunter breezed past us eating a burger.

His sister grabbed his arm and he spun around to face us, mouth smeared with ketchup and slightly unsteady on his feet.

'Oi, Hunter,' Fran said. 'Why don't you introduce me to your new little pals? I've not seen these two around before.'

Hunter wiped his mouth with the back of his hand and looked Austin up and down.

'Yeah, I vaguely know this one,' he said.

'How's it going, mate?' Austin said.

Hunter's mouth curled into an evil half-smile when he turned his attention to me, and he peered at me through squinty eyes. Then he shook his head.

'Nah,' he said finally, 'I've never set eyes on this one before. But welcome anyway, boys. Enjoy yourselves!'

He smiled and slapped me on the shoulder and then took a bite out of his burger and walked off. I felt myself blush; not just my face but my entire body was blushing. Why would he say he'd never set eyes on me? What was that about?

'He's an idiot, my little brother,' Fran said, as if she'd read my mind. Then she stalked off to answer the door again, leaving Austin and me to our own devices.

I turned to Austin.

'I thought you said we were invited. That was mortifying.'

'Who cares,' he said. 'You heard Fran, the guy's an idiot. Let's just get a drink and enjoy ourselves, shall we?'

He dropped the bag he was carrying at his feet and fished around in it, eventually pulling out a bottle. I glanced down at what he was holding and then looked back at him, appalled.

'Baileys. You've got to be kidding me, bloody *Baileys*? You stole the bottle of Baileys Irish Cream my mum had last Christmas? Like we can walk around drinking that. We're not a couple of sixty-year-old librarians, mate.'

'Well . . . I just grabbed the first things that came to hand. They had the dimmer switch down in the living room, didn't they?'

I wondered in that moment whether I was ever going to be cool in any given situation. It certainly didn't feel like it. Just then, Austin produced another bottle from the bag.

'I got this one as well. Cider. Better than nothing, right?'

'Yeah, cider's OK, I guess,' I told him. 'Let's go get a

couple of glasses from the pool house and then circulate. It's time to party, Austin. Time to party.'

A couple of hours in and things were pretty sweet. It was one of those warm spring nights that makes you feel like summer has already begun. We'd managed a couple of laps of the event, not really spoken to anyone, but spotted some people who looked like they might be a good laugh had we spoken to them, plus a few hot girls who we decided we might come back to later if the mood took us. I have to be honest, nobody looked like they might be interested in hearing about a fantastic new website and video channel, but then again the night was still young. Typically, we'd found Sai and Ava sitting far from the action, way behind the pool in a quiet part of the garden under a tree. They were hanging out with a long-haired kid I recognised from school who was strumming a bright blue acoustic guitar and singing something that sounded a bit subdued compared to the rousing dance tracks the DJ was spinning. I noticed he had a pretty good voice, though, and the lyrics to his song, 'One Moment', were actually very cool. Ava was watching him in awe.

'This is Cooper,' she said. 'He goes to our school. Have you guys met?'

I shook my head. I'd never spoken to him, just seen him around school a few times: usually on his own, just him and a guitar case. I sat down with them and Ava offered me a sip of her beer, then offered it to Sai, who put his hand out and shook his head.

'I don't do that,' he said. 'Religious reasons.'

79

'Yeah, well if you're that religious, you wanna learn to clear your internet browsing history, mate,' Austin said, which brought laughter to the group and even caused a brief giggle from Cooper in the midst of his angst-ridden ballad.

'So do you fancy yourself as a bit of a singer, Ava?' I asked.

'Not me,' she said. 'I appreciate music, but it's not my thing. Cooper's amazing, though. He's going to the Royal Academy of Music next year, right, Coop?'

Cooper nodded. 'I hope so,' he said, putting his guitar down.

'So when did you two lovebirds get together?' Austin asked. 'Is this a first date we're interrupting?'

Everyone sniggered and then Sai said, 'You have to be kidding, right?'

Austin looked at me and shrugged.

'What am I missing?' he said.

'We met at the LGBT student mix and mingle at the start of term,' Ava said.

'Yeah, and?'

'We were *both* there,' Cooper went on.

Austin screwed up his forehead and I wondered if he had a clue what they were talking about. Austin was really smart but sometimes he could be really slow, if you know what I mean.

'Sorry, you lost me,' he said, confirming my speculation.

'He's gay, dude,' I said, then I looked at Ava in surprise. 'And you too?'

A smile spread across her face.

'It looks that way, yeah,' she said.

Austin looked mortified.

'What the . . .? You mean you're a lesbian and you didn't even think to tell me? I thought we were mates.'

'I'm sorry, I needed to sort it out in my own head before I told anyone. I was just waiting for the right moment,' Ava said.

'Oh, and sitting under a tree with Sam Smith here, strumming his guitar, was the right moment, was it?'

I wondered for a split second if Austin might have had a bit of a thing for Ava that he hadn't told me about, but then he started to laugh.

'You're a complete head case, Ava,' he said. 'But of course it doesn't matter to me who you fancy.'

'Or me,' I said.

'Well thanks very much, boys,' Ava said. 'Now, shall we go join all those rich idiots at the party? I feel like dancing.'

For a while, Sai and me stood watching Austin, Cooper and Ava strut their stuff on the patio, making total fools of themselves as far as I was concerned, but then my eyes began to wander around the rest of the guests at the party. There were people dancing wildly in their swim gear, still wet from the pool, and others who had paired off and were wrapped around one another, kissing. Over in a far corner I spotted Hunter, swigging from a bottle of Bud. His face was lit by the flicker of a lantern, which made him look mysterious and slightly sinister, it has to be said. He was smiling but looked a bit lost somehow, and I wondered if, deep down, he knew all the kids at the party were just there because he had shedloads of dough and a lifestyle so many of them aspired to. Surely that was the only reason he was one of the elusive populars, right?

Seconds later, I was startled by the sight of someone else moving through the crowd. It was Ella. My heart literally somersaulted at the sight of her. Yes. Yes. *Now* we were talking. Now the evening was going to pick up. I looked around to see Sai's dark eyes burning at me, his mouth half open as if he had something important to say.

'What's up, Sai?'

'You really like her, don't you?' he said.

'Who?'

'Taylor Swift . . . Who do you think I mean? Ella,' he laughed.

'Oh, is she here?' I said, with as much innocence as I could muster.

'Don't give me that, man, you were practically foaming at the mouth when she crossed that patio,' Sai said.

I began to laugh and then told him that I was going to get one quick drink before going over to speak to her. Dutch courage.

'Just be cool,' he said, 'and be careful.'

That struck me as weird at the time, but I brushed it off.

'I'm Mr Careful,' I told him. 'I'm Professor Careful.'

For a while I lost sight of Ella, so I scanned the party for the unmistakable blue dress I'd seen her float past in, my eyes darting around the crowd. She was nowhere to be found and for a few minutes I lost hope – maybe she'd been on her way out when I saw her. Then in the distance I spotted a blue and gold smudge blurred by disco lights and I knew it was her. I took a deep breath and pushed through the crowd, which seemed to be getting bigger as the night went on, crossing the patio where most of the revellers were dancing, weaving in and out of sweaty arms and wet clothes and trying not to spill my drink. Finally, Ella spotted me and flashed a massive smile. Result. She was pleased I was there; in fact she looked very happy indeed.

'I had no idea you were coming, Jack,' she said as I reached her.

She was leaning against one of the white Roman-style pillars that flanked one side of the pool and she looked like a total goddess.

'Well I haven't really seen you much to tell you, have I?' I was trying not to sound resentful. 'I thought you might have been abducted by aliens.'

She looked down at the floor, slightly embarrassed.

'I know, I know,' she said. 'I have been a bit distracted the last couple of weeks and I apologise for that. Trust me, though, I'm so into GenNext and I'll be back on form from next week, ready for the launch.'

'Really?'

'Absolutely! Now give me a sip of your drink, Jack Penman,' she said. 'What is it, anyway?'

'I'm not actually sure,' I warned her. 'It came out of a big bowl and it's a funny brown colour, but it tastes nice enough.'

Ella sipped from my glass, then licked her lips and smiled. I didn't know if it was the alcohol I'd had earlier, but I definitely felt light-headed.

'Sweet,' she said.

'What?'

'Very sweet,' she whispered, her lips almost brushing my ear.

'I . . . I . . .'

'The drink, I mean,' Ella said. Then she threw her head back in a laugh, just as Ava, Sai and Austin rocked up behind me, being annoyingly lairy. This was obviously not the right time, but the evil look I gave the three of them clearly hadn't conveyed that, because they stayed put right where they were.

For the next hour or so, the five of us hung out on the patio, watching the chef-in-Speedos flip burgers and somehow manage to skilfully avoid the hot cooking oil spitting or spilling over any delicate areas. We laughed, we danced a bit and we all got slightly tipsy. Then there was the moment when I decided it was now or never. I mean, how much longer could I leave it before I made my move and told Ella how I felt? What was stopping me? That was an easy one: it was the thought of her knocking me back or telling me she wanted to be 'just mates'. Still, if I didn't have the courage to do it then, after a couple of drinks, when the hell would I? I walked over towards Sai, who was doing his best to hit the top notes of Sia's 'Chandelier', which was blaring out of a giant speaker to our left.

'I'm going in,' I said.

'What?' He stopped singing. 'Going in where?'

'Ella,' I said. 'I'm going to ask her out, or kiss her or something. I haven't quite worked it out yet, but I've got to take action.'

Sai looked slightly anxious, panicky even.

'Mate, there's something I've been meaning to tell—'

'Can you just hang on a minute, Sai. I need to think.'

I took a slug of whatever it was in the glass I was holding, then spun around to face Ella, who was standing about ten feet away from me, her eyes closed, swaying to the music. God, she looked amazing: lightly tanned skin, soft lips, the gold of her hair floating around her bare shoulders . . . but hang on a minute, what was this? Suddenly an arm slid around her waist from behind, then another arm, coming out of the night like a snake, wrapping itself around her body, the glint of a gold watch caught in the pulsing lights – a guy's watch. What? Ella's head tilted back, and she smiled as the face behind her emerged from the darkness, just about visible as their mouths moved closer together.

I didn't notice that I'd let go of the glass I'd been holding until I heard it smash on the floor at my feet. Everyone turned to look at me as I tried to get a grip on exactly what I was seeing, and then it hit me. Like some Stephen Spielberg push-pull camera effect, everything came suddenly and terribly into focus. Ella was in the throes of a deeply passionate kiss . . . with Hunter.

THE AFTERMATH

'I was going to tell you, mate,' Sai said. 'I even tried to up on the roof the other day. I wasn't sure, though, you know what I mean?'

I was sitting on what seemed to be a large inflatable dice, a few feet away from the pool. The music, which had sounded so amazing an hour ago, now sounded like a muffled banging in my head, the buzz of the bass distorted and ugly. Ava, Sai and Austin were standing around me looking suitably sympathetic and my head was still spinning, although I wasn't sure if it was the alcohol or the shock that was making it happen.

'Tell me what, Sai?' I snapped at him. 'How the hell did you know that was going to happen? How could you have . . . Wait, no. Don't tell me this is an ongoing thing. That was a one-off, right? She's not actually . . .'

'Their parents have known one another for years,' Sai said. 'They've been on family holidays together and they're always at one another's houses. I went to the same primary school, so . . .'

'They were like childhood sweethearts or something equally revolting,' Ava said softly. 'Then since Ella came back from Hong Kong it's been this sort of on-and-off type of thing, but I had no idea it was back on. I mean, we've become pretty good mates but she never said a word to me.'

'It's only been back on over the last couple of weeks,' Sai said sheepishly. 'I only know because Hunter owed me money for some coursework I'd done for him and when I went round to collect it, Ella was there. It was kind of obvious. I should have said something, Jack, but I didn't know what to do for the best. I hoped it might go away, you know?'

Ah, the last couple of weeks. Of course. That explained pretty much everything as far as I was concerned.

'Well I wish you *had* said something, Sai,' I said. 'I feel like such an idiot.'

'To be honest, I totally thought it was all in the past, so why bring it up?' Austin said. 'I thought you might freak out if you knew. I'm sorry, mate.'

'Yeah, it's not like they've been all loved-up at school or anything,' Sai added. 'They sort of keep it under the radar. I mean, I've got no idea if they've had sex or done anything or—'

I stood up quickly and put my hands up; I really didn't want to hear any more.

'You know what, guys, I think I just want to hang out on my own for a while.'

Austin put his hand on my shoulder.

'Come on, mate, don't be a drama queen. It's a party.'

I glared at him like I might kill him, and he nodded as he clocked that I really meant it before turning around to face Ava and Sai.

'Let's go, guys,' he said. 'This party's had it.'

Finally alone, I sat back down on the giant dice. I've no idea know how long I stayed there, but the party began to disintegrate around me, with more and more people either leaving or falling down on the soft grass, unable to stand the pace any longer. The pounding house music set had gradually morphed into a blissed-out break beat selection, softer and easier on the ears at whatever time of the morning it was. There were several people still floating around in the pool on inflatables and a fair few couples kissing in dark corners or on the sunloungers scattered around the patio. I wondered where Ella and Hunter might have gone, and then a picture of them climbing that fantastic staircase in search of an empty bedroom flashed violently through my mind, making me cringe and shake my head to banish the thought. I wondered if she'd seen my look of horror as she locked lips with that idiot, or whether she was too wrapped up in what she was doing to even care what I thought. I didn't know, and right then I didn't care. And yeah, I know I sound like I was wallowing in self-pity and milking the drama, but come on! Think about how you'd feel in my shoes. It wasn't pretty in my head, I'll tell you that. Sure, I fought valiantly against the sharp stinging behind my eyes, and tried desperately to unravel the knot that was twisting tight around my stomach, but it was no good. I was heartbroken.

I was still sitting there trying to work up the energy to get up and head home when a voice startled me out of my thoughts.

'Hey, mister. All on your lonesome? Where're your playmates?'

I looked up to see Hunter's sister, Fran. Still no shoes, still smoking, still gorgeous.

'Could you possibly be any more patronising?' I said, laughing. 'My mates have all gone home.'

'Not you, though?' she said, blowing out perfect rings of smoke as she exhaled. 'You're the hardcore one of the group, are you?'

'Not exactly. I . . .'

'I was going to go to bed, but I have to make sure everyone leaves and nobody nicks the family silver,' she said.

'Family silver?'

'So I thought I'd go for a dip in the pool instead. Fancy joining me?'

I realised suddenly that somewhere along the line I'd lost the bag that had my board shorts and towel in.

'I haven't got any . . . I mean, I've lost my swim stuff.'

'Just take your shoes off like me,' she smiled.

'What, jump in with all my clothes on?'

'Or take them off, whatever. It's a lovely night and the pool's heated.' she said. 'I double-dare you.'

She looked straight at me, and in one mad, determined moment I kicked off my trainers, took my phone out of my pocket and jumped up, standing by her side and holding her hand. As we walked towards the pool's edge, she turned to me and grinned.

'After three. One . . . two . . .'

The water felt incredible, but I hadn't bargained on the pool being quite as deep as it was, and because I was mid-yell when I hit it, my mouth filled with water as my head disappeared under the surface and I came up coughing and spluttering, with a mini-fountain of chlorine-infused water shooting out of my nose. Yeah, I know, really attractive. After I'd pushed my hair out of my eyes and composed myself, Fran swam towards me, laughing.

'I can't believe you jumped in the bloody pool with all your clothes on,' she said, moving up close to me.

'Well, it's been that kind of night,' I said. If you want the God's honest truth, I couldn't believe I'd jumped in the bloody pool with all my clothes on either.

'Oh really?' she said, wrapping her arms around my neck. 'And what kind of evening is that?'

'Unusual,' I said.

Then she leaned in and kissed me.

We stayed there for what seemed like ages but was probably only a few seconds: kissing and treading water. I tried to take in the moment – God, I really tried – but it wasn't as easy as you might think. I mean, there I was kissing an incredibly sexy older woman in a swimming pool in the middle of the night, and yes, it was all pretty awesome. Trouble was, all the time it was happening, there was this nagging thought at the back of my mind – as if a tiny little bloke was standing on my shoulder hammering at my head with a tiny little hammer – and I kept wondering what this moment would feel like if it was with someone I had feelings for. What would it feel like if it was with Ella?

Once Fran had stopped kissing me, she sighed and shook her head, smiling.

'So pretty, but so young,' she said, touching my nose with the tip of her finger.

'I'm not that much younger than you, am I?'

She shrugged and then let her head fall back to float on the water, staring up at the stars.

'Shall we get out?' she said after a while. 'It's not as warm as I thought it would be.'

'I'm going to give it another minute,' I said. I was probably blushing like a tomato with teeth.

Fran kissed me, very lightly, on the lips, then swam to the edge of the pool, pushing herself up on her arms, her wet clothes clinging to her body as she clambered out. Yeah, that was all very . . . nice.

Back on dry land, it occurred to me that I hadn't really thought it through, plunging into the water with all my clothes on. No minicab was going to take me home soaking wet, and I certainly didn't feel like walking. Luckily, on the way out, I spotted my bag sitting under one of the sunloungers, so I grabbed the towel from it, dried myself, and changed into my dry board shorts. Then I wrapped the towel around me and called a local cab service.

It had been an epic night, but now I was knackered, and as I left, quietly stepping over sleeping teenagers as I went, I wondered how I'd got it so wrong with Ella. I felt angry and stupid, not to mention hurt. Then my mind slipped back to the last thirty minutes with Fran, and that at least raised a smile. Although I couldn't say for sure that Hunter's older sister had completely salvaged my evening, she had most definitely repaired a little piece of the damage.

THE BAD MONDAY

Trust me, the Monday morning after Hunter's party won't go down in history as one of my all-time favourite mornings. If anything, I should have been on a high: GenNext was going live that very morning, and I'd ended the previous week in a swimming pool being kissed by a gorgeous woman. Most people might say those two items alone added up to a pretty decent result, but any positive vibes I managed to conjure up in my head that morning soon evaporated every time the grim vision of Ella and Hunter kissing re-emerged. It literally made my stomach turn over.

When I hurtled downstairs at 7 a.m., I found Mum sitting at the breakfast bar in her robe, staring out into the garden.

'Hey, Mum.'

It was like she didn't hear me.

'Is there a cup of coffee going?'

She suddenly came to life, as if somebody had just switched her on at the plug socket. Jumping up, she grabbed a cup from the cupboard and flicked on the kettle.

'Sorry, Jack, I was miles away.'

She'd been a bit weird all weekend and I started to wonder if there was something going on between her and Dad that I didn't know about. I sat down and inhaled a bowl of Crunchy Nut Cornflakes while I thought about it.

'Are you worried about something, Mum?'

'Don't eat so fast!' she said, sitting down next to me with two cups of coffee.

'That's not an answer.'

'The only thing your dad and I worry about is you,' she said, touching my arm.

'We've been through this. I'm fine this time, I told you.'

Mum got up again and started unloading the dishwasher, which had a cup and about two teaspoons in it. She was definitely distracted.

'I guess . . . Sometimes I worry that you don't think I can handle myself, Mum. You know, 'cause of what happened.'

'What do you mean?' she asked, still at the dishwasher.

'Well . . . does Dad think I should have fought back a bit harder? Or do you, maybe?'

At that she spun around, a look of concern on her face.

'No, Jack, don't ever think that. We think you did exactly the right thing. You can't win with people like that, with bullies. I'd rather you ran away from a fight than had someone stick a knife in you, like you see on the news every other week. God forbid. I'm proud of the way you handled it all.'

I was about to answer when Dad interrupted us, bellowing from upstairs: 'You'd better get a move on, love, the traffic will be murder!'

I shot Mum a puzzled look. Where the hell were they going together first thing on a Monday morning? Didn't he have to be at the office? Wasn't she opening the hair salon?

'Your dad's just running me up to the doctor's,' she said. 'I've been feeling a bit tired and Dr Murrell said I might need to take some iron tablets and something else I can't remember the name of, so I've got to pop in and get a prescription.'

'But . . . what kind of—'

'It's nothing to worry about, Jack. I've just been working long hours and I need to take some time off.'

'You do work too hard, Mum,' I said. It was true. Mum was a brilliant hairdresser and had loads of loyal clients, so she was always taking on extra last-minute jobs here and there because she didn't want to let anyone down. I looked at her. She didn't seem sick but I couldn't help but feel a little worried.

'Well, I can't trust anyone to hold the fort,' Mum said, laughing to herself. 'I've put that young girl Shanice in charge this morning, God help me. She nearly burned Mrs Hamilton's head off the other day, leaving the peroxide on for too long.'

I smiled weakly at her and got up from the breakfast bar, dumping my bowl in the freshly unloaded dishwasher.

'Yeah, well you need to chill out and look after yourself, Mum, do you hear me?'

'I hear you, Jack,' she laughed. 'Now get yourself off to school.'

Walking to the bus stop, I tried to shake the notion that Mum might have something seriously wrong with her. Even though she was playing the whole thing down, it was going to niggle away at me until I knew for certain she was OK. I looked up into the bleak grey sky as I wandered past the long line of semi-detached houses on my road, and wished the sun would at least come out. It was supposed to be spring, after all. A bit of sun would make everything seem better. Maybe.

So you know when you're thinking that you really don't want something to happen, and then that's exactly the next thing that happens? Well that's how my morning went. I spent the bus journey to school making notes on my iPhone and formulating plans for the next stage of GenNext: a) to take my mind off my conversation with Mum that morning, and b) to stop my mind from wandering back to thoughts of Ella, because by this point, quite frankly, I was beginning to feel a bit pathetic about the situation. Yeah, so she's dating a total idiot, big deal. Get over it, Penman, there are other girls out there and there's nothing you can do about it anyway. Right? Right.

Just as I thought I was beginning to get it all sorted in my head, at least for the time being, I jumped off at the bus stop closest to St Joe's and who do I almost crash into? Yep, Ella and Hunter. Holding hands – I kid you not. It was like someone had dropped me in the middle of some sick and twisted parallel universe. All these weeks they'd apparently been dating and today was the day I had to come face to face with it. Not only that, but there was absolutely no avoiding them as they were coming out of Caffè Nero and literally walking towards me. So I set my face to 'don't give a crap' and hoped for the best.

'Hey, Penman.'

Was I going a bit mental or was Hunter kind of semi-smiling at me?

'What's going on?' I said, walking alongside them towards school.

95

'Nothing much. Did you have a good time Friday night?'

No, I wasn't losing it: he was actually being pleasant, though probably only because Ella was with him.

'Yeah, it was cool. I haven't been to many parties like that.'

'I bet,' he said smugly.

Ella, meanwhile, was noticeably sheepish, sipping her skinny latte and avoiding meeting my eye, and I wondered if she felt at all guilty. Had she even realised what this was doing to me? You know what, I really don't think she had.

'Look, I know you guys haven't exactly hit it off, but all that needs to change right now,' she blurted out in a fairly demanding voice. 'I can't have my boyfriend and one of my best mates not being cool with one another, right?'

'I've told you, babe, it's all cool with us. Right, Penman?' Hunter said, slapping my shoulder.

So that was why Hunter wasn't being his usual repulsive self: Ella had obviously had a word with him. When I looked into his face, however, there didn't seem to be even a modicum of sincerity in this new nice-guy demeanour of his. He clearly didn't mean a word of it; it was just to keep Ella sweet.

'What about you, Jack, are you cool?' she said.

'All good, buddy,' I said.

'Excellent,' Hunter said, grinning. 'Any friend of Ella's an' all that malarkey.'

He turned to face Ella, kissing her on the lips, and I'm fairly certain some of that morning's Crunchy Nut Cornflakes made their way from my stomach back up into my mouth.

'Look, I've got to run, babe, I've got some business to attend to before lessons,' he said. 'I'll see you later.'

Then he was gone and I was left alone with Ella. Awkward.

As we continued towards St Joe's, our pace naturally slowed until eventually we stopped outside the gates. It was like we both knew that something had to be said before we walked any further, so I went first.

'Well this is . . . I mean, why didn't you say anything?'

'About what?' She looked at me wide-eyed, brushing her hair off her face with her right hand.

God, was it possible she really didn't know how I felt?

'Why didn't you tell me about you and Hunter is what I mean,' I went on. 'Seemingly it's been going on for a while and we were together, like, every day, working on GenNext and the media production project, so I'd have thought you'd have given me the heads-up on who you were—'

'Look, Jack, I am sorry, really. It was only the last couple of weeks that I realised . . . I mean, by the time I suspected that you kind of . . . you know . . . liked me in that way . . . you know, in a more-than-mates type of a way . . . by then it was already back on with me and Hunter, and I know you're probably not a fan of his, but we've known each other a long time; we have a lot of history together. That's why I kept out of your way for the last week or so; I didn't want you to feel bad or upset and . . . I'm just sorry, OK?'

Ah, so she did know after all. I shrugged and gave her a look as if I had absolutely no idea what the hell she was going on about.

'You . . . you do like me, right, Jack? This is what this is about, isn't it?'

I shrugged again, looking back at her as if she were babbling a load of utter nonsense. It threw her, I could tell.

'Oh God, I'm really embarrassed now,' she said, looking

down at the floor. 'I thought . . . well, it seemed like . . .
Sorry, Jack, I've read this completely wrong, haven't I?'

'Er . . . slightly, yeah.'

I have to tell you, I felt pretty low at that moment. Even
after everything that had happened, I still cared about this
girl so much, and the last thing I wanted was to make her
feel stupid. I was on a self-preservation roller coaster, though,
and there was no jumping off.

'All I was saying was, because we're mates and working
together, I didn't get why you kept your boyfriend a secret,
that's all.'

'Oh! So you're OK with it, then?' She sounded surprised
and hopeful. 'And you're OK with us still working on
GenNext together?'

'Why wouldn't I be all right about it?' I said. 'Like Hunter
said, it's all cool with me, *babe*.'

I wasn't exactly sure how convincing I was being or if she
was in any way fooled, but it was too late by then.

'Right,' she said, 'why wouldn't you?'

'Anyway, I'd better get to class,' I said. 'Loads on today.
I'll see you later, I expect.'

'Yeah, see you later.'

Ella looked slightly dumbstruck as I turned and walked
away from her, leaving her standing alone at the school gates.
And yeah, of course I wanted to turn around and shout at
her like a nutter: demand to know why the hell she wanted
to be with an idiot like Hunter and not with me. But I didn't.
I just kept walking. And I'd like to tell you that it felt good,
walking away like that, but it didn't. It felt bad. Really bad.

THE HEROES

When I walked into the sixth-form common room that lunch-time, I was met with a trio of anxious faces. Austin, Sai and Ava all looked as if they'd just come back from a funeral, and I knew it was for my benefit.

'Don't even,' I said to Ava, as she wrapped her arm around my waist and rested her head on my shoulder. I looked down at her wrist, delicately tattooed with a red-haired mermaid, and smiled at my new friend's concern for my mental well-being.

'We were worried when we didn't hear from you all weekend,' she said.

'Yeah, Austin said you'd probably topped yourself,' Sai added.

'Oh did he now?' I laughed. 'But you didn't think about calling my parents to find out?'

They all shook their heads.

'You absolute muppets.'

'Seriously, are you OK?' Austin said. 'I mean, not to be selfish but things are looking so good with GenNext, I'd hate for something like this to screw everything up before it's even got off the ground, you know? Not after the result we had this morning.'

'Something like what?' I said. 'Look, don't worry. Me and Ella are cool, and— What result? What are you talking about, Austin?'

'Sai, grab your laptop,' Austin said urgently.

Sai complied, banging away quickly at the keyboard as we all sat down around a coffee table.

'We went online at nine a.m.,' he said, flashing the screen at me, 'and look at the views since a couple of YouTubers put a link to GenNext in their video descriptions.'

'And look at the comments about the interviews; about Ella,' Austin said, pointing at the screen.

'Are they good?' I said, trying to speed-read a few of them while Sai waved the laptop around.

'They're amazing.' Ava smiled. 'People love her. Look, I've taken a screenshot of some of the comments.'

@LoupyLou777
OMG Loving @EllaGenNext reporting on @GenNextOnline she so beaut ☺

@DwayneGT
Just watching @GenNextOnline looks like a cool website

@*_*SaraB*_*
The @GenNextOnline footage of @YearsandYears gig is awesome wish I'd been there *sob*

'And that's why we're worried,' Austin said. 'I mean, if you and Ella fall out . . .'

'Don't worry, Austin,' I assured him. 'As I said, we're cool. At least I think we are.'

Ava grabbed my arm, tugging at me urgently.

'But this is all really good news, right, Jack? These figures and stats? We're on our way, aren't we?'

I perused the information once more: thousands of hits in just a few hours and traffic coming from all over the world. A sudden rush of excitement surged upwards, like it had started from my feet and was now shooting out through the top of my head. For just a moment, the misery of the last few days melted away and I felt my mouth curl into a massive grin.

'Are you kidding me? Guys, we so are on our way; this is amazing!' I said. 'OK, so now we need to figure out what's next.'

'Exactly,' Austin agreed. 'Now we've hooked people in, we can't sit back and just hope they keep coming back. We need to ramp it up a notch. I think we should give it a week or so and then drop The Gloves interview. Show everyone we really mean business.'

'Totally!'

After that, the three of us just stood there for a while, grinning at the stats and one another like lunatics. And why not? This was pretty amazing stuff, you know?

Our brief moment of glory was interrupted by a commotion in the hall outside the common room: shouting and swearing – it didn't sound too friendly. A few people, including Ava, headed towards the door to find out what was going on.

'Hey, what's your problem?' Ava called out as she reached the corridor. 'Leave him alone.'

I followed her across the room, and when I stuck my head outside, I was somewhat surprised to see Cooper crouching down on the floor nursing his guitar, which looked like it had been broken in about three places.

'What the hell is this?' I said, slightly stunned. 'Cooper, what happened?'

There were a couple of guys standing over him shouting insults.

'The kid's a homo!'

'Nasty little faggot!'

Unsurprisingly, they were pals of Hunter's; I'd seen them hanging out with him a bunch of times. A handful of other students were standing around, but nobody seemed to be doing much to help, so before I knew what I was thinking, I was pushing through the gathering crowd and picking up the smashed guitar before helping Cooper to his feet.

'What's he ever done to you, anyway?' I said.

I was standing in between Cooper and the bigger of the two guys and dearly hoping the dude wasn't thinking about beating the crap out of me.

'I don't like what he is, and I don't like the way he looks at me,' the guy said.

I knew this boy, vaguely; he was in a couple of my classes and quite smart, if I'd remembered rightly. I couldn't believe he was behaving like such a dick.

'The way he looks at you – are you kidding?' Ava shouted from behind me. 'You need to go home and clean your bath-room mirror, mate, because you're not exactly Taylor Lautner. You do realise that, don't you?'

'He just got in our way,' the chunkier of the two piped up.

'So you smashed his guitar?' I said. 'Really nice.'

'He dropped it, didn't you, fag?'

Cooper said nothing; just stood there looking unsure, so I stepped forward, squaring up to the two guys but bricking it the whole time.

'Look, just back off and leave him alone, all right?'

That was when I spotted Hunter, grinning and shaking his head at me from the back of the small crowd.

'Ooh, Penman, you're pretty scary when you're angry,' he said, smirking. 'Is there something we should know about you and the travelling minstrel?'

So Hunter being cool with me had lasted what? Three hours? I knew it was just a front for Ella.

'Dudes, you need to walk away,' Hunter told his friends. 'You're embarrassing yourselves and me. Just leave it. Let's go get some food.'

That was when Ava stepped forward, furious.

'So as these are your stupid mates, Hunter,' she spat, 'what I want to know is, do you agree with them?'

Hunter looked at his pals and then back at Ava, confused.

'What are you bleating on about?'

'I mean, do you think like they do? Those names they were calling Cooper?'

The corridor was full of people but you could have heard a pin drop at that moment.

'Whatever,' Hunter said. 'I haven't got time for this.'

'Is that right?' Ava said, her eyes burning. 'Because I'm the same as Cooper, do you hear? I'm gay too, and if he's all those things, then so am I. And me and Cooper and people like us are going to shut that crap down in this school.'

She looked over at the two boys. 'Do you understand? We're going to shut you down.'

As the small crowd slowly scattered, Ava sat Cooper down in the common room while I surveyed the damage to his guitar.

'Thank you, guys, but I think I'm OK,' Cooper said. 'I did worry I might be toast there for a minute, but they're usually all mouth, people like that. Of course, I could have done without the smashed guitar.'

Within seconds, Sai and Austin had joined us, closely followed by Ella, who ran straight over to me, looking slightly horrified.

'Jack, are you hurt? Someone said you were in a fight?'

'Hardly a fight,' I laughed. 'Not even a minor scuffle.'

By this time, Hunter and his friends were nowhere to be seen and Ella smiled at me proudly.

'Jack, you little hero,' she said.

I was a split second away from telling her about her boyfriend's part in all of it, but I stopped myself. Why make her feel bad? She'd find out what he was really like soon enough without my help, plus it would have just sounded like sour grapes after seeing them together that morning.

'Jack, that was pretty brave, mate,' Sai laughed. 'Those were some big-ass dudes, man.'

'Nah. If you want to talk brave, look no further than Ava,' I said. 'She just came out in front of half the school.'

'Oh God, I did, didn't I?' she giggled.

'Yes you did, bitch,' Cooper said.

I don't know if it was relief or shock or what, but within a few seconds all six of us were in stitches, arms around one another in a circle, laughing our heads off.

THE RISE AND RISE

The next couple of weeks were pretty much a whirlwind as we handed in our remaining coursework, knuckled down to some hardcore revision, and prepared for the onslaught of exams. Meanwhile, we had to keep up GenNext's social media, and with the site getting more and more hits every day, that was a massive task on top of everything else. I have to say, I felt pretty positive about my media production AS level – Mr Allen had given my and Ella's project an A, which was half the grade – and I worked my ass off to cram for my other subjects, too. As nail-biting as it all was, when the exams finally arrived, they didn't seem too bad. OK, so I might not come out with the world's most amazing results, but given that I'd switched schools in the middle of sixth form, I felt pretty positive. The other four members of the team moaned and groaned about the amount of work just as much as I did – especially Austin, who'd left most of his revision until the last minute and then crammed like a nutter – but when it came down to it, they were all so bloody smart they would probably end up acing every single exam.

Once the exams and all things study-related were done and dusted, we only had a few weeks back at school, and before we knew it the summer holidays were upon us. And that was when everything really started to go crazy and my life as I knew it was literally turned upside down. Sure, there may have been a summer happening out there somewhere, but there certainly wasn't much of a holiday going on; well, not for me, Sai, Austin, Ava and Ella, anyway. In fact things were going so freakishly well with GenNext that we hardly had time to take a breath. Everyone at school seemed to be talking about us online, and we found ourselves being bombarded with messages and texts from students, either telling us how much they loved the site or wanting to get in on the action.

We'd decided to hold The Gloves interview back until we'd really built up our subscribers and whetted their appetites, so when we did eventually upload it, everything suddenly went completely bat-crap crazy. Just the mere mention of the band's name on the site caused a massive buzz and a huge amount of traffic, but once The Gloves put links to GenNext on their Facebook page, Instagram account and Twitter feed, we were getting tens of thousands of hits a day, plus a ton of new subscribers who seemed hungry for more. After that, the info@GenNext mailbox was bursting at the seams with emails from managers and agents practically begging us to interview their hot new acts and future stars. For the first few weeks, Ella and I tried to shoot segments with as many of them as we could – at least the ones we thought had something cool or original about them – just to stockpile plenty of good content. After a while, though, I could hardly keep up with the emails, and I found myself trotting out the same polite reply, telling people that we just couldn't accommodate any more requests at the present time and we would get back to them as soon as we could. It was utter madness.

Poor Mum and Dad must have started to forget what I looked like. For the previous few months, on the rare occasions I'd actually been at home and not sleeping, I'd either been locked in my room studying or flying past them in the hall on my way out of the door. Family mealtimes had completely gone out of the window, and the only time I ever found myself actually sitting down to eat was after midnight in front of a computer screen. Of course, they were both very proud of what I was doing and told me so whenever I phoned or messaged them from HQ with the next exciting bit of news. To tell you the truth, I think they were even happier about the fact that I now had a good bunch of friends and I was no longer the social recluse they'd spent so many sleepless nights worrying about. That said, I could tell they had concerns about how fast GenNext was moving and how insanely busy my everyday existence was becoming, even though they never actually said it out loud.

'You've still got your A levels to think about next year, Jack,' Mum reminded me on a regular basis.

Yeah. I wasn't so sure about that. I was much too busy becoming the face of a hugely successful website and online channel. We'd get our AS level results soon enough, later on in the summer, and to be honest, with all that was happening, the daily onslaught of teachers banging on about higher education seemed like a distant memory now. Exam results somehow just didn't seem as important now as they had done while we were still at school.

Actually, Ella was much more the face of GenNext than I was in those first weeks. I have to be honest, I didn't feel massively confident about being on camera in the beginning. Still, as time passed, I started finding my feet and feeling more confident – I even started to enjoy it a bit. I actually got a few personal mentions on Twitter, which made me chuckle to myself on more than one occasion.

@Babycakes595
OMG @JackGenNext doing the @TRexFootball team interview is EVERYTHING

@Anna_banana_
Is it just me or is @JackGenNext srsly fiiiiiine?

I mean, who'd have thought it, eh? The geek who nobody even spoke to a year ago. It was all very weird and wonderful.

The first time it truly sank in how fast things were moving was when Cooper phoned Ava to tell her that he'd received some serious attention from several record labels after we'd uploaded a video of him playing a low-key acoustic set – and not tiny obscure ones either; I mean record labels that I'd actually bloody heard of. We were all really chuffed with the news, of course, but on that same boiling hot Saturday, Ella came bombing down the stairs to HQ brandishing the shiny new iPhone 6S that Hunter had bought her for her birthday the previous week, and sounding flustered.

'Seriously, you have to look at this, guys!'

'What's up?' Ava strode towards Ella and threw an arm around her neck as she looked down at the phone screen.

'Look at the number of followers on my Instagram all of a sudden,' Ella said.

Now I already knew how good Ella's Instagram was – let's face it, I'd spent enough time studying it over the past couple of months – so I wasn't exactly surprised that she'd picked up a few new followers now she had a bit of an online presence.

'How many?' I asked.

'Well,' Ella said, 'it's gone from just under three thousand last week to . . . and you won't believe this . . . two hundred and fifty thousand.'

'What?! When did this happen?' Ava screamed.

'I don't really know,' Ella said. 'I mean, I've been so busy on GenNext I haven't even looked at my personal account for a few days, but then today it's just . . . and it's pretty much the same with Twitter.'

She tapped and swiped and then tapped her phone again as Sai and Austin leapt up from the sofa to join us.

'Look' she said, holding her phone up. 'I mean, I've been tweeting The Gloves interview, but this morning the followers are jumping up by the second. I've literally got hundreds of tweets from people saying how much they love GenNext. It's just—'

She stopped dead, a look of astonishment sweeping across her face.

'Oh my God, that's why. Oh wow!'

'What is it?'

'Katy Perry only retweeted my message and the link to GenNext late last night,' she said. 'I mean, how did she even . . . ?'

'Yeah, that'll do it,' Ava laughed. 'She has over eighty million followers.'

'This is legit crazy, guys,' Austin said. 'It also explains

why I've just had an email from some hipster cosmetics company saying they'll pay us proper coinage if we get Ella and Jack using some of their hair wax, sludge, clay, whatever, and mention them by name on camera. I thought it was a piss-take, but—'

'How much money?' Sai jumped in.

'Two grand a pop.'

'Tell them we'll do it for three,' I said, thinking fast.

'Yeah?'

'Hell, yeah!'

Of course I was going to do it – wouldn't you? Look, as far as I was concerned, GenNext wasn't just a cool after-school project or a hobby any more. Now it was something to build on; a way to make money and start carving out a career, just like I'd always wanted.

It didn't stop there, either; as the summer rolled on, there were more and more opportunities to turn GenNext into a viable business, and in the end Sai suggested we let his dad's youngest brother, AJ, take us under his wing and manage us as a team. AJ was only in his early thirties and looked even younger, but he was very shrewd and extremely successful. Amongst other things, he was a partner in a cool talent agency called Metronome. When Sai put it to us, we all agreed that the business and promotional side of GenNext was getting too complicated for us to handle while we had the technical and creative side to look after. It was time to take things to the next level.

Later that afternoon, Ella pulled me to one side saying there was something she wanted to ask me, so the two of us headed out for a walk. Now I have to tell you, it had been quite some time since I'd been on my own with Ella, and that was something of my own engineering. Much as I enjoyed being close to her, I was worried that being alone with her might be too difficult. Like, I wouldn't know what to say or how to behave, you know? When other people were around it was a doddle to be natural, but alone . . . well, I just didn't know. For a start, it all still felt a little raw, even though it had been a couple of months since I'd found out about her and Hunter. What if I ended up taking her hand or telling her how amazing she was, or something utterly embarrassing like that? I might not be able to stop myself. I was apprehensive to say the least, and what could she possibly want to ask me that couldn't be said in front of the others anyway?

We headed out into a gorgeous, bright day, taking a leisurely stroll around the streets near Austin's place, lost in banter about how fast everything was happening and how excited we both felt. After a while, Ella suggested we go to the park and sit down for a while, so I grabbed a couple of Diet Cokes from a newsagent and off we went. It was scorching, but so good to be out in the sun, especially after living like moles in Austin's cellar. Ella grabbed a small bottle out of the patchwork shoulder bag she was carrying and started spraying it at me.

'What the hell is that? Get off!'

'You'll end up like a radish with your fair skin if you sit out in this sun for too long,' she said, giggling. 'Just let me put some on; we don't want you developing a nasty skin complaint, now do we, Jack Penman?'

'I suppose not,' I said.

Just hearing her call me by both my names like she did the day we first met made me feel horribly nostalgic, and the thought flashed through my mind that maybe things might have been different if I'd just . . . No. I wasn't going to go there again. That subject was done.

'How's it going with Hunter?' I asked instead. I didn't really want to know, but it just sort of came out.

'Oh, we have our moments. You know,' she said evasively.

'Actually I don't know,' I said. 'You never talk about him much and you never bring him along to any of the gigs we film or anything, really.' Then, seeing as we were on the subject, I thought I might as well go for broke and ask the question that haunted me. 'I mean, are you guys in love . . . or is it just a casual thing?'

She went silent for a moment, thinking about it. 'I thought I was in love with him for a little while, maybe . . . back at the start of the year,' she said. 'Then we had a break from one another and then we fell into this casual dating thing and then . . .'

'Then what?'

'Then you came to St Joe's.'

She smiled so sweetly at me and I swallowed hard, my heart suddenly thumping in my chest. What was she trying to tell me?

'And that made things different how?' I said softly, daring to put my hand on hers.

'Oh, you know,' she said.

'I don't know, I'm actually really dumb,' I said. 'People have to spell things out for me generally, otherwise . . .'

Ella lifted her hand and softly touched my cheek.

'You absolute nutter,' she laughed. And then she leant forward and gave me a friendly peck on the cheek.

It was only a quick, harmless kiss, but as she pulled away, the shock of what she'd done registered in her eyes. She stared at me for a moment, her face softening, and then she leant in again, closing her eyes, and before I knew what was happening, she'd kissed me again – on the lips. Only this time it wasn't harmless. It was sweet-soft and amazing. It was what I'd been waiting for from the moment I set eyes on her that day in Mr Allen's class. It was everything.

OK, so it's probably been said a million times, but when I kissed Ella, every single part of me felt weak, as if I'd completely surrendered. It was *the* most fantastic thing imaginable for a few moments, but then she jerked away from me as if some electric current in my lips had given her a shock.

'No, no, no,' she said. 'I am *not* going to be that person, no way.'

'What person?'

'Jack, I'm with Hunter. I'm sorry. Wow, I shouldn't have done that; what an idiot.'

She jumped up from the grass and I followed suit, grabbing her hands.

'Ella, if that's how you felt, then why is it wrong?'

'It's not fair on you or Hunter or anyone,' she said. 'God, I really need to sort my crap out; I'm so, so sorry, Jack. Can we just . . . forget it ever happened, please?'

And the moment was gone. That tiny, blissful moment when I felt like she was mine again – as if she ever had been

– was over. As we crossed the park and made our way out of the gates we didn't speak for a while, then once we were back on the noisy high street, Ella broke the ice.

'OK, let's rewind all that and talk about what I wanted to ask you in the first place,' she said, giggling nervously. 'It's actually about Hunter.'

Jeez. 'What about Hunter?'

'Well, it's kind of an invitation actually. Hunter's dad is having a big event this weekend at their house, to celebrate some massive business deal he's pulled off, so you can imagine how swanky it'll be. I mean, he's having the house set up like a 1950s Las Vegas nightclub, with a casino, and live entertainment, and all sorts of crap. You know, Rat Pack style. He's so well connected and, like, richer than God, so there'll be all sorts of people there.'

'And you want me to go?'

'No, *Hunter* wants you to go. He thinks you're cool, Jack. He says you're smart and most of his mates haven't got anywhere near the nous you have and he'd like to get to know you better. He's heard me banging on about GenNext and how well we all work together, so I guess he wants to feel a bit more involved, do you know what I mean?'

'Involved?' I didn't like the sound of that too much. Nor did I believe for one second that Hunter thought I was cool.

'Look, I know he's going to invite you, Jack, so when he does, please say yes. You'll have a blast, I know you will.'

'I suppose,' I said, half-heartedly. 'Are you going?'

Ella shook her head. 'It's not strictly a boys-only night, but I think that's the general vibe. I don't think many of

Hunter's friends are taking their girlfriends, so I'm not going to cramp his style.'

'So why do you care if I go?'

'Maybe it'll make my life a little bit easier,' she said with a nervous laugh.

How could she even think that after what had just happened, let alone say it? My brain suddenly felt like it was on a final fast-spin cycle and I was totally confused. I had to say something.

'Ella, we can't ignore what just happened. You can't just—'

'No, Jack,' Ella said firmly. 'Not now. I need to think. I need to sort my life out.'

Then she smiled, half closing her eyes as if she were studying me.

'Now, have you got a tux, Jack Penman?'

'I think my dad has.'

Yeah, I know. That was possibly the uncoolest thing I could have said, but this was a bit of a freaky proposition and a pretty wide curve ball. I mean, aside from the meteor-hitting-the-planet-sized event that had happened less than fifteen minutes before in the park, Hunter was a guy who a couple of months back pretended not to even know me and then semi-threatened me in the school corridor. Inviting me into his inner sanctum with all his best mates was a complete 180-degree switch-around, and as far as I was concerned there had to be more to it than Hunter suddenly deciding that he and I should become BFFs. And as for Ella, as for that kiss . . . Well, there had to be more to that, too. I was just going to have to be patient and wait for the right moment to find out what it was.

THE KEY

As I left my house that Saturday night, it crossed my mind how annoyed with me Austin would be if he knew what I was about to do and where I was headed. He wasn't at all happy that I'd been invited to Hunter's dad's casino night, but from what I could tell that was mainly because he hadn't been. Sour grapes, you know? We even got into a stupid argument about it, to the point where I said I wasn't that fussed and wouldn't go if it bothered him that much. So yeah, as far as Austin knew, I was having a rare night at home, binge-watching *The Walking Dead* and filling my face with Domino's finest. And honestly, that was my plan. There was something about the whole idea of spending an evening in the company of Hunter and his rich pals that didn't exactly sit right with me, whether Ella wanted me to go or not. However, when the official invitation to the event was hand-delivered to my house in a black and silver envelope by a fully suited and booted chauffeur, I kind of thought again. In fact, my interest was well and truly sparked.

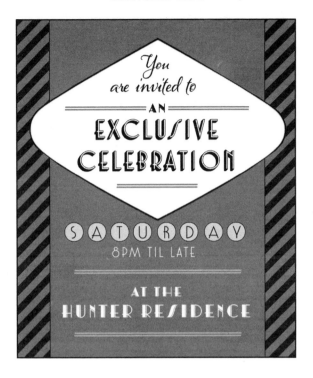

You are invited to AN EXCLUSIVE CELEBRATION

SATURDAY
8PM TIL LATE

AT THE
HUNTER RESIDENCE

Even more enticing was the shiny gold key included in the slick package. I mean, what was that about? You'd want to know, right? Attached to the key was a label with a message: *Jack Penman. For your eyes only. Hunter.* Yeah, I was more than a little curious.

When I jumped out of the cab at Hunter's place, the house looked dark, but when the butler – yes, you heard me right, *butler* – swung open the heavy wooden door, I could see it was full of life despite the dim, moody lighting. As I crossed the hall I passed a mirror, and I have to say, for my first time in a tux I looked pretty darn good. And no, it wasn't my dad's, OK? I bought it online from Top Man with some of the money we'd got for promoting those hipster hair products on GenNext, which I'd also used to slick my hair back so I might come close to achieving that Leonardo DiCaprio, *Great Gatsby* vibe. Just the thought of that made me smile, remembering the first day I met Ella, my wet hair dripping all over her prized copy of the novel. I'd even bought a proper bow tie, not one of those crappy clip-on ones, and I'd learned to tie it myself from a YouTube tutorial.

As I wandered around the party – which as far as I could tell was just a load of flashy blokes a lot older than me drinking whisky from heavy tumblers or puffing on cigars out by the pool – I couldn't see Hunter or anybody else I knew. Ella was right: there weren't many girls in attendance either. Crap, maybe I'd made a mistake coming to this shindig. I mean, there I was, standing in the middle of this huge room surrounded by people I didn't know, without any idea of what to do next. Then I slipped my hand into my pocket and felt the key and suddenly remembered why I was there.

'Cocktail, sir?'

A young woman dressed like a 1950s waitress shoved a silver tray under my nose.

'Er . . . not right now, thanks.'

'OK, well there are beers over at the bar if you'd prefer,' she said.

That sounded like a better idea, so I made my way across the room and out on to the patio, where the bar was set up. For a fleeting moment, my mind flashed back to Hunter's birthday party and I found myself staring at the spot where I'd seen him kissing Ella. I put a stop to that thought pretty fast. Nothing good ever comes of dwelling on bad memories, right?

'Just a beer, please,' I told the barman, who was wearing a better tux than I was.

'Of course, sir.'

Once I'd taken a few gulps, I finally felt relaxed, well, sort of. The thing was, I literally couldn't see a single person I recognised. I mean, where were all Hunter's mates, the guys from school? Come to that, where was Hunter? I looked back into the house and watched as people shoved their chips on to roulette tables and turned over cards, guzzling champagne all the while. It was very over-the-top and, I had to admit, pretty impressive. Were all these people as filthy rich as Hunter's family? It was hard to tell with everyone in tuxedos. I mean, some of them might have been postmen or builders and not rich tycoon types at all. I could have been an heir to a billionaire fortune as far as anyone here knew. I was just pondering that idea when someone cleared their throat, loudly, right next to me.

'Are you Jack Penman?' he enquired.

I turned to see a small, pimply kid I recognised from school – Year 10 – kitted out in an old-fashioned bellboy get-up.

'Seriously?' I said.

'I know, I know, just go with it,' he said. 'Are you Penman or not?'

'You know I am.'

'Do you have your key, sir?'

'Yes.'

'Then would you like to follow me?'

I followed him into the house and up the impressive stair-case to the upper floor, where he walked me along a hall and through another grand lounge – this one deserted.

'Sorry, I've forgotten your name,' I said, quickening my pace to keep up with him.

'Just Bellboy,' he said, and he gestured for me to go straight through the double doors at the end of the lounge.

'That's not your name,' I said.

'It is tonight, Mr Penman,' he said. Creepy. I wondered how much Hunter was paying him, or if he'd just bullied him into it.

I found myself in another, smaller hall with three doors running along it. I took the key out of my pocket and stood there for a moment, thinking that it surely must open one of them. But which one, and why? Knowing Hunter, I'd suspected all along that this might be some elaborate prank to make me look like an idiot, but I was determined to find out either way. I turned around to ask Bellboy which door the key unlocked, but he'd vanished. I was on my own, and as I wandered over to the first door I have to say I felt a bit stupid. There was something rather 'Goldilocks and the Three Bears' about the whole thing: trying the doors, one by one. In the end, I ignored the first two and went straight for the third, and bingo . . . I was in.

'You found us, then, Jack.'

Again, the large room was dimly lit, but I spotted Hunter right away, sitting at a solid square table surrounded by a few of his regular sidekicks plus a few I didn't recognise. Others were milling about the room with drinks in their hands. The room was like a proper old dude's study, with antique furniture, floor-to-ceiling bookshelves, a small, old-fashioned bar, heavy drapes at the window and a Chesterfield sofa on one side where a trio of pretty young women were sitting, all staring at me as if I'd just walked in without any clothes on. I hoped one of them might be Hunter's sister, Fran, but no such luck, so I turned my attention back to Hunter.

'Come in, Jack. Shut the door before my old man finds out where I am,' he said.

I closed the door and moved into the room, coughing slightly with the cigar smoke.

'I feel like I've walked into some kind of secret society or something,' I said, laughing nervously.

'Well, you sort of have,' Hunter said with an arrogant smile.

'What's with all the mystery, then? The secret key and the Year Ten kid dressed up like something out of *The Grand Budapest Hotel*? Couldn't you have just said "Upstairs, first on the left"?'

'There's no fun in that,' Hunter laughed.

'So how come you're not downstairs, schmoozing with all your dad's mates?'

'Oh man, that's exactly what the key and this room is all about, not having to schmooze with my dad's friends. They're totally boring,' Hunter said. 'Only very special people get a key to this room. Only people I choose. The thing is, Jack, my dad doesn't even know this little cubbyhole exists. As far as he's concerned it's the dusty old library nobody ever goes in.'

'So what goes on in here?' I asked.

'Pretty much anything you want,' Hunter said. 'Come and sit down. Have a drink. Have whatever you like.'

OK, I know what you're thinking: that Hunter wanted something – I was thinking the same thing. There was something odd about this whole scenario and part of me wanted to turn around and walk out of the room and out of the party, but a bigger part of me felt compelled to stay.

'Jack, I want you to meet my uncle Callum, fresh off the plane from New York,' Hunter said, steering me over to a thickset guy who looked a bit like Phil Mitchell from *EastEnders*. 'He's kind of in the same game as you, the whole online media thing, but on a much bigger scale, of course.'

'Of course,' I said.

'You guys should chat,' Hunter said, patting me on the shoulder like we were old buddies.

Callum pulled a chair out from under the table next to him, so I grabbed a beer from a nearby ice bucket and sat down between him and Hunter.

'Hunter's been telling me all about your GenNext project,' he said cheerfully. 'I did some research; you guys are getting a lot of attention from the press.'

'Yeah, it's going well,' I said, loosening my bow tie in an attempt to feel a little more relaxed.

'It's good to see young people being entrepreneurial and having success – I like it.'

Young people? Hunter's American uncle looked about thirty at the most. He had an almost-shaved head and piercing blue eyes, but his lips were so thin they were almost non-existent, and although his mouth was smiling, those steely eyes most definitely weren't. He was one of those dudes who just looked immediately untrustworthy; in fact he could have been dressed as Woody from *Toy Story* and holding a basket of kittens and I'd have had him down as dangerous.

'So what does your company do?' I asked.

'We're experts in social media, but what we do best is help people like you,' Callum said.

'How so?'

'Investment, advice, that sort of thing. We help up-and-coming media companies grow,' he clarified.

'Callum's done some pretty amazing stuff over the last couple of years, Jack,' Hunter said. 'Joint projects and partnerships with Google and YouTube . . . all sorts.'

'Oh, right,' I said. 'Cool.'

So was this it? Was this why Hunter had invited me to his super-secret room? A two-pronged attacked to get in on some GenNext action? That must have been what Ella meant when she told me how Hunter would love to feel more involved. I glanced around the room to see what was going on around me, and there was definitely a weird vibe. People kept coming and going from a small room off the one we were sitting in, and when I looked over at the sofa, two of the young women had disappeared while the other was being leched over by one of Hunter's idiot mates.

The rest of the conversation with Callum went pretty much how I'd expected, with him laughing and slapping my back and banging on about how amazing he and his company were, but it was all leading up to the million-dollar question and I knew it was coming.

'So would your GenNext crew be up for talking to me about a helping hand? See what I could do for you? Just an idea, Jack, if you want to move on to the next level.'

I could have written his script myself, and after a few beers I was more than ready for it.

'The thing is, Callum, I'm pretty sure the reason GenNext is so successful is *because* of my GenNext crew, as you put it,' I said confidently. 'We're a team of young people communicating with an audience of young people, and that's why it works. That was our vision and the whole point of it. As things stand, I think we're doing pretty well on our own.'

'Well I'm sure you are, but—'

'Look, I appreciate your interest, Callum, but it's supposed to be a party and I find business discussions at a party a bit boring, do you know what I mean?'

I surprised myself with my bluntness. Callum's eyes were blazing and his thin lips had practically disappeared. He stared at me for what seemed like ages until his face suddenly changed, moving into something almost resembling a smile.

'You're right, Jack,' he said. 'Let's just have a drink, shall we? A proper drink.'

This guy made me feel seriously uncomfortable, but I didn't really see how I could refuse, so I said, 'Sure.'

Hunter yelled over to his barman to rustle up some amaretto sours, which I thought might be gross but actually weren't bad at all.

'Here's to no business talk at parties,' Callum said, holding his half-empty glass in the air. 'Cheers, Jack.'

I clinked my glass to his. 'Cheers!'

'Another?' Hunter asked, grinning. 'As I said earlier, you can drink whatever the hell you like here.'

*

The party sounds cool, right? Wrong! Cut to me waking up on a massive pink sofa with a banging head, feeling disorientated and horribly sick at eleven o'clock the next morning – at least I really *hoped* it was the next morning; I had the sense that time had passed but I had no idea if it was hours or days, or just how drunk I'd got. There was this panicky flutter high up in my chest like something bad had happened, but for the life of me I couldn't think what it might be. In fact, I couldn't remember anything much about the previous night after a certain point. It was weird. I mean, you hear stories about people my age getting crazy drunk and blacking out, but that wasn't something I could imagine happening to me – no way.

It took a while for the fog to clear and for me to realise that I was actually in the upstairs living room I'd walked through the previous evening. There was no one else in the room and no sign that there'd even been a party – the place was pristine. I also had no fricking idea how I'd got there or why the hell I hadn't made it home to my own bed – did someone just dump me here? Was I that much of a mess? I desperately tried to unscramble my thoughts, trying to figure out what the very last thing I remembered was. Was it the second, or the third cocktail? Sure, I could remember being in Hunter's den and the conversation with his creepy uncle, but did we stay in that room for the whole night? I had a weird feeling that at one point I'd been outside in the fresh air, and I had flashes of people shouting and cheering, but those flashes didn't connect to any specific memory I could pinpoint.

I was properly awake now, and the more I thought about

it, the more panicky I felt. I tried to tell myself that I was fine and there was no harm done – except where the hell was my shirt and jacket? OK, something had clearly happened that night, but as hard as I tried, I just couldn't find the missing pieces of the puzzle, and the way I was feeling at that moment, perhaps it was better that way.

THE VIDEO

Sophia Chance-Addison wasn't exactly what you'd call a star, despite what she might tell you, but she was one of those people you just sort of knew because she was on the front of at least two of the celebrity gossip magazines every week. Even if you couldn't quite remember her name, you knew her face, and if you were a young, straight guy, you might be familiar with certain other parts of her body, too, as she wasn't afraid to ditch the vast majority of her clothing for a photo-shoot if the mood took her. She'd originally made her name as 'the blonde bitchy one' on one of those scripted drama-slash-reality TV shows – you know, where a group of mostly attractive friends all sleep with one another and then argue about it in posh restaurants before jetting off to Marbella or Ibiza – but since the show's decline in popularity, Sophia seemed to be aligning herself with anything cool or slightly edgy in an attempt to cast off its cheesy reputation. I guess that's why her agent had asked us to interview her for GenNext back when the site had really started to take off at the beginning of the summer.

Don't get me wrong, we were very happy to get Sophia, as long as she agreed to our terms on the style and content of the interview, which I conducted and which proved amazingly popular with much of our male audience. Ava filmed the segment and spent the entire afternoon rolling her eyes, tutting and insisting that Sophia was shamelessly flirting with me and that I was lapping it up and couldn't keep my eyes off her. I'd argued that as we were both in our swim gear in a bath of chocolate milk, it was very difficult for me to look anywhere else and/or even concentrate. I know, I know, but it was Sai's twisted idea, not mine, and thank God Ella wasn't around that day or I probably would have bottled it completely, but the up side was we got a ton of hits from the interview, plus a nice wad of cash from the company who made the chocolate milk.

Now the reason I'm telling you all this is because the morning after my lost night at Hunter's dad's party, Sophia Chance-Addison started tweeting me – publicly, not privately – saying how much she loved GenNext and how cool it was and how she'd been thinking about me and would love to see me again and that we should get together for dinner sometime. OK, so I'm not dumb; I knew there was a good chance she might just be latching on to me because I was part of something she saw as cool and different, but then I thought, why the hell not? Sophia seemed like a fun girl – if a tad overconfident – and it was about time I stopped mooning over Ella and went out on a proper date, you know? And no, I didn't let Austin's blatantly envious taunts of 'she'll eat you for breakfast, mate' and 'you're punching well above your weight' get to me either. In fact my first date with

Sophia went pretty well, I'd say, once she'd finally got off the phone to her agent, her ex-boyfriend (awkward, lots of shouting) and her mum, and despite the fact that the restaurant she chose served the smallest portions of food ever in the history of the world and I had to go get a Five Guys Bacon Cheeseburger and Cajun fries after I dropped her off in the cab afterwards. We did share a pretty passionate kiss goodnight, though, and although it didn't have quite the shiver-down-the-spine factor that Ella's had a couple of weeks before, it wasn't exactly dog food either. Plus Sophia said she definitely wanted to see me again, and soon, so I'd say it was all good, right?

That same evening, while Sophia and I were just finishing our tiny desserts, I had a disturbing phone call from Hunter's uncle Callum, who was about to board a plane back to the States and was very keen to talk to me about his 'little company' getting involved with GenNext with a view to helping us get to the next level, whatever that was. Initially his tone was friendly enough, so I didn't see any real harm in a quick chat.

'Hey! You're a switched-on guy, Jack. I know you can see the potential in what GenNext could be with the right help and investment,' he said, over the noise of Heathrow airport.

'I suppose so,' I said.

'Exactly. I knew you were smart.' Callum was clearly trying to sound friendly, but there was an urgency in his voice that unnerved me.

'I guess there are all sorts of possibilities when you think about it,' I said.

'And you should grab them, Jack.' Callum laughed, but

it sounded forced. 'Don't get left behind, man. Ventures like GenNext are a dime a dozen; it's only the smart cookies like us who rise to the top.'

'Yes, well I think I'm smart enough to know that GenNext is about the five of us – my team – doing what we do best. It's grown organically and that's the way it needs to continue,' I said. 'We're just fine as we are right now, thanks.'

To be honest, I felt a little bit out of my depth even having that kind of conversation, and it wasn't that I didn't like the idea of GenNext getting bigger or having someone help us. There was just something about Callum that I really didn't like, and that wasn't even taking into account the fact that he was related to Hunter, who, despite his recent efforts to be friendly, was about as genuine as a snake in a suit selling double-glazing door-to-door. The whole thing stank and I wanted nothing to do with it.

'You know, it would probably be a big mistake to dismiss this without seriously considering all the options, Jack,' Callum said, after another speech about how amazing he and all his pals were.

'Look, Callum, I'm really not interested in getting involved with your company or any other company,' I said, putting it as firmly as I could. 'We're cool with the way things are, OK?'

He went quiet; all I could hear for the next few seconds was breathing and the sound of a bustling airport. When he finally spoke again, his tone had changed from smarmy to extremely pissed-off.

'Do you know what I don't like, Jack? I don't like it when I try to be helpful and friendly to someone and they throw it back in my face – that really gets my back up. Don't you hate that?'

'Look, Callum—'

'You know, you'll regret it in the long run,' he said. 'I'm not someone who gets along well with the word *no*. Do you see what I'm saying, Jack?'

There was clearly no telling this guy, and by this time he was coming across like something out of a Guy Ritchie movie, so I bit the bullet and told him to get a life and then hung up. Yeah, I know that might sound all very brave and cool, but trust me . . . I'd just made one of the biggest mistakes of my life.

It must have been about two in the morning when I heard the ping on my phone that signified a text, followed by an email alert on my phone, laptop, desktop computer and iPad one after the other. Then Facebook Messenger beeped its signature beep, followed by WhatsApp. WTF? Somebody was clearly trying to get through to me, so I picked up my phone, staring at it until my eyes adjusted to the light of the screen, then hit play with my thumb and stared down at the blurry moving image.

I jumped out of bed and headed over to my desk, scrabbling round in the dark for my iPad. I tapped the screen, bringing it to life, and quickly located the message with the video attached. Now I could see it properly, but as far as I could make out, it was just some drunk guy stumbling around at a party, drinking out of a bottle, shouting and climbing on to a table, then taking his jacket and shirt off – basically making an absolute idiot of himself.

What the hell was this, and why send it to me? Did somebody expect me to upload it on GenNext or what? Only there was something familiar about the scene, as if I should have known what I was looking at but couldn't quite put my finger on what the hell it was. Then it hit me: the bookshelves and the heavy drapes. This was Hunter's secret room, and it was clearly the night of Hunter's dad's party, so I was there, right? But surely I'd have remembered . . . I would have . . . I would . . .

As the video rolled, I suddenly felt the blood drain from my face and my stomach lurch like I was on the world's tallest drop-ride. The half-naked drunk was now in full performance mode on the table. And yes . . . it was me. It was me on the table. But how was that possible? I mean, can you imagine watching a movie of yourself doing something that you have absolutely no idea you did? It was surreal and scary. And do you know what the worst part about it was? I was singing a One Direction song at the top of my voice, that's what. I was shirtless on a table, singing into a champagne bottle and pretending to be Harry Styles. There's pretty much no coming back from that, reputation-wise, you know?

Eventually the guy . . . I mean, *I* fell off the table and staggered into another table full of glasses, knocking everything flying. The others around me were laughing and pointing and then a couple of them lifted me up, practically dragging me out of the room with my feet scraping along the floor. Then the screen went dark for a couple of seconds, but there was still more to come. When the picture resumed, the camera was close-up on me and I was sitting in the driver's seat of a car, with the sound of people around me cheering and egging me on with cries of 'Do it, Penman. Do it!'

I couldn't believe what I was looking at. It was impossible to comprehend that I could have got myself in such a state, and worse still, got behind the wheel of a car. It was right there in front of me, though, and as the jerky iPhone footage zoomed in and out of focus, I realised that someone was very intent on capturing every single embarrassing moment. I felt sick, and the sheer panic I'd experienced the morning after the party roared back with a vengeance.

As the camera pulled away, I could see that the car was no less than one of Hunter's dad's Ferraris, and I was just sitting there shaking my head and looking ill. All of a sudden, a member of the cheering crowd jumped into the passenger seat and leaned across me, trying to start the ignition. Surely I wasn't going to try to drive the bloody thing? Please, no, I wouldn't have . . . would I?

'Do it, Penman, do it!'

My cheerleaders were getting louder and more aggressive, but in the end I was relieved to see myself stumbling out of the car before throwing up all over Hunter's driveway, the laughter finally fading as the screen went to black.

Once the video was over, I just stood there in the dark of my room in my underwear, desperately searching every corner of my mind for a single scrap of recollection and wondering what the hell this was all about. At that moment every gadget in my room lit up, bleeped and buzzed with a follow-up message.

> **Made a bit of a fool of yourself there, didn't you Jack?**

133

It was obviously a sick joke. I mean, who would even think of doing something like that? Only one person I could think of. I grabbed my phone, furious, but I didn't recognise the number the text came from and there was no contact name on the WhatsApp. So I texted whoever it was a brief message back. Just two words and an exclamation mark; I couldn't be any clearer than that, could I?

Anyway, I couldn't sleep the rest of that night, wondering how it could have happened. I was sure Hunter was behind it, but what was he hoping to achieve? And how did I get in such a mess in the first place? There was more to it than me just having a few drinks, I was sure of that, but at the end of the day, I was the one who'd idiotically put myself in a position to let it happen, and that just made me feel stupid and scared. That wasn't me in that video, or at least any version of me I could ever imagine. Only it was.

I spent the remainder of the night praying that Hunter hadn't shown the video to Ella – or anyone else for that matter, but especially Ella. As it turned out, that was the least of my worries.

Austin was on the phone at 8 a.m., which was ridiculously early for him and not great for me as I hadn't slept a wink.

'What is it, mate? I'm knackered,' I said, yawning and trying to unglue my eyes.

'I don't even know where to start,' Austin said. He didn't sound massively happy, it has to be said.

'What's happening, Austin?'

'What's happening, are you kidding me?' he repeated in an unnervingly high-pitched voice. 'OK, J, I'm going to give you enough time to get up, go online and then call me back. You've got ten minutes, tops.'

Austin hung up the phone and I grabbed my laptop from the floor next to my bed and opened it up. What did he want me to look at? GenNext? Twitter? What? As I opened my Facebook page, the dread was already washing over me, but somehow I just couldn't imagine that Hunter would actually . . . Oh. He had. The video of out-of-control Jack Penman behaving like a complete and utter dick and jumping behind the wheel of a Ferrari was all over my Facebook, with ten thousand views and counting. Twitter was the same, with retweets of the video stacking up before my eyes, and however I tried to spin it in my head, it just didn't look good. It wasn't cool or even funny – well not to me, anyway – it was just reckless and embarrassing. The worst part about it was that the end of the video, with me climbing out of the car and throwing up, had been edited out, so as far as anyone watching was concerned, I might have started the car and driven it away once the camera had stopped rolling. Nice, huh?

By 10.30, I was down at HQ chugging a Starbucks double-shot macchiato and desperately trying to explain to Austin, Sai and Ava that my drinks must have been spiked and that Hunter was behind it because I told his slimy uncle to get lost, and because he'd been out to get me from day one. Sai and Ava listened to me, but they looked sceptical, and I was conscious of the fact that everything coming out of my mouth probably sounded like the paranoid babblings of a madman trying to detach himself from a bad situation. Austin, meanwhile, sat staring at his computer screen with his back to me. He'd warned me not to have anything to do with Hunter and I'd told him I wasn't going to – I'd lied to him. For a moment I tried to imagine how he must have felt watching the video. He was my best mate and I'd hurt him and our friendship. Well played, Jack, well played.

'The question is, why did you even feel you had to hang out with Hunter and his crew?' Sai asked. 'Are we not good enough for you now you're famous?'

'Steady on, mate, of course you're good enough, and I'm not bloody famous.'

'Look, there's absolutely no point in having a go at Jack; that's not going to do anyone any good, is it?' Ava interrupted. 'The main thing is damage limitation. We need to assess what harm, if any, this is going to do to GenNext, right?'

Austin spun around on his chair.

'Well I can assess that for you right now, Ava,' he said flatly. 'I'm looking at an email from the company who were about to pay us a big sum of money to review and feature their new range of sportswear and trainers over the next few months. It says: "We don't feel it would be a viable option for us to associate with a website that endorses the sort of behaviour we witnessed on the video." Great! The hair wax people also want to pull their latest mention offline. Is that a good enough assessment for you so far?'

Before anyone could answer, Ella was at the bottom of the stairs, out of breath.

'God, Jack, are you OK?' she said.

'Is he OK? That's a laugh,' Sai said.

'Ella, it was bloody Hunter,' I blurted out. 'He obviously spiked my drink and this was the result.'

'I'm not sure about this spiking drinks malarkey, Jack, it all sounds a bit too spy-novel to me,' Ava said.

'Jack, I know Hunter can be a bit of a tool, but come on,' Ella said.

'I'm telling you!' I yelled. 'His uncle was trying to muscle in on GenNext and I basically told him where to go, and the next thing I know—'

'Well it sounds feasible to me,' Sai said. 'Somebody went out of their way to film this for a reason.'

'Look, there were loads of people at that party, anyone could have done it,' Ella snapped. 'There's no way Hunter would do something like that for some sort of stupid revenge thing, for God's sake. Maybe you just need to take responsibility and own it, Jack.'

'Or maybe you should go and ask him if he did it,' I shouted back, losing it completely. 'Maybe you need to wake up.'

Ella looked stunned and everyone else just stood there staring at me. I knew it was time to go.

'I'm really sorry, Austin,' I said, calmer now. 'If you guys want me out, then I'll go. Just let me know what you decide.'

And with that I was out of there.

Over the next few days, my escapades at Hunter's dad's party were all over the place. The amount of heated social media discussion meant that, for the first time, GenNext caught the eye of the mainstream media – and not in a good way. There were several articles, online and in the press, commenting on and questioning the behaviour of teenagers in the public eye and making me out to be some sort of devil teen. It got to the stage where I didn't even want to turn on my computer or look at my phone ever again. I pretty much felt like everyone was pissed off at me: my friends, Ella and especially Mum and Dad, who'd hardly said a word to me and seemed completely preoccupied. Everyone, in fact, except Sophia, who didn't seem to have even noticed all the madness online and just kept WhatsApping me to find out when our next date might be.

I didn't know what to do for the best, but I knew I couldn't just sit there and rot in my bedroom, so I pulled myself together and filmed a short apology that I could upload on GenNext. It was nothing too dramatic, just a few words telling everyone how ridiculous my behaviour had been that night and that it wasn't something I was proud of or endorsed in any way. I also made sure everyone knew that even though I had no business sitting behind the wheel of a car in that state, I absolutely did not drive it or even attempt to. What was it Ella had said – take responsibility and own it? Well that's what I was doing.

Two days later, I met Austin, Sai and Ava in a little café near my house for a full English, and I was pleased and somewhat surprised to hear that, after putting their heads together and talking about it, they were unanimous in their conclusion that Hunter was indeed responsible.

'I think it was a set-up from the start,' Sai said, waving his fork in the air. 'If he couldn't get in with GenNext in a legit way, he was obviously prepared to play dirty.'

'I think that's why he invited you in the first place,' Austin said. 'All that mysterious key crap and welcoming you into the fold. It was part of his master plan, and when it didn't work, he resorted to Plan B.'

'The thing is, it's backfired on him massively,' Sai said. 'I mean, yeah, we've had some negative press, but most of the younger GenNext subscribers seem to love you even more, Jack.'

'Seriously?'

'Yeah, deluded,' Austin laughed.

'Have you not seen the comments under the apology you uploaded?' Ava said, putting down her mug of tea and showing me her phone.

'I've tried not to look,' I said.

'There're hundreds of them, and 99.9 per cent are in support of you.'

'The kids all think you're cool and funny, Jack, and our media profile has sky-rocketed. You couldn't make it up,' Sai said. 'Yesterday our subscribers went up massively. I reckon by tomorrow we'll have reached the one million mark.'

'You're kidding me.'

'That's not to say you weren't still a massive tool,' Austin said, punching my arm.

'I know, I know,' I said. 'I'm just glad you guys are still talking to me; that was the worst thing about all this. I'm not sure about Ella, though, after the way I shouted at her.'

'There's something going on with her, but I don't know what it is,' Ava said. 'She's been acting a bit weird the last couple of days. I'm seeing her tonight, though, so with any luck I'll get to the bottom of it.'

I smiled, hopefully, and then the four of us dug into our

plates of egg, bacon and sausage, with half of me feeling like a massive weight had been lifted off my shoulders, and the other half realising that there was no way Ella and I would ever be together. Not while Hunter was on the scene.

THE LOST MOMENT

Sai's uncle AJ turned out to be a good person to know. As well as his partnership in the talent agency, he was a share-holder in The Abacus – a swish private members' club in Shoreditch – and when Sai announced that AJ wanted to throw us a little party to celebrate GenNext signing to the management team at Metronome, I was over the moon. After all the crap I'd been through with the video, I really felt like blowing off some steam and just hanging out with my mates and having fun. In fact we were all well up for it, and for the first time since I'd been friends with the GenNext team, literally everyone was taking a date. It's funny, maybe there was something about having a bit of success that suddenly made us more attractive, I don't know, but all of a sudden girlfriends seemed to be coming out of the woodwork.

That being the case, I fired Sophia a casual text to see if she fancied coming along, without making a big thing of it. Of course, Ella was going to be there and I had mixed feel-ings about seeing her. I mean, half of me was nervous about facing her after I'd yelled at her a few days before, and the other half was still angry that she seemed incapable of grasping the idea that Hunter might be involved in my very public shaming. I also knew there was a distinct possibility that I was going to have to face Hunter himself at the party, but screw worrying about that. If he was there, he was there. I certainly wasn't going to give him the satisfaction of knowing that he'd almost wrecked everything for me and everyone else on the team. We'd pulled it back from the abyss and had come back bigger than ever, and that was all he needed to know.

I caught the train down to London that Friday night, mainly so I could catch up with some of the GenNext emails I'd missed when I couldn't face looking at my computer. The rest of the gang travelled down by minibus, driven by AJ. By the time I got to The Abacus, everything was in full swing: the music was banging, the drinks were flowing, and it looked like it was going to be an epic party.

'As it's my own private soirée tonight, I might have accidentally left a bottle of something fizzy on your table,' AJ said as he greeted me at the neon-blue door of the club's entrance. 'Just keep it on a low one and don't get too lairy, OK?' He winked at me as I headed inside to look for the rest of the GenNext gang.

'You're a star, AJ,' I said, laughing.

As promised, AJ had organised a prime table for us, in a much better spot than the trio of *Hollyoaks* actors who were stuck over on a duff table near the dance floor next to a massive speaker, and as I got closer to our booth, I was relieved to be greeted by a sea of happy faces, all dressed in their finest attire and seemingly in the mood to celebrate.

Ava appeared especially pleased with herself, which was hardly surprising given the cool and rather gorgeous Japanese girl sitting next to her. Ava looked a bit more sophisticated than I was used to. She was wearing her pastel hair up in an artfully messy bun and she had on a short blue skater dress with pumps. Her date looked effortlessly elegant in a loose off-the-shoulder black top over skinny jeans and spiky heels. The two of them were smiling at each other and giggling.

'This is Suki. She works in promotions at the label Cooper has just signed to,' Ava yelled over Calvin Harris. 'Suki, this is Jack Penman – our glorious leader.'

'Good to meet you, Suki,' I shouted back. 'Wow, has Cooper signed his deal already? That's amazing!'

'We had to get in quick; there was a lot of competition from other labels,' Suki said, leaning over the table so I could hear her. 'He's got such a massive following online – it's all pretty crazy. We're dropping his first track next week because there's such a demand.'

I noticed Suki had a tattoo of a swallow on the back of her shoulder, then I remembered Ava's mermaid tattoo and smiled to myself – I had a feeling those two were going to get on just fine.

Austin's date was a Year 13 girl from school, Jess. Yes, she was one of the populars, but then I guess Austin counted as one himself these days, thanks to GenNext. He'd been going on about Jess for ages but had never plucked up the courage to ask her out, especially as she was in the year above and therefore officially out of his league. Then, three days before the party at The Abacus, I received a series of excited WhatsApp messages from him: one telling me how he'd spotted her buying T-shirts in Hollister, the next telling me he was seconds away from walking over and asking her out, and then a final one that just contained about a million happy emojis.

Sai, meanwhile, was on a sort of blind date with a very pretty Scottish girl called Chloe, who he'd met on Tinder and who was studying at the Royal College of Music. Typically, he was being very methodical about the whole thing, telling me in an email earlier that day that it was more of an experiment than a date at this stage, like something out of *The Big Bang Theory*. Still, whatever it was, he looked like he was enjoying himself.

Austin and Sai had scrubbed up pretty well, both looking good in jeans and smart ironed shirts, for once, and with new haircuts. In fact, looking around the table, it was obvious that the success of GenNext had given everyone that extra little bit of sparkle. This certainly wasn't the same group of misfits I'd stumbled upon in the sixth-form common room only a few months before – everyone seemed to have blossomed and gathered a bit of confidence. Yeah, maybe that was why we all had dates that night. Except Ella, that was. She was Hunter-less and on her own, which was a little weird as we were supposed to be celebrating the success of a company that she was the face of, but as she didn't appear too unhappy, I certainly wasn't going to lose any sleep over it. I mean, we hardly ever saw them together anyway; why should tonight be any different? Maybe Hunter was just keeping a low profile because he knew we were all wise to him and his epic failure of a plan to screw us over. Yeah, that was about right; when it came down to it, the guy was nothing more than a sly coward. Poor Ella. Could someone as smart as her really be so blind to the real Hunter?

After a quick-fire round of 'hellos' and 'what's happenings', I sat down and poured myself some champagne – a reasonably small glass to start with, given how badly my last brush with alcohol had gone. Austin leaned across the table, chinking his champagne flute against mine.

'Ah, Jack Penman! Not so long ago we were sneaking Baileys Irish Cream out of your mum and dad's drink cabinet, and now look at us: celebrating our success and sipping champagne at our own private event.'

'Mate, you were the Baileys burglar,' I laughed. 'Can't trust you to do anything right. But I'm happy we stuck together, because as you said, look at us now.'

'Are we going to have a dance later, Jack?' Ava interrupted. 'I'm dying to see you wiggle that cute little ass of yours.'

'I'm not sure I'm prepared to wiggle anything, Ava, but I might join you on the floor, yeah,' I smiled.

Ella threw her head back and laughed.

'I'm really glad you're here tonight and everything's OK, Jack,' she said.

She was smiling, but there was something a little weird about the way she said it. Maybe it was because I hadn't seen all that much of her lately outside of GenNext, or the fact that the last time we did see one another we'd both been so angry. Anyway, I shrugged it off, mainly because Ella did seem genuinely pleased to see me and looked utterly beautiful. I had to admit it to myself, after all these months my feelings for her were still just as powerful as ever, and however much my confidence had grown as far as women were concerned, when it came down to it I still felt tongue-tied when she was around.

Things got even stranger later on when Ella grabbed my hand from behind as I was halfway across the dance floor on my way to get some water, pulling me backwards and spinning me around to face her.

'Jack, where are you going?'

'To the bar; I need a bottle of water. Do you want some?'

'Oh. Well I just wanted to tell you something, that's all,' she said nervously.

'Can it wait? I'll be back in a sec.'

She shook her head. 'Not really.'

'What is it?'

'God, I don't know why, but I actually feel a bit nervous telling you this,' she said.

The club lights were flashing in my eyes, the music was blaring, and the dance floor was packed with people gyrating and twirling and generally throwing themselves drunkenly around to Rudimental, yet there we were in the midst of it all, just standing facing one another like two mesmerised statues.

'Nervous? What are you going on about? Is it something to do with GenNext? Because you know I usually think your ideas are great.'

'No, it's not that.'

She took both my hands in hers and smiled, and then I smiled too, like it was catching or something, and then—

'Jack! Jack, babe, I'm here!'

The happy expression on Ella's face quickly morphed into something quite different and she stopped smiling.

'What's *she* doing here?'

I spun around to see my date for the evening waving at me from the edge of the dance floor. She was almost two hours late; in fact I'd kind of forgotten she was coming at all.

'Sophia, you're here!' I shouted. 'That's . . . that's amazing.'

Yeah, I know. Awkward. And just when Ella was clearly about to lay something mind-blowingly important on me – or at least that was what it felt like. Maybe she was ready to finally acknowledge the fact that we'd kissed, that we'd had a moment that meant something. Whatever it was, it was going to have to wait a while.

I made my way to where Sophia was standing and greeted her with a kiss just as Ella swept past me with a face like a bulldog chewing a wasp. I knew I'd blown the moment. Whatever she wanted to say, it certainly wasn't going to happen while Sophia was around – I was sure of that.

It didn't take long for Sophia to make her presence felt at the party; that seemed to be one of her more blindingly obvious talents.

'Hey, bitches!' she yelled as we reached the table, air-kissing everyone and no one in particular.

Ava looked up at Sophia and then at Ella and then at me.

'Oh, hi, Sophia, how are you?' she said weakly, but Sophia barely registered it.

'OMG! Trust me to get it wrong,' she yapped, looking everyone over and giggling. 'I feel totally overdressed. Jack, you never told me you were all going to be so dressed down and casual.'

Yeah, that didn't go down too well, as you can imagine. Ava and Suki's faces were like a couple of thunderclouds, and Ava's arms were crossed defensively. For a nanosecond, my mind flashed back to the interview I'd done with Sophia, and how unimpressed Ava had been at the time.

'For those of you who haven't met her, this is Sophia,' I said nervously. 'My, er . . . date.'

I clocked another weird little look flash between Ava and Ella – what the hell was going on?

Sophia sat down on my lap, throwing her arms around me and kissing me, and as she pulled her lips away, I could feel the remnants of a gummy smear on my cheek. Ella had this uneasy, fixed half-smile on her face, and suddenly this kind of annoyed me slightly. Yeah, so Sophia was a bit of a live wire, but why should Ella care, especially given her own dodgy romantic choices? Wasn't I entitled to bring a date like everyone else?

'Oh, are you guys like properly seeing one another now?' Ava said, trying to sound bright and breezy but clearly a bit taken aback. 'I thought Jack was coming on his own tonight.'

She hadn't meant anything by it, but it was a bit like banging a tiger's cage.

'Well sorry to disappoint you, darling. I can leave if you'd prefer.' Sophia smiled like she was joking . . . but she actually wasn't.

'Oh no, I just meant—'

'And what does that even mean, "seeing one another"?' Sophia said, talking over Ava. 'It's such a ridiculous expression, don't you think, Emma?'

'It's Ella,' Ella said icily.

'Of course we're "seeing one another",' Sophia went on. 'I think, Ava, what you really meant to ask is are Jack and I—'

'Er . . . she just meant that Jack hadn't mentioned bringing anyone tonight, that's all.' Sai jumped in just in the nick of time.

'Well don't worry, sweetie, I can afford to buy my own drinks, you know,' Sophia said, stroking her Marc Jacobs handbag exaggeratedly.

'Help yourself to champagne, of course,' Sai said.

'I don't need telling twice, babes.' Sophia snatched a champagne flute off the table. 'Are we getting another bottle?'

Austin did the honours and poured Sophia a glass while Ava caught my eye and drew her hand across her throat as if she were pretending to slash it with a knife.

'What do you think of my uncle's club, Sophia?' Sai asked.

'It's all right, darling, but there's nobody here, is there?' she said, and we all glanced around the room, which was positively heaving. 'No one worth knowing,' she clarified.

I guess I'd realised by then that as gorgeous as she was, Sophia's sharp tongue was one of her less appealing qualities. It was pretty confusing for me. I mean, there I was with this gorgeous, sexy young woman who was all over me, but it was happening so fast and I wasn't sure what it even meant, to me or to her. And yes, I knew that half the straight male population of the country would have swapped places with me in a millisecond given the chance, but next to Ella, Sophia was just . . . Well, there was no comparison.

Anyway, things quietened down after that, and in the end there was some good-natured banter across the table. Suki,

Jess and Chloe were all very cool, smart women, and I was happy to sit back and watch my friends enjoying themselves for a while. Ella, on the other hand, did not look like she was enjoying herself and had gone seriously quiet, so when Sophia headed off to the bathroom to touch up her make-up for what seemed like the millionth time, I leaned across to talk to her.

'What was it you were going to tell me?' I said gently. 'It sounded pretty important.'

'Do you know, it clearly wasn't very important at all,' Ella said.

It was one of those statements that us boys never seem to be able to grasp. You know, where a girl will say something and the boy knows that a) there's a hidden meaning in there somewhere and he better figure it out fast or he's dead, or b) she means the exact opposite of what she said and he'd better realise *that* fast or he's dead.

'No, go on. I want to know.'

'Look, we'll talk tomorrow or whenever,' Ella said. 'I was obviously—'

At that moment Sophia marched back into the booth and stood directly between Ella and me.

'Let's take a selfie, babe!' she shouted, waving her iPhone above our heads and pouting. 'I've not posted anything for hours; there'll be sixty thousand Instagram followers out there who'll think I've literally dropped down dead.'

'If only,' Ava muttered, probably a bit louder than she'd intended.

Ella got up suddenly and grabbed her jacket.

'I think I'm going to go,' she said.

'No, don't go,' I protested, but she'd clearly made her mind up.

Ava stood up and hugged her.

'Are you sure you're OK?'

'I'm fine, really,' Ella said. 'I'll call you, yeah?'

Then she was gone and suddenly I wasn't happy any more. I felt like something really bad had happened and it was all my fault, but I had no idea what it was. Out of Sophia's earshot, I scooted up close to Ava to find out.

'Is Ella OK? She looked a bit—'

Ava covered her face with the palm of her hand and shook her head slowly.

'You absolute knob,' she said.

'I'm sorry?'

'She was about to . . . It's what tonight was all about for her, Jack.'

'I don't understand. What was tonight all about?'

'She wanted to tell you that she confronted Hunter about the video and she believes you,' Ava said. 'Before Miss Reality TV was all over you like a cheap coat, she was going to tell you that she's broken it off with Hunter. She dumped him. Because of you.'

Before I knew what I was doing, I was jumping up from the table and sending glasses flying. I practically skidded across the dance floor and up the stairs, out of the club. Maybe she was still outside, waiting for a cab. Maybe she was . . . No. Too late. Gone. I took out my phone to fire her a WhatsApp message, and then I stopped myself. That wasn't going to cut it. Whatever I had to say to Ella, and whatever she had to say to me, it had to be face to face. It would just have to wait until tomorrow. I would make it up to her then, I was sure of it. Oh, and just in case you were wondering, that was the last time I ever saw Sophia Chance-Addison.

THE VERY BAD THING

I came home to find Mum and Dad still up talking in the living room, and as it was after two in the morning, I knew I was in for a grilling about where I'd been and what I'd been up to. OK, so I'd literally had about four mouthfuls of champagne that evening, so they certainly couldn't have a go at me about being drunk. Then again, I guess I couldn't blame them for being a little bit pissed off at me. I mean, I'd done my best to avoid them as much as possible since the video debacle; in fact I'd barely seen them for the past week, and aside from a couple of texts I hadn't even been in contact that much. I sneaked in quietly and was halfway up the stairs, thinking I might just have got away with it, when they came out into the hallway. Dad jumped in first, sternly as he always did – bad cop.

'You're having a laugh if you think you can start wandering in at this time every night, son. Can you come down here and speak to us, please?'

'Ah, Dad, I'm seriously knackered.'

To be honest, I just wanted to get into bed, go to sleep

and forget the whole evening. I was gutted about what had happened with Ella, and the sooner I was unconscious and didn't have to keep turning it all over in my mind, the better.

'Now, please,' Dad said, in a tone that made it clear there was no argument.

When I faced them in the living room, it was Mum's turn, this time with the softer approach – good cop.

'Jack, we've hardly see you for the last few days; what have you been doing with yourself?'

'I've just been staying at Austin's and hanging out with the GenNext team,' I said, shrugging. 'Surely you haven't waited up this late just to ask me that?'

'No, we were up talking anyway,' Mum said, 'but we have been a bit concerned about how fast all this GenNext stuff is moving, and let's face it, your behaviour hasn't exactly been in character lately, has it? Staying out late, and all that stuff in the video: partying, drinking and running around like a mad thing.'

'I told you about that; my drinks were spiked,' I said, defensively.

'Yes, but the fact is you shouldn't really have been drinking so much in the first place, should you?' Dad said. 'Look, I know it's normal for blokes your age to be experimenting with drinking – I get that, Jack, I really do. But given that this company of yours has thrust you into the public eye – really quite unexpectedly – you do need to be careful about how you conduct yourself. At the end of the day, you're still a teenager who has a year of school left to go.'

This was a reasonably calm demeanour for him, and I was quite surprised he wasn't going nuts at me. As I sat opposite them on the armchair, clocking the deadly serious looks on both their faces, I knew they meant business. Mum sighed, and shifted in her seat.

'Look, I know your project is going really well and we are really supportive of that, but Jack—'

'The thing is, Mum, it's not really a project any more, it's a business,' I said softly. 'We're actually earning some serious cash, I've told you that. I can't think of another job I'd be able to walk into at the moment with these kinds of prospects.'

'What prospects?' Dad said.

'Dad, I spend almost all my time working on GenNext. We've got a company account now and we've even taken on management because we can't do it on our own any more.'

'How much cash is "serious"?' he said. 'Because your idea of serious cash and mine are probably—'

'Almost forty thousand last month.'

They both sat in stunned silence for a few seconds.

'For what?' Mum said. 'Are you doing something illegal?'

'No, Mum,' I laughed. 'It comes through featuring certain products on the channel. We get people reviewing stuff, or just name-checking it, and we get paid by the companies who make it.'

'Well that all sounds very impressive, but you've got to keep us more in the loop,' Mum said.

'And can we agree that you'll cool it with the playboy lifestyle from now on?' Dad added.

'OK, Dad.'

I smiled and nodded. I knew how lucky I was to have the parents I did. They were pretty cool and so easy-going compared to a lot of my mates' parents. I mean, Sai's mum and dad were super-strict, and Ava was always having stand-up shouting matches with her mum.

'Well I'm glad we've cleared the air about that, Jack,' Mum said. 'Your dad and I do worry about you and we want to know what's going on in your life, especially with all these big developments happening every five minutes. It's just because we love you and we care, you know that, don't you?'

I nodded and gave her the best smile I could manage given the evening I'd had, but just as I was getting off the sofa, ready to hug her goodnight, she spoke again, almost in a whisper.

'The thing is, Jack . . . well, there's something else that your dad and I need to talk to you about. Something important.'

I sat back down again. There was something about the look on her face that set alarm bells off in my head. She looked pale, and Dad mirrored her expression with his own look of dread.

'I told you I'd been feeling extra tired with all the long hours at the salon,' Mum said. 'I suspected something wasn't right, but I couldn't put my finger on what it was.'

I nodded slowly, a sense of dread creeping over me like a black fog.

'Anyway, when I went to the doctor, he suggested I went to see a consultant at the hospital. Now, I've still got a couple more tests before anyone can say anything for definite, but—'

'Anything definite about what?' I said, swallowing hard. 'And how come this is the first I'm hearing about you having to go for hospital appointments?'

'There was no point in worrying you if we didn't have to,' Mum said.

The fact that she was telling me about it now told me that there wasn't going to be a good ending to this conversation.

'The thing is, if it was just the tiredness, I might not be so worried, but then . . .'

She was struggling to get the words out, and Dad moved closer to her on the sofa and put his hand over hers gently.

'I discovered . . . I found a lump,' she said.

'A lump? What do you mean?' I almost choked on the words, my breath quickening.

'A lump in my left breast, Jack.'

There was a certain way my mum used to look at me when I was a little kid, whenever I was upset or scared. It was a sort of warm-eyed smile designed to reassure me that I was safe and everything was going to be fine. She was giving me the exact same look now. Only it wasn't working like it always had when I was little. It wasn't working at all. I felt numb, like someone had just hit me really hard.

'So . . . so what does that mean exactly?' I said finally.

'Well, it's not looking like it's going to be good news, Jack. I'm sorry. I just wanted to let you know so you can prepare yourself.'

'Prepare myself, right,' I said in a daze.

This was insane. How could anyone possibly prepare themselves for something like this? I looked up at my loving, kind, beautiful mum and I wanted to shout out in anger and smash something. How was it fair that someone who spent their whole life caring for and looking after people could be facing something as terrible as this? I felt tears pricking against the back of my eyes, but I didn't want her to see me cry. I wanted to be brave because I knew she would be.

'So it's not definitely . . .'

'It's not definitely cancer, no.'

Dad was the first one to actually say the word, and when I glanced over at him, he looked almost as wiped out as Mum did.

'Your mum knows her own body better than anyone, and she knows something isn't right,' he said.

'I'm going in for a biopsy next week. Then we'll know one way or another,' Mum said.

I looked down at the floor and watched as a rogue tear-drop escaped from my eye and fell, hitting the carpet next to my foot.

'I'm sorry, Mum. I'm really sorry for everything I've done in the last few weeks. I feel like I've mucked so many things up lately, but it's all going to be better from now on, I promise. Dad and I are going to look after you, aren't we, Dad?'

Dad and Mum both got up from the sofa to come and sit next to me and put their arms around me, and I couldn't help it – more tears welled up in my eyes.

'We certainly are, son,' Dad said.

'Don't start, you'll have me at it,' Mum sniffed, half laughing.

The three of us sat there, arms round each other, for several minutes, while I struggled to get my tears under control. Eventually Mum gave us both a gentle squeeze and pulled away.

'I think we should all get off to bed and talk about this tomorrow,' she said. 'Let's not get all drama queen about it until we know for definite.'

I stood up and gave her another hug, taking a deep breath and pulling myself together.

'You're right,' I said. 'It might not be as bad as we think.'

'Exactly,' Dad said. 'Let's keep positive.'

Up in my room, I lay awake until it was light with a hundred terrible scenarios rampaging through my head. To think that I'd come home imagining that blowing my chances with Ella that night was the absolute worst thing that could have happened, only to be faced with the possibility of something so much worse. I couldn't even begin to get my head around it.

I must have dropped off about half eight in the end, and then I slept. I slept longer and deeper than I had for months, years even. I slept until it was almost dark again.

THE EXIT

With my body clock now completely out of whack, I spent that following Sunday evening in the living room with Mum and Dad, watching whatever they wanted to watch on the Sky planner and talking about everything apart from the actual thing we were all thinking about – the dreaded C word. Halfway through *House of Cards* I got a text from Ava asking me a) where I'd been all day, b) to call her, and c) if I'd seen the pictures from Friday night all over Twitter.

To be honest, I hadn't seen much of anything that day. In fact the only time I'd even picked up my phone was to send Ella a couple of WhatsApp messages asking her to call me. I didn't go into any detail; just said I had to talk to her. As Mum's news really started to sink in, I knew it was Ella's voice I needed to hear – and not even in a romantic way. Forgetting all the other feelings I had for her, Ella was my mate and I knew she'd know the right words to say and the right advice to give me, because she always did. Only my WhatsApp messages were going unread, and by 9 p.m., when Ava texted, there was still no reply from Ella.

To be honest, the last thing I needed that night was to get into a conversation with Ava, who would probably just keep telling me what an idiot I was when I really didn't need to hear it. I'd see her and the rest of the GenNext team the following morning and whatever she had to say could wait until then. I did head straight to Twitter, however, only to discover that the pictures Ava was referring to were mostly of Sophia and me at The Abacus together: Sophia sitting on my lap, Sophia kissing me, Sophia's selfie of us pouting into the camera, directly lifted from her Instagram feed. There were a couple of other candid shots of us holding hands on our previous date thrown into the mix, too. The general twist on the story was that we were the new hot couple, and there were plenty of quotes from her to confirm the rumours, plus with her profile being what it was, I was bound to find myself plastered over the cover of *Heat* or *Closer* the following week, even though our brief relationship was already done and dusted.

I dropped my phone on to the chair next to me and pondered for a minute how completely my life had changed in the space of a few weeks and how utterly bonkers it all was. I mean, was I really sitting there telling myself that my face was going to be all over the covers of national magazines in the next few days like it was nothing? How did that happen to someone like me – and with Mum's news hanging over my head, should I even really care any more?

When I got out of bed that Monday morning, my eyes and my head felt heavy. In fact my whole body felt as though it was being dragged down with lead weights. The fact that there was still no reply to my messages from Ella wasn't helping matters either. I spent twenty minutes in the shower, just letting the water run over my body as hot as I could take it, and while I was shaving I told myself that however bad I felt, and however worried about Mum I was, I couldn't let myself go under. Dad said we had to stay positive until we knew for sure what Mum was going to have to deal with, and he was right. I just had to try to carry on as normal, whatever the hell that was these days. I also had to talk to Ella . . . as soon as possible.

When I arrived at HQ, Austin and Sai were buzzing around like crazy while AJ was pacing around in a slim-cut suit with his Samsung glued to his ear, yapping away and sounding very animated. In the midst of it all, Austin's brother Miles came bounding down the stairs, followed by his mum. 'Sounds like a lot of noise and plotting is going on this morning,' she said, laughing, as she set down five cups of tea and a huge plate of bacon rolls on the coffee table.

'Yeah, it's like CSI Hertfordshire down here,' Miles added.

'So what *is* going on?' I said, after Austin's mum had gone back upstairs. 'Can somebody fill us in, please?'

In the end, Austin did the honours.

'So last night, AJ gets a call from CTA in LA . . .'

'Are you talking in code, mate?'

'It stands for Creative Talent Agency, which is a massive talent agency in Los Angeles,' he clarified. 'Anyway, they have this artist, Harriet Rushworth, who's sold, like, a hundred billion records . . .'

'That many?'

I knew of Harriet Rushworth but I'd only heard one or

two tracks. I vaguely remembered watching a bit of one of her super-high-budget videos on Vevo, but that was as much as I could tell you about her.

'Yeah, she's like cool pop, a bit like a slightly more edgy Taylor but with red hair. She's huge over there and in most of Europe . . . but she's not as big here yet . . . and they want to build her profile, so . . .'

Austin sounded like he could hardly breathe, so Sai shoved a bacon roll in his mouth and took over while AJ continued his ever more urgent-sounding phone conversation.

'They want to promote Harriet in the UK, but they want people to discover her rather than forcing a whole cheesy marketing campaign down everyone's throats . . . and they think GenNext is the perfect tool.'

'They think the direction we've taken is sick and they've asked if we could fly over and film an interview with her for the site ASAP,' Austin said, his mouth still full of food.

'Seriously?'

'Totally!'

'We're going to LA?'

'We're going to LA!'

It took a few seconds for the data to unscramble in my brain, and when it did, I could hardly believe what I was hearing. This was huge. The chance for GenNext to actually go global and really make its mark – our little project that we'd started right there in that basement. It was incredible, only . . . I wasn't exactly sure how I was supposed to jet off to America with Mum's health hanging in the balance. OK, so maybe that part required some thinking, but right then and there I was simply going take a moment to bask in the glorious news and drink a cup of celebratory PG Tips. Surely I deserved that after the last couple of days, right?

'It's all set,' AJ announced, finally off the phone and grinning like a fool. 'We can fly out on Thursday morning. My people at Metronome will coordinate the details with CTA and we'll do the interview with Harriet on Saturday. It's going to be big, fellas, in front of an audience going out live online worldwide.'

'Get in!' Austin said, fist-pumping the air.

Miles wasn't quite as thrilled. 'You guys are so lucky – I want to go to LA.'

'Maybe next time, little bro,' Austin smiled, ruffling his brother's hair.

'Somebody needs to phone Ella,' I said – and yeah, that was pretty much where my happy moment ended.

'I wouldn't bother phoning her, guys.' Ava had just arrived and was standing at the bottom of the stairs, hands on hips, looking like she was about to burst into tears.

'What's going on, Ava?' I said, worried by the expression on her face. 'Where's Ella?'

'She's gone, Jack. I spent half of yesterday trying to persuade her that she was making a massive mistake, but she wasn't having it.'

I put my cup down on the desk in front of me and stared back at Ava, my heart rate rising by the second.

'What do you mean, she's gone? *Where's* she gone?'

Ava sighed and sat down on the bottom step, running her hands though her bleached hair nervously.

'Come on, Ava, this is important,' Sai said urgently.

'You know her dad was about to go to Canada on business?

Well, he asked Ella if she wanted to go with him, and she said yes,' Ava said. 'At the moment she feels like she's done with GenNext; it's all been too much. She knows she screwed up big time with Hunter and she feels like an idiot, and then there's the whole situation with . . . well, you know.'

'We don't bloody know,' I snapped. 'The whole situation with what, Ava, *what*?'

'Look, don't shoot the messenger, right?' Ava yelled, jumping off the step and striding over to face me. 'She felt stupid because she was trying to let you know how she felt about you, and there you were with Sophia all over you like chickenpox, and now she just wants to run away from it all, OK? Do you understand now?'

I suddenly felt like an icy fist was squeezing my heart.

'But there's nothing between me and Sophia; what was she thinking?'

'Try telling her that after she saw all that "hot new couple" crap online,' Ava said. 'Look, Jack, it really isn't your fault. I'm not yelling at you, honestly. I'm just upset because after all these years of being the girl nobody wanted to hang out with, I finally had a best friend and now she's gone and it'll probably be ages before we see her again.'

Ava started to cry, tears spilling out by the bucketload, so I put my arms around her and pulled her close. I'm not going to lie, I felt absolutely gutted, but at the same time I couldn't stand to see Ava breaking her heart like that – it was awful. As Ava let it all out and I did my absolute best to hold it all in, we were joined by Sai, Austin and even Miles in a sort of weird GenNext group hug that seemed to go on for ages, while poor AJ just looked on, bewildered.

Ten minutes later, I left the others to fill Ava in on the news about LA and stumbled out of Austin's house into the greyest of days, and it really was grey in every single way. I felt dizzy and for a while I thought the bacon roll was going to make a reappearance right there on the pavement in front of me. I took a few deep breaths and then I walked for a while, just trying to get my head around the fact that Ella was gone and as far as I could figure there was nothing I could do about it. Not right then, anyway, and maybe not ever. A hundred thoughts flashed through my mind, one morphing into another and then another until I couldn't keep up with any of them. I mean, how was it possible for the universe to make so many bad things happen in such a short space of time? Could someone please answer me that?

As I reached the park and the spot where Ella and I had kissed just a few weeks before, my phone beeped and buzzed in my pocket and I pulled it out. It was a text.

> I'm sorry Jack. I can't do this anymore. Love always. Ella. X

THE THREAT

So what now? There seemed to be a lot of questions that needed answering and not very much time to answer them before we were due to jet off to America to interview one of its biggest pop stars. No one actually said it out loud, but the major question on everyone's mind was, could GenNext even survive without its front woman? I mean, Ella had been the face of the whole thing; she'd been the one that everyone was talking about when we first took off – she was the star – and while Austin, Ava and Sai all seemed convinced that I could step up and take over, I wasn't so sure. Any confidence I'd gathered in the last few months had been shredded in a matter of days to the point where I felt like I didn't know what I was doing any more. All the drama with the video leak, and then Mum's terrible news, and now Ella . . . I'd sort of lost my way, to be honest. The only thing that didn't seem to be going downhill was GenNext's popularity.

After a few heated discussions with the management team at Metronome, it was decided that Austin and I would be the ones taking the trip across the pond, with AJ accompanying us to oversee everything. As much as Ava was dying to go to LA, she said she couldn't even consider missing her dad's fiftieth birthday party, which was that same weekend – particularly as she was taking Suki along and introducing her to the entire family. Poor Sai agreed to stay behind and hold the fort at HQ because his ridiculously strict parents weren't happy about the idea of him going, even though there'd be a member of the family with him.

We were only going to be out there for four days, but I felt pretty indecisive about taking the trip right up to the last minute, what with everything going on at home. After a heart-to-heart with Mum and Dad, who insisted I get myself 'on that bloody plane', I eventually caved. They might have had some reservations about the speed with which GenNext had taken off, but even they recognised that this would be a massive opportunity for us – and one that might not come around again. Mum was due to go for her tests the day after I left, but she insisted that I'd be back before the results came in, and that she'd keep me up to date with everything via WhatsApp and FaceTime. In the end, I told Austin I was good to go. I made a deal with myself that I wouldn't tell him – or the other GenNext members – about my mum until we got her results. I didn't want to put a massive dampener on the trip . . . plus, saying it aloud to my friends would have made it feel even more real and frightening, you know?

The evening before we left for LA, Austin, Sai, Ava and I sat on the abandoned sofa on the roof of Sai's building so we could put our heads together one last time and agree on the vibe of the interview and the kinds of questions Austin and I were going to ask Harriet Rushworth. Earlier that day we'd completely immersed ourselves in her YouTube channel, watching all her music videos plus a bunch of her interviews from American TV shows and a guest slot she did on *Saturday Night Live*. I had to admit, she was pretty amazing. I mean, apart from being a talented writer and performer who made great pop music, she was smart, quirky and emphatic about giving back to her fans and empowering girls and young women. She certainly wasn't the type you could interview in a bath of chocolate milk. No, that wasn't Harriet Rushworth at all.

'The one thing it can't be is boring,' Ava said after we'd run over the questions for the thousandth time. She was frowning and waving her finger at us like a teacher reprimanding a class of naughty five-year-olds. 'It's still got to be us; it's got to be edgy and quirky. Don't go all Hollywood just because that's where you are. At the end of the day it's still got to be GenNext, OK?'

Austin and I both nodded, and I felt a whole swarm of butterflies crashing around in my stomach.

'We'll keep it cool,' I said.

'And you are going to FaceTime or Skype with us every day, right?' Poor Sai looked like he was going to cry, and I felt crap about leaving him behind.

'Yes, Sai, how could I go a single day without seeing that cute little face?' Austin laughed.

Ava jumped up and stood in front of us, looking deadly serious and even more like a teacher.

'Joking aside, this might be make or break for us,' she

said. 'Yes, we were lucky to pull everything back after Jack's little escapade – no offence, mate – but now we've got to withstand losing Ella and that might not be easy, because she was just . . .'

Nobody answered and nobody had to; we all knew what she meant. Everyone stayed quiet for a few seconds; all I could hear was the sound of birds and distant traffic. Then Ava made for the door.

'Right, I'm off to scope out a pressie for my dad's birthday. Good luck, boys; you'll kill it, I know you will.'

Austin followed suit and jumped off the sofa.

'Yeah, and I need to take Jess on a second date before I head off, just to make sure she realises what an all-round amazing dude she's landed.'

'Lucky Jess,' Ava laughed, rolling her eyes.

'Look, I need to leave her wanting more of this,' Austin said, lifting up his T-shirt and exposing what he clearly felt almost passed for a six-pack.

'Tell them what you're *actually* doing with her, though,' Sai said.

Austin looked down at the floor sheepishly.

'My mum's making us a lasagne and we're watching *Avengers Assemble* on DVD with Miles.'

Ava and I laughed, and that felt good, you know? After everything that had happened in the past few weeks, I was determined to get my act together for this trip to LA. To make it the start of something great for GenNext.

We said our goodbyes and then I headed home. There was no question about what I was doing that night, aside from packing, of course. I was simply going to hang out with my mum. Yeah, I know it doesn't sound very rock 'n' roll, but that was all I wanted to do.

Just as I reached my house, a car blasted its horn and almost scared the crap out of me. I whipped my head around to see a white Beamer with blacked-out windows parked opposite my house. I scanned the area to see if there was anyone else around that the blast might have been aimed at – there wasn't. Weird, right? Deciding to ignore it, I turned back and started walking toward the house, but then the car horn blasted again, only this time it was relentless, so I headed over to find out who the idiot was behind it. As I got closer, the driver's seat window lowered slowly, and there it was . . . of course . . . Hunter. He was grinning like a maniac and doing this stupid little wave, like he was greeting a toddler.

'Hey there, pretty boy,' he said, just as I reached the side of the car.

'No Ferrari, Hunter? You must be slumming it,' I said.

'Must be, driving around this neighbourhood,' he said.

I wasn't in the mood to play games. 'What do you want?'

'Not much,' he said, leaning out of the car. 'I just wanted to see how you were getting on after that embarrassing little performance of yours leaked online. What an unlucky coincidence that someone just happened to have their iPhone camera on at the moment you were making a total mug of yourself.' He shook his head in mock disapproval.

I'd been right all along, of course. Who else would have gone to so much trouble to make me look like an idiot for all the world to see? Who else would want to screw everything up for me like that?

'Why did you do it?' I said. 'Why does somebody like you even care about me and what I'm doing? You've got a big house, loads of money; what possible reason could there be for you to start messing around with my life?'

'As usual, you're proving what I've always known about you, Penman: that you've got a very high opinion of yourself,' Hunter said lazily.

'Whatever,' I said. 'Was there anything else I can help you with?'

'There is actually,' he said, his false smile falling fast as his jaw tightened. 'I want to know if it's true about Ella.'

'If what's true?'

'That she's gone; left the country or some rubbish.'

'You mean she didn't tell you?' I gasped in mock surprise. 'Isn't that strange . . . Oh no, wait! She dumped you, didn't she, Hunter? That's right, she dumped you because she found out what a complete and utter loser you are.'

By the end of the sentence I was almost shouting, and Hunter had such fury in his eyes I had no idea what was going to happen next. I could only ever remember someone looking at me with that much hatred once before: the time those two idiots attacked me at the back of the bus, putting me in hospital. It crossed my mind that Hunter might be about to try the same thing, but instead he just sat there in his car, fuming.

'It was your fault she finished with me,' he spat finally. 'It's your fault she's gone, and don't think for a minute I'm going to forget that.'

'If that's what you need to tell yourself to help you sleep at night,' I said, turning to walk away.

I was over this now; I just wanted to get indoors, back to my family. As far as I was concerned, this chapter of my life – the chapter that contained Hunter and anything in his world – was closed.

'You can walk away with that smug grin on your face if you like, Penman, but trust me . . . it won't last long.'

I stopped in my tracks and turned around to face him again.

'What's that supposed to mean?' I said.

'You know me, Jack.' There was a sudden eerie calm in his voice. 'Watch this space; the fun's not over yet.'

He started the engine and I felt my blood run cold. Now I really did feel like I was back on that bus. Surely he was just spouting off, right? Surely all this crap was over now. Still, I wasn't going to let him have the last word. Not this time.

'You're no gangster, Hunter; you're just a rich kid with too much time on his hands. Pathetic. Do everyone a favour and go drive that thing of a cliff, will you?'

This time there was no retaliation from Hunter; he just chuckled to himself and shook his head like I was some sort of idiot. He revved the car loudly and then pulled it into reverse so suddenly that I had to jump backwards out of the way. I watched him speed off, following the car with my gaze until it was out of sight around the corner, leaving me standing in the middle of the road feeling extremely unnerved.

OK, so I was fazed for an hour or two by Hunter's threats – wouldn't you have been? By the next morning, though, after I'd thought about it with a clearer head, I realised how weak and pathetic it all was. I truly almost felt sorry for the guy; I mean, what was he going to do anyway? I certainly wasn't going to put myself in a position to be caught up in any more of his scams to ruin GenNext. Hunter was over; he just didn't want to admit it. In fact, as far as I was concerned, the minute the chauffeur-driven black Jag XJ pulled up outside my house at 7 a.m. to take me to the airport, it was a case of Hunter who?

'I like your style, AJ,' I said, climbing into the car after dumping my bag in the boot.

'I thought we should start as we mean to go on,' AJ laughed from the passenger seat.

Austin had been picked up first, and I scooted on to the back seat next to him. He looked a bit bleary-eyed and tired, but gave me a smile as if to say, *yeah – this is actually happening*, so I nodded like I'd read his mind.

As we headed along the motorway towards Heathrow, AJ took us through the details and schedule of the trip. It was just four nights, but pretty full on.

'First off, Harriet Rushworth is throwing a launch party tonight and we've been invited,' he said. 'Now, you know LA is eight hours behind the UK, so by tonight you'll be like zombies if you don't get a few hours of shut-eye on the plane. That shouldn't be a problem, though, because you'll have a nice flat bed to sleep on.'

'Seriously?' Austin perked up.

'We're being flown out Virgin Upper Class,' AJ said, grinning. 'Now tomorrow morning, not too early, I've agreed to a meeting with a company called Herald Media. I've checked them out and they're a very big deal out there, with a ton of money and an impressive client base. I've got an idea they want to talk about partnering with GenNext or something along those lines. I'm not certain that's something we want at this stage, but I spoke to Angela Linford, the company president, and she seemed very keen to meet with the two of you. In fact she's paying a pretty decent fee just for us to turn up at the flipping meeting. It seems like overkill if you ask me, but they're enthusiastic – *very* enthusiastic – so I've agreed to go with a proviso that we don't have to commit to anything, fee or not.'

This was a surprise to me, and not necessarily a good one. I'd already staved off one company with an interest in GenNext and now here was another one already. Still, instead of blowing AJ's idea out of the water without at least hearing him out, I decided to bide my time and keep positive.

'I suppose the more people we get to know out there the better,' I said. 'It can't hurt to listen to what she's got to say.'

Austin agreed, and I sank back into the warm leather of the Jag's back seat, listening to AJ reel off the rest of the itinerary. For the next thirty minutes I sleepily watched the world whizz past me, wondering what would be in store for us when we got to LA, speculating how two young guys from Hertfordshire would cope in a situation with real superstars in actual Hollywood, worrying about my mum's test results – although I tried not to dwell on that one for too long, as it scared the hell out of me – and yeah, you guessed it, thinking about Ella. What was she doing now? I wondered. Was she missing GenNext? Did she even know all this was happening? Was she thinking about me? And just how bloody far was it from Hollywood to Canada?

THE LA LIFESTYLE

Wow! What wasn't there to like about Los Angeles? Everywhere I turned, I felt utterly dazzled. The glorious sunshine, the palm trees, the beachfront properties in Malibu, the criss-crossing freeways with four lines of traffic, and, of course, that iconic Hollywood sign, nestled up in the hills above. There was so much to take in, and when I looked over at Austin as we pulled into the underground parking lot of our hotel in West Hollywood, I knew he was feeling exactly the same.

That afternoon, AJ surprised the hell out of us when he announced that Harriet's management had rented us a car so we could do a spot of sightseeing before the party that evening – an actual Ferrari. As you can imagine, Austin and I didn't need telling twice, and before long we were bombing around LA, taking in the sights, cruising past the swanky shops on Rodeo Drive, stopping for 'Double-Doubles' at In-N-Out Burger, and then parking on Hollywood Boulevard so we could jump out and peruse the stars on the Hollywood Walk of Fame. I can tell you, sitting in that Ferrari in our

Ray-Bans with the warm Californian wind in our faces felt totally incredible. If someone had told me six months ago that I'd be doing this during my summer holidays, there's no way I'd have believed them, and of course I couldn't resist taking a couple of pictures and uploading them to Instagram.

Just a couple of hours later we were walking into The Blind Dragon – the venue where Harriet Rushworth was throwing the launch party for her new single – and that was something else altogether. Austin and I strolled down a red carpet, roped off and lined with security guards who were holding back a growing crowd of eager fans, all dying to catch a glimpse or grab a photo of the star of the evening or one of their favourite celebs who might be in attendance. By the time I got inside, I had spots floating around in front of my eyes with all the camera flashes going off in my face, and Austin looked like he was about to faint. AJ was close behind us, and while Austin and I just stood in the foyer of the building, stunned and not quite knowing what to do next, he ushered us through quickly.

'Will we get to meet her today? Harriet, I mean,' Austin said breathlessly. 'And will she even know who we are? Well, she might know who *you* are, Jack, because she'll have seen you on GenNext, but she won't know me, will she, the guy behind the scenes? Will you introduce me, AJ? Will you make sure you do that, because I don't want to look an idiot, do I? And also I promised Miles I would, like, get a picture and something signed or . . .'

Austin was doing what he does best: talking. In fact he was positively babbling. I gave him a stern look as we left the foyer and entered the bustling main room.

'Austin, if you ask Harriet Rushworth, or anyone else, for an autograph, I am going to kill you, do you hear me? We need to look like we belong here, not act like fangirls.'

Austin looked to AJ for support but AJ shook his head. 'Not cool, Austin, not cool,' he said.

'Sorry, boys, I can get a little bit star-struck,' Austin said sheepishly. 'It was the same when I met Ant and Dec after a charity footy match once – I could hardly speak.'

It was total chaos in the room, with more and more people swarming into the swanky bar area, which was fitted out with plush red furniture and oriental-style lanterns hanging down from the ceiling.

'It's not exactly exclusive, is it?' I said, referring to the sheer volume of people as the crowd swelled, but then I spotted a young woman in square geek-chic glasses waving energetically at me as she headed towards us. She was wearing a plain white T-shirt and faded jeans, so she was clearly staff and not one of the glammed-up party guests.

'Hey, guys, you're here!' she said in a chirpy American accent, shaking our hands vigorously. 'I'm Millie, Harriet's PA – it's so great to meet y'all!'

Austin looked at me with a raised eyebrow and I tried not to smile. Why was everyone in America so bloody enthusiastic?

'You need to follow me and put these on.' Millie handed us silver plastic wristbands and set off through the crowd, her brown ponytail bobbing behind her.

We followed her to a smaller room off the main bar with a couple of security guards flanking its entrance. Millie held up her silver-banded wrist, and once we followed suit, they opened the doors into a softer, darker atmosphere.

'This is the VIP room,' Millie said. 'It's completely crazy tonight, so just kick back and enjoy yourselves in here. We'll catch up on Saturday afternoon at the interview, then Harriet will have a chance to say a proper hello, OK?'

She gave us a wide smile and AJ thanked her while subtly preventing Austin, who was holding a five-dollar bill, from trying to tip her. When we ventured further inside, we found that this room was indeed a lot less manic than the main bar, but within seconds of sitting down at a table in the quietest corner there was already someone heading towards us, trying to get our attention. This time it was a heavy-set guy with dreads, wearing a quilted silver jacket and wrap-around sunglasses – despite the fact that it was pretty dark in there – with what looked like diamonds on either side of them. Nice!

'Hey, guys, Justin asked if Jack would like to join him at his table over there,' he said. 'And the rest of your party, of course, Jack.'

The guy turned and looked back across the room. I followed his eyes to the table in question and nearly choked.

'We don't know any Justin, thanks,' Austin smiled. 'But tell him we said hi.'

The guy shrugged and walked away and I stared at Austin like he was an alien.

'What are you doing?' I said, in a ridiculously high-pitched voice.

'Look, you're bound to meet fans and followers, J, but we can't go mingling with everyone. You said it yourself, we need to be a bit elusive and look like we belong here.' Austin clearly felt like he was finally getting into the Hollywood show-business vibe.

AJ started to laugh. 'Who do you think you are, Austin, Lady Bloody Gaga?'

'But . . . but . . . the Justin he was talking about was Justin Bieber,' I said, pointing over at the table. 'Look! What is he going to think now we've blown him out?'

Austin wasn't listening, though. As soon as I mentioned the Bieber, his veneer of cool completely vanished and he was halfway across the room before I could take a breath or even finish the sentence. AJ and I got up and followed, and by the time we reached the table where Justin and his entourage were hanging out, Austin was gushing about how we'd love to join them, what a big admirer of Justin's tats he was, and how he was dying to get seriously inked himself, just as soon as his mum gave him permission. Yeah, kill me now – that was what I was thinking. Justin didn't seem to care, though. He just smiled and invited us to sit down and join him and his friends, which of course we did.

The rest of that evening was like some kind of crazy hallucination. I mean, I was actually sitting chatting with one of the biggest pop stars in the world, who actually knew who I was and what we'd created, and what was more, he loved it – it was insane. About half an hour after we'd sat down, there was some kind of big commotion over at the entrance to the VIP room; the space lit up with camera flashes and a bright beam of light coming from the film crew who were backing into the room.

'It's Harriet,' Austin said, as half the room jumped out of their seats to get a better look.

For the next five minutes, I watched in awe as Harriet

glided effortlessly around the room, smiling, chatting with guests, greeting friends and answering questions from the TV crews and journalists who clustered around her. She looked totally gorgeous in a short, strapless gold dress decorated with tiny beads, and her distinctive mane of hair tumbled down over her shoulders like a red waterfall. In the midst of it all I could just about see Millie, her ponytail sporadically poking out of the crowd as she darted around, efficiently, making sure Harriet didn't get stuck with the same reporter for too long.

'She's kind of amazing, isn't she?' I said, glancing over at Austin, whose eyes were out on stalks, like a cartoon animal.

'She's coming over,' he said, elbowing me, and before I could open my mouth to answer, Harriet and half her entourage were upon us and once again I was temporarily blinded by the flash of half a dozen cameras.

Millie pushed through the photographers and took charge. 'OK, guys, that's enough for now. Let's give Harriet some time to enjoy the party; there'll be more opportunities for questions and photos later.'

As the flashes subsided and Millie ushered the scrum of followers out of the VIP room, Harriet leaned across our table and blew a friendly kiss at Justin, rolling her eyes as if to say, 'How crazy is all this, dude?' while he nodded in empathy. She looked down at Austin and me with a smile that could have lit the whole room and held her hand out to me – to be honest, I wasn't sure whether to shake it or kiss it, like she was royalty or something – but then she changed her mind and went in for a hug before pulling up a chair and sitting down next to me.

'Well you're just as good-looking in real life as you are on screen,' she said, still beaming. She touched my arm lightly. 'Nice physique, too.'

'Oh . . . thanks.' I was more than slightly taken aback by her directness. 'I'm trying to watch what I eat – not too much sugar, you know?' OK, I don't know why I said that. What was I, a bloody Victoria's Secret model?

Luckily, it made her laugh. 'You wanna try wearing this dress for half an hour,' she said. 'I've eaten nothing but lettuce for two days in preparation, but as soon as this launch party's over and done with, there's a tub of Ben and Jerry's Caramel Chew Chew with my name on it up in my mini-fridge.'

'Sweet,' Austin said, and Harriet spun around to face him.

'Sweet indeed,' she said, nodding approvingly. 'You must be Austin; named after the city I was born in.'

'That's me,' Austin said, just as Millie returned, hovering over Harriet with a cocktail.

'They sure breed 'em sexy over in the UK, huh, Millie? Just look at you two,' Harriet said, leaning in towards Austin. 'Are you boys, like, together? Because you would make a *really* cute couple.'

Austin looked horrified and I giggled. It was weird; I knew Harriet was just playing her part, being the perfect pop-star host, but there was something so warm and charismatic about her, and her upfront, flirty nature was funny as well as sexy.

Millie knelt down beside her boss with a slightly pained expression. 'Harriet, I know you've only just sat down, but the guy from *Rolling Stone* has *finally* turned up and wants to say hello. If it were anyone else I'd tell him to take a hike, but we are doing the cover shoot next week, so . . .'

Harriet sighed and stood up. 'Duty calls, boys, but it was lovely to meet you – short and sweet though it was – and I'm so looking forward to our live chat on Saturday. I'm real excited about being on GenNext.'

I stood up just as she did and she planted a soft kiss on my cheek.

'We're excited too,' I said, 'and it was great to meet you. Enjoy your Ben and Jerry's.' I gave her a wink and she flashed one more amazing smile at me before disappearing into the crowd again.

After that, Austin and I were up and working the room like pros and it felt like everyone knew who we were and why we were there. I laughed, talked, listened and learned and I seriously couldn't remember a time when I'd ever felt so alive. It was *the* most fantastic buzz and I couldn't wait to show everyone what GenNext was really all about when we did the big interview in a couple of days' time.

By the time we got back to the hotel, I felt completely shattered. I'd heard about jet lag but had no real idea what it was, and what it did to your body . . . by then my body was telling me that it was 9 a.m. UK time and I seriously needed to crash. The trouble was, once my head hit the pillow, my mind was crammed full of that evening's events and I still couldn't get off to sleep. In fact, right at that moment I felt so alive I thought I might never sleep again.

THE OFFER

So there we were the next morning, sitting around a weird space-age-looking glass table loaded down with a massive box of Krispy Kreme doughnuts and cartons of Tropicana orange juice, in the offices of Herald Media in Universal City, Burbank. To be honest, I wasn't feeling good vibes from the minute we walked out of the elevator into the unfriendly, sterile environment, but maybe that was because by that time my brain and body didn't seem to know whether it was morning, noon or night. Whatever happened, I'd told myself I was going to keep an open mind. Just like AJ said on the car journey over there, the people at Herald Media had offered to pay for our time, so we at least had to be professional and show our faces.

'You might be the hottest thing since Netflix right now, boys, but we don't want to slam the door in anyone's face at this stage,' he told us. 'That would be a big mistake.'

Austin, who was looking very sharp in a shirt, jacket and slim-cut khaki chinos, seemed a little more intrigued about the whole thing than I was, and while we sat making introductory small talk with the company president, Angela Linford, and her male counterpart, it dawned on me that he might be more open to some kind of involvement. In fact, I wasn't really sure what he thought. Jeez! Maybe I should have discussed it with him before we walked in; maybe we should have had a game plan. Typically, I'd just imagined he'd be on the same page as me – sure that GenNext didn't need anyone else – but I didn't really know.

Angela was a tall, self-assured blonde in her mid-thirties with the whitest teeth I'd ever seen. Her business partner, Tyler, looked like Will Smith, only a bit younger – tall, super-confident and totally slick. They were exactly the kind of people you'd expect to meet in Hollywood and both looked like they could have been movie stars themselves, or at least robot versions of movie stars. They were a bit too perfect for me and I found it all slightly disconcerting.

'Jack, Austin, we are truly thrilled about the prospect of working with you guys,' Angela said. She gave us a shiny white smile so wide I imagined you could see it from space. Hang on, what the hell? She seemed to have assumed that working with us was a definite. Beside me, AJ looked a little taken aback.

'Sorry, can you explain what you mean by that?' I said, doing my best to sound polite. 'You're a big company out here in LA and we're working out of a basement in Hertfordshire. I mean, what's the attraction for you guys?'

'We may be thousands of miles apart, but we know something hot when we see it, Jack,' Angela said, her eyes gleaming. 'Yes, you may be a small operation, but you're already known all over the world. You've tapped into a way of presenting and interviewing and reviewing that people love. It's captured the zeitgeist; the essence of now. I'm talking about an investment on our part, Jack, a coming together of ideas. We would love GenNext to become a part of what we have here at Herald, and we feel we can offer you something in return. Something we have that you don't.'

OK, now I was convinced that Angela was an actual robot. Her patter sounded so rehearsed and phoney; it was like she'd reeled it off a thousand times and just changed the names to suit the occasion. My stomach was tying itself into a knot just listening to her. I looked over at Austin, who was nodding along with Angela as she spoke, and my heart sank like a stone when I spotted the eager expression on his face.

'And what is that?' I said, finally.

'I'm sorry?' Angela said, smiling pleasantly.

'What is it you have that we might want?'

'Money, for one thing,' Tyler jumped in. Jeez, this guy didn't beat around the bush.

'GenNext is doing pretty well financially,' AJ said calmly. 'If it's just a money thing, then—'

'Our clients are some of the biggest companies out there, Mr Perera,' Tyler said. 'Soft-drinks companies, fast-food chains. Waving a few hair products in front of a camera for a couple of hundred bucks is an impressive start for Generation Next, but we're talking a whole different ballgame here. This is about us seeing the potential for development in this project, and providing you with the resources to take it into the big league.'

Tyler definitely wasn't as nicey-nice as Angela was clearly trying to be; in fact, he was pretty bolshie. I wasn't at all keen on him, and I think Angela sensed my discomfort because she jumped right back in to smooth things over.

'What Tyler means by development is – well, you guys have some rough edges that we could help smooth out. You're still inexperienced, but there's a charm in what you do. It's won you such a big audience so far and it's something we can really tap into. Let me tell you a bit more about the sort of vision we have for you.' She sat forward and smiled again. 'Ultimately we're talking about creating a fresh new brand for Generation Next that we could sell to one of the big networks out here, with, eventually, the prospect of a major new prime-time TV show. Ella Foster certainly has a great face for the small screen, so the idea is that she and you, Jack, could even end up anchoring the project yourselves. The possibilities are endless; you see that, don't you?'

I flinched at the mere mention of Ella's name, and Austin shot me a worried glance. We hadn't mentioned her sudden departure, obviously. And what did Angela mean – that Herald would sell our brand, and that Ella and I could 'even' end up anchoring the project ourselves, like that wasn't a certainty? Surely she didn't imagine we were just going to hand GenNext over to them and walk away, did she?

'Look,' Tyler said, 'Herald Media are in the business of building brands and commercial success. That's where we can really help you guys.'

'Well, we definitely like the idea of commercial success, right?' Austin said nervously. AJ nodded.

'And what about connecting with your audience?' I said. 'What about that?'

'That goes without saying,' Angela said, the toothy grin making a sudden reappearance.

'You see, the thing is, I think we know our audience better than anyone,' I said.

Angela and Tyler gave each other a swift look. 'Well *of course* you know your audience, Jack,' Tyler said patronisingly. 'Our plan would be to expand that demographic; make GenNext really fly. There's a lot of money to be made if you—'

'We're talking *a lot* of money where you're concerned,' Angela said, smoothly cutting her partner off before he could get my back up any more. 'A life-changing amount, in fact.'

Austin was still nodding, like he'd been hypnotised or something, and I looked over at AJ, who'd stayed eerily quiet throughout, just to see what he might be thinking. I couldn't read his expression, or make out what his reaction to this pair was. What was it Angela had said? Smooth out the rough edges? Network TV? The whole point of GenNext was that teenagers could dive in and watch whatever content they wanted whenever they wanted; it wasn't some lame weekly programme you could nestle between a crappy game show and *The Real Housewives.*

It suddenly hit me that I didn't have anything else to say to these people – I'd had enough. It was just like Callum all over again, but now I was in a fancy office instead of at a fancy party.

AJ picked up the slack just as I clammed up. 'It's very important to the guys that they feel they still have full control over their own company,' he said, firmly. 'GenNext is something they've built from the ground up; they don't want to let go of it just when things are getting exciting.'

'Mr Perera, we wouldn't dream of having it any other way. Isn't that right, Tyler?' Angela put her hand over her heart, her eyes wide and innocent.

Tyler nodded, slowly and, to me, unconvincingly.

Angela went on, 'It's clear to us that Austin and Jack here are extremely talented and informed – how else would they have created such a phenomenon? If they were to partner with Herald, they would of course retain full creative input and control.' Her voice was laden with an insincerity that seemed lost on Austin and – worryingly – on AJ, who looked like he believed her.

'What do you think, guys?' Tyler leaned over the desk towards Austin and me. 'Can you see yourselves living in a nice pad in West Hollywood? Great car, beautiful weather, successful global company?'

Austin's eyes widened at this. He was smiling like something amazing was going on, clearly entranced by the possibilities.

'Look, why don't the three of you grab a coffee and read through our proposal, and then if everyone's happy we can move forward and get some contracts under way?' Angela said, sliding sheets of paper across the desk towards us.

'What, *now*?' I sprang into life again, practically yelling the words.

'We'd like to move quickly on this.' Angela flashed another megawatt smile, as if the deal was already in the bag. 'It's an amazing opportunity for all of us, and it would be great to get the paperwork signed whilst you're in town.'

There was definitely a control panel somewhere under her smart black dress, I was sure of it. I sat motionless, horrified at the prospect of being strong-armed into a deal right there and then, hoping that AJ would put the brakes on this madness.

'No, Jack's right,' AJ said eventually, getting up from his chair. 'This is something we need to digest properly and discuss with the other members of the team.'

I felt a massive surge of relief sweep through my body as he spoke.

'Well don't digest for too long, Mr Perera,' Angela said, the fixed smile slipping slightly. 'As you'll see from the figures, this kind of partnership deal doesn't come along every day. I'm afraid that with such an enormous investment involved, I can only extend the offer for a limited amount of time.'

'I see,' said AJ, frowning. 'And how long would that be?'

'The offer will stay on the table for the duration of your stay in LA. Any longer and we'll be obliged to withdraw it,' Angela said pleasantly. She glanced briefly at me, her gaze momentarily cool. 'I do advise that you consider it *very* carefully. You may not find another quite as generous.'

'Right.' AJ looked a little uncomfortable. 'We certainly will. Thank you very much for your time, Ms Linford, Tyler.'

'You'll be hearing from us very soon,' Austin added eagerly, clearly unable to help himself. I could practically see the cartoon dollar signs flashing in his eyes.

'I'm sure we will, Austin,' Tyler said smoothly, gripping Austin's hand like they were old friends. When he shook my hand, it was a different story – cold and indifferent. He'd obviously realised that I wasn't quite as sold on the virtues of Herald Media as Austin seemed to be.

We said our goodbyes, smiled politely and then, finally,

we were in the elevator, heading down. I was so happy to be back out on the street again, soaking up the gorgeous California sunshine. I'd felt as though I couldn't breathe in that room, but even out in the fresh air, the sense of dread I had about Herald and their plans for GenNext was growing by the second.

The moment we were outside the building, Austin confirmed my worst fears.

'Oh my God, wasn't that incredible? Boys, we've been in LA for less than a day and we've been offered a partnership with a major media company. Sweet!'

'Sweet? Are you kidding me?' I snapped. 'I couldn't wait to get out of there.'

'What do you mean?' Austin looked horrified at my outburst of negativity.

'I mean they don't get what we're about. They want to change us – didn't you understand that, Austin?'

'I understand that they want to develop GenNext, but why is that such a bad thing?' he said, slightly bewildered. 'Isn't that what we wanted, to get bigger and better? Isn't that why we came here in the first place?'

'Yes, of course, but those people, they were just . . . just . . .' I felt like I was losing the plot and couldn't believe I was even having to explain this to Austin when it was so obvious.

'Just what, Jack?'

'They were . . . there was just something dodgy . . . they wanted to move way too quickly. GenNext should be about the five of us and our philosophy, not some big corporation. We've still got a long way to go before we start thinking about someone else coming in and taking over. We've . . . Oh, I don't know.'

'No, you obviously don't know,' Austin said, shaking his head. 'Sometimes I don't get you at all, J, I really don't.'

'OK, let's not argue the point right outside their office,' AJ interrupted, ushering us away from the front of the building towards a nearby coffee shop. 'You boys are clearly coming at this from different angles; we need to sit down and talk it through.'

'Come on, J, we've got to at least think about it,' Austin said.

But I'd thought about it already and I knew that I wanted absolutely nothing to do with Herald Media.

Once we were inside the coffee shop, the debate got even more heated, to the point where AJ gave up trying to referee between the two of us and went to grab us some lattes. I was horrified that Austin could see anything good about this proposal, but he seemed completely into it. What was up with that? Didn't he have any faith in what we were doing, in what we had already done? AJ wasn't much help either, telling us that he could see both sides and wanted to look through in detail what Herald were actually proposing before he decided which side of the fence he was going to come down on.

I sat there for a while, sipping my coffee and brooding about the meeting, and then I reminded Austin that we'd agreed not to make any decisions about anything until we'd Skyped Sai and Ava. That was one of the coolest things about the GenNext team – everybody got to say their piece, and every decision we made had to be a unanimous one. I tried to banish the thought that our fifth member wasn't around to be a part of the decision-making process this time. I felt sure that Ella would totally get where I was coming from and that she'd agree that there was something weird about Herald and their insistence that they wanted a piece of us.

AJ took his laptop out of its case and connected to the coffee shop's Wi-Fi.

'Let's do it right now,' he said. 'I did tell them we'd make contact late their time, right after the meeting, so they'll be waiting.'

It was good to see Ava's face flash up on the screen in front of us as we all huddled around AJ's laptop, waving like idiots. Sai was peering over Ava's shoulder, grinning.

'I'm so jealous right now, guys,' he yelled. 'It's bucketing down with rain here and you're out there – I'm well depressed.'

Everyone laughed, and then I blurted out what was really on my mind.

'Have you heard anything from Ella, Ava? Has she messaged you? How is she?'

'Just this,' Ava said, tapping at her phone and then holding it up for me to read.

> Missing your face, babe. Hope everything is cool with you and Suki. Canada is a bit boring but a change of scenery much needed. Send my love to the boys. xoxoxo

'Is that it?' I said, a little deflated.

'I'm afraid so,' Ava said. 'What's happening out there? How was the meeting?'

'It was awful,' I said.

'It was amazing,' Austin said, almost simultaneously.

Sai and Ava looked confused as Austin made an attempt to elbow his way in front of me and hog the camera, shoving me out of the way.

'So which was it, amazing or awful?' Sai said.

'Awful!'

'Amazing!'

I shoved Austin back and he flew sideways off his chair.

'I think we'd best start from the beginning,' AJ said, helping Austin up off the floor. 'It's a long story and we're going to need to go through every detail.'

Over the next fifteen minutes, Austin and I talked Ava and Sai through the meeting, argued our points, and generally yapped over one another while the two of them watched us attentively through the screen. I was almost out of breath by the time I'd finished my diatribe on how awful and manipulative I felt Herald Media was, and I thought I'd done a bloody good job of convincing them I was talking sense. I was wrong.

'Look, Jack, this is something we need to at least consider,' Ava said. 'OK, so we don't jump into it without further talks, but this seems like a massive opportunity to me.'

'Me too,' Sai said, nodding furiously from behind her.

'And that's what I've been saying,' Austin said, banging the table. 'We just need to think about it. And we need to think about it *fast*, because we've only got three days to make up our minds before they withdraw the offer.'

I suddenly realised I was losing the battle, and that was when I got angry.

'Ava, you weren't there,' I said, raising my voice. 'Herald are, like, the opposite of everything we stand for: corporate, controlling . . . I had a really bad feeling about it and you of all people would hate it, I know you would.'

'Maybe I would, but I still want to know more,' Ava said. 'I think we should at least move forward and talk to them; let AJ get to grips with what the offer consists of.'

'We've all potentially got university fees to think of. We could set ourselves up with a deal like this, man. Maybe buy our own flats and cars,' Sai agreed. 'We can't just dismiss it.'

'Don't you think I want a flat and a car, Sai?' I said, jumping out of the chair. 'I want all that but I want it on *our* terms, not like this.'

After that everyone just started shouting, all desperate to be heard. In the end, we were politely asked to leave the coffee shop because we were disturbing the other customers, but not before I'd reminded everyone of the GenNext rule regarding decision-making – it had to be unanimous if we moved forward, and this very definitely wasn't.

'If you want to keep me as the face of GenNext, then this isn't happening,' I said firmly.

I could sense that everyone was getting increasingly pissed off with me, and it wasn't a good feeling, I can tell you. Apart from the brief fall-out after my leaked video, we'd barely even had words before, let alone a transatlantic shouting match. Still, this was important. GenNext, and everything it stood for, was at stake and I wasn't going to keep my mouth shut no matter how annoyed the rest of the team were.

'So you're happy to hold us all back, are you?' Ava snapped.

'I've got nothing else to say,' I yelled, walking away from the table. 'That's my final word.'

I didn't wait for AJ and Austin to come out of the coffee shop. Instead I got out my iPhone and ordered an Uber before firing Austin a text telling him that I'd be back in a couple of hours. I just needed to be on my own for a while, you know?

I took the Uber to Venice Beach and then I hopped out and walked along the boardwalk, which stretched out in front of me, side by side with the Pacific Ocean. I watched the skaters and the rollerbladers, the bodybuilders and the buskers. There were street vendors and performers everywhere I looked – everything from break-dancers to people walking on bits of broken glass, mime artists and musicians. It seemed so lively and beautiful, and yeah, I felt happy and excited being surrounded by all that, I really did.

There was something else, though: a weird melancholy feeling pulling inside me, right down in the pit of my stomach. Have you ever experienced that? Waves of happiness and sadness all at the same time – optimism and a sense of doom hand in hand. The euphoria of last night paired with the horrible meeting of this morning. The thing was, just at that moment, I couldn't even work out exactly what it was that was making me feel like that. Was it the fight with my friends about Herald? Was it my mum? Ella?

All I knew was that I had to pull myself together, because over the next couple of days the stakes were going to be high and I was expected to shine. Only right then and there, I didn't feel very shiny at all.

THE GOOD NEWS AND THE BAD

I hung out on Venice Beach a lot longer than I'd planned to. In fact, I only decided to leave when I remembered Ella's warning that my skin was the kind that burned easily and it dawned on me that the last thing I needed on top of everything else was to look like a bloody tomato interviewing a massive pop star the following day. I'd thought long and hard about messaging Ella, or even calling her, as I sat on the wall overlooking the beach, just staring out to sea. In the end I didn't. Mainly because I couldn't stand the thought of her ignoring my call or not wanting to speak to me, or anything else that was going to make me feel any more alienated than I already did. I wasn't ready to go another few rounds with Austin and AJ either, but deep down I knew we had to come to a fast decision about the Herald Media offer, so I stood up and took a breath. It was time to face the music.

When I arrived back at the hotel, AJ and Austin were hanging out in the lobby drinking coffee, and let's put it this way, neither of them looked especially joyful. I sighed and trudged wearily across the deep carpet towards them, expecting another argument or at least the cold shoulder from Austin.

I decided to sound as upbeat and breezy as humanly possible, even though I felt like crap. 'What's happening?'

'Sit down, Jack,' AJ said, and I complied, dragging a seat from a nearby empty table and facing them both. Austin was looking at the floor rather than at me, which I took as a worrying sign that something bad was about to happen.

'Look, we've had another conversation with Sai and Ava,' AJ said. 'We've all agreed that you didn't exactly cover yourself in glory in the way you handled the situation, but we also know how passionate you are about GenNext and that you only behaved the way you did because of it.'

'Like a spoiled brat,' Austin said, looking up and peering at me through his floppy fringe – and hang on, was that a sly smile I saw flicker across his mouth? 'We all agreed – Sai, Ava and even me – that if you were so against Herald then we really couldn't go ahead with it. As good as it sounded, it's not worth fighting about, not with the Harriet interview right under our noses. Ava reckons if Herald want to invest then other companies will too. Maybe someone we're all happy with next time. You know, I wasn't exactly delirious about the way it all went down, J, but when I thought about it, Ava's right – what we've done is amazing and it's only going to get better. Plus, we've already lost Ella; we can't lose you too.'

'That's . . . that's amazing,' I said, nodding humbly. 'I mean, I never wanted us to fall out like that, Austin; it's too good, what we all have together. I just had this gut feeling, a bad feeling, do you know what I mean?'

Austin shrugged and nodded, and I wanted to jump up and down and run around the hotel lobby whooping and cheering, but I decided that might be a bit much so I just quietly thanked them both for understanding.

'And now we have to let Angela and Tyler know that we're turning down their very generous offer,' AJ said.

'God, I didn't even look at the paper,' I said. 'Exactly how much have we turned down? Actually, don't tell me. I don't think I want to know.'

'No, you really don't,' AJ said, getting up and shaking his head.

'Actually, AJ, I'd like to call Angela myself, if that's OK with you,' I said. 'She did give me her cell number.'

AJ looked more than slightly relieved. 'Be my guest,' he said. 'That was not a call I was looking forward to. Be nice, though – no gloating.'

'It's all cool, AJ. I'll be totally professional.'

AJ smiled mysteriously and rubbed his hands together. 'Now, in other news, you'll need to pack your suitcases again in the morning.'

Austin and I looked at one another, confused. 'What . . . why? We're not leaving till Sunday evening,' I said.

'You guys are leading a charmed life,' AJ went on, chuckling. 'The Harriet interview is now taking place at The Four Seasons, and because you were both such a big hit at the launch party last night, her management team at CTA have reserved us some rooms there, just for tomorrow night. Boys, we've been upgraded.'

'What?!' Austin said, jumping up and slapping my back. 'That's fricking amazing.'

That was when I felt the terrible pressure of the day evaporate from my body, hover above my head for a moment and then disappear into the atmosphere. Thank God!

Once AJ and Austin had gone up to their rooms, I sat quietly in the lobby for a moment, absent-mindedly twirling Angela Linford's business card around in my hand and thinking about what I was going to say. Sure, I was going to get a huge amount of satisfaction from telling her and that smarmy Will Smith clone to get lost, but at the same time I wanted to stay true to my word and remain completely professional. Eventually I took a deep breath and dialled the number Angela had scribbled on the back of her card, and waited . . .

'Hello, Angela? It's Jack Penman. Yes, I'm well, thank you. Look, I'll cut to the chase. I just wanted to let you know as soon as possible that I've talked your offer over with my colleagues and after great consideration we've decided that GenNext is not ready to partner with Herald Media or anyone else at the present time . . . Yes, you're hearing me correctly . . . Yes, I'm clear on what that means and everything you said, but . . . No, I'm absolutely not crazy; I know exactly what I'm doing. I'm positive. We're fine on our own, more than fine, and we won't be taking this offer any further . . . Well, you can call Mr Perera but he'll tell you the same. Look, I'm sorry, I have to go, Angela, we have this big interview to prepare for and . . . I'm sorry, I really do have to go.'

And that was it. The deed was done and the Herald Media

offer was no more. To be honest, I'd been expecting more
of an argument, maybe even raised voices, but that wasn't
the case. Yes, it was clear that Angela Linford was angry,
but there was a steely coldness about her that was more
unsettling than anything, all the bright and phoney enthusiasm of this morning blown away like smoke.

After I hung up, I took a couple of deep breaths, put my
phone back in my pocket, then stood up and headed out of
the lobby with a tight-lipped but relieved smile on my face.
Now I felt better. Much, much better.

It didn't last long. That lovely little buzz of elation I
experienced as I stepped inside the elevator and hit the button
for the fourth floor was to be short-lived.

After a quick meeting in the corridor outside our rooms, we
all agreed that room service and a rented movie was the
order of the night. Austin and I were both still jet-lagged
and knackered and knew we had to be razor sharp the
following day for Harriet. Part of me wanted to ignore the
restraints of my tired body and hit the town – I mean, we
were only in LA for a few days; surely we should be making
the most of it, right? In the end, common sense and a few
stern words from AJ won out, and once I'd shut the door
of my room and fallen back on to the exquisitely soft bed,
I knew we'd made the right decision. In fact, I didn't even
make it to dinner time – I was asleep before nine.

Sometime later I was jolted awake, sitting bolt upright
and breathing hard. I'd had one of those dreams – you know
the type – where your brain is throwing all kinds of weird,
panic-inducing stuff at you. I was swimming in the middle

of the ocean, completely alone, and diving down into the deep, dark water. Every time the water closed over my head, the panic would surge up and I'd be frantically turning, searching for the threat I was sure was just behind me . . . And then bam! A great white shark streaked through the water towards me, its enormous mouth wide open, rows and rows of needle-sharp teeth ready to tear into my flesh . . .

I awoke from the nightmare with a heart rate like a marathon runner, drenched in sweat. I looked over at the clock radio next to my head; it was 1.47 a.m., and that was it, I was wide awake. I don't know why, but even as the memory of the dream slipped away and subsided, there was still this sense of panic hanging over me, as if something was very wrong but I couldn't quite put my finger on what it was.

I sipped some water and then fumbled about on the nightstand, locating my phone and holding it up to my face to check for messages – nothing. I decided to call home and speak to Mum, find out how she'd got on at the hospital the previous afternoon. OK, so she probably wouldn't have any results yet, but I just wanted to make sure she was all right. I was thousands of miles away and I knew that if I just heard her voice I'd feel better – calmer, somehow.

When she first answered, Mum's voice was a croaky whisper, but the second she realised it was me, it brightened.

'Jack! It's so good to hear your voice; your dad and I have been itching to know how it's all going and what you've been up to. When's the big interview?'

I was relieved to hear that familiar chatty quality in her tone. It was a happy sound and that gave me hope. The news was going to be good, surely – or at least, not terrible.

'Never mind me, Mum, what happened at the hospital? How did you get on – did it hurt?' I wasn't entirely sure what the tests entailed, and if I'm honest, I didn't really want to know. I hated the thought of Mum going through anything that involved needles and pain.

'Oh, it was just, you know, the usual,' Mum said, as casually as if she'd just been queuing in the post office for a book of stamps. 'Everything takes ages – you hang around to see a nurse, and then you wait even longer to see a doctor, and then you come away none the wiser; it's always the same. Then there's all that medical jargon; you need a degree just to understand what it is they're talking about half the time. My head was spinning by the time I got out of there.'

Mum was talking but she wasn't really saying anything that had any meaning. She chattered on a bit more about the friendly receptionist who'd checked her in and the uncomfortable chairs she and Dad had to sit on for ages, and it was then I noticed that her bright tone had a brittle edge to it – there was something slightly manic in her delivery. She was keeping something from me.

I sat up in bed. 'Mum?'

'We spent almost an hour just waiting in the canteen,' she went on. 'Actually, the food there's not bad, for a hospital canteen. Your dad had a jacket potato and—'

'MUM?' Now there was silence on the other end of the line and all my hope fell away. 'What did the doctors say, Mum? What's happening? Please tell me.'

She sighed, long and slow. 'We wanted to wait until you got home, Jack, that's why I didn't phone yesterday. We didn't see any point in ruining your trip because, well, what can you do anyway?'

My heart felt as though it was caught in my throat and I swallowed hard to push it back down. 'It's fine, Mum, just tell me.'

When she spoke again, the brightness had disappeared completely. 'I'll just . . . I'll just get . . .'

There was some muttering and rustling on the line and the next voice I heard was Dad's.

'Jack, your mum has breast cancer.' He spoke softly, like he was trying to comfort a child. 'We suspected as much but now it's been confirmed. They got the results back practically straight away as they didn't want to keep us hanging on.'

I bit my lip and gripped the phone tight. 'Right.'

'It's in her left breast,' Dad went on. 'She'll go in for an operation, probably the middle of next week, to remove all the bad stuff and then she'll have chemotherapy, probably six doses over the next few months, then they're talking about possible hormone treatment.' There was a brief pause, and then I heard him sigh. 'This is going to be very hard for your mum, and it's going to be tough on us as a family, too. I'm sorry to do this over the phone, son, I really am. As Mum said, we wanted to wait until you got home, but here you are calling home, so . . .'

For several seconds I was speechless. I felt as though I'd been pushed off the top of a very tall building and I was falling fast, the g-force pummelling my face, waiting for the inevitable crash.

Then Mum was back on the line, her voice more purposeful now.

'Jack, I'm going to beat this. It's operable, and the treatment these days is amazing, so I'm going to get through it, do you understand?'

I nodded as if she could see me, but the tears were falling so fast that I was scared to speak in case it all came tumbling out and she heard me crying. I really didn't want that. So I just whispered a 'yes' and then listened to her talk about the inconvenience of going into hospital, about Dad's inability to grasp the most basic of culinary skills and the fact that she'd have to prepare and freeze dinners before she went so we didn't starve; I listened to her tell me that I'd have to download *Game of Thrones* and *Midsomer Murders* on her iPad for when she was recuperating because she still hadn't got the hang of how to do it, and I listened to her tell me how lucky she was to have the family around her that she did. See, that's my mum. Even at a time like this, there she was telling me how lucky she was.

Then her voice lowered to almost a whisper. 'Listen, Jack, while your dad's popped to the kitchen, I need to tell you something, something very important.'

'I'm listening, Mum.'

'Whatever's happening here, with me, you have to carry on with your life,' she said. 'You've done amazing things over these last few months and you've *got* to keep on; work harder than ever and be the absolute best you can be, do you understand me? That's really, really important.'

'I . . . I think so,' I said.

'Good,' Mum said, with a smile in her voice. 'I don't need to be worrying about you as well as me, do I?'

'I suppose not,' I said.

Before we hung up, I told her I loved her and that I'd see her in just a couple of days. After that, I sat in the darkness wondering how the hell I was even going to get through the next couple of days. I was completely gutted: hollow and heartbroken. How could this be happening to my mum? I just couldn't get my head around it. Everything else that had happened that day – the Herald offer, the fight with Austin, Ava and Sai – suddenly seemed so trivial and stupid.

What seemed even more stupid was the fact that I hadn't had the guts to call Ella and tell her any of this: about Mum, about my real feelings for her. That was going to have to change. To use that ridiculous TV expression, I was going to have to man up. I had to call Ella, hear her voice, speak to her. I had to tell her how I felt about her, because life was too bloody precious not to. And I *would* call her. Just as soon as the interview with Harriet was out of the way and I could think straight, that was exactly what I was going to do.

THE BLACKMAIL

The following morning – you know, the one at the start of the most important day of my life so far – well, I wasn't feeling too great. You can understand that, right, after the news I'd had. The thing is, no matter how hard I tried to concentrate on all the positive stuff that Mum had told me during our phone conversation, my mind just kept tripping over into the negative, the sad, and the downright terrifying. So once I was up and out of bed – and that took a while – I just sort of blundered around like a trapped moth: banging first into the bathroom door and then the wardrobe door and then treading on all my crap, which was strewn about the room as I tried to pack, ready to move hotels. In the end, a cup of strong coffee followed by a long, hot shower helped bring the world into focus a little, while the chirpy buzz of *Good Morning America* in the background distracted me from my dark thoughts long enough for me to get my act together. I just needed to get today done and dusted and then I could get home to Mum, to my family, where I belonged right now.

Finally packed and still swathed in a complimentary fluffy

white bathrobe and slippers, I grabbed my phone to call AJ and find out the schedule for the day and what time we were leaving for The Four Seasons. That was when I spotted the text message; it must have come in while I was in the shower.

> **You might want to reconsider our offer, Jack.**

WTF? No contact details, and the number was a complete mystery, but surely it could only be from Herald Media, right? I mean, what other offer was there to reconsider?

As I was staring down at my phone, trying to fathom out what the message even meant and why on earth Angela Linford or Tyler would embarrass themselves by sending me such a random text, it buzzed with life again. Another message – same number.

> **We have something you might not want the world to see.**

This time the message was immediately followed by a photo of a girl and a guy – actually it looked more like a screen grab than a photo. The girl was on a bed, half naked, and the guy was . . . Hang on . . . I widened the photo with my fingers, enlarging it as much as I could, my heart thumping in my chest. It was a bit blurry and the guy had his back to the camera, but . . . the blonde hair, the nose ring . . . I couldn't be one hundred per cent certain, but the girl looked like . . . like Ella. Exactly like her. But how? How the hell would Herald even have such a photo? Was this a joke? Had some hideous Internet troll photo-shopped Ella into some tacky porno shot?

I stood there, my wet hair dripping on to my iPhone screen, trying to piece together a jigsaw of haphazard information in my head. Then another message arrived with another screen grab, this one more explicit than the last but the face, the features, much clearer. It *was* Ella. It was her. What the hell was going on?

> There are more where these came from. A whole video. Reconsider the offer or this goes viral.

My mind was all over the place, and I seriously expected to wake up at any second. What was this anyway – some kind of James Bond, Bourne trilogy blackmail crap? Was I actually supposed to take it seriously? I mean, how was it even possible that Herald could have got hold of a video of Ella in that kind of situation? Surely she couldn't have known there was a camera – no, of course she didn't. I wanted to throw up, the whole thing was so sick and revolting.

I glanced back down at my phone, my heart rate going up a notch – as if that was even possible – as I looked again at the guy in the screen grab. It was just the back of his head in one shot and a shadowed profile in the next, but could that be him? Could that be Hunter? Oh. My. God. Jack, you idiot! Of course it could be . . . of course it *was*.

Within a few seconds, I'd thrown my phone down on the bed and was hunched over the desk in one corner of the room, hammering the keys of my laptop, filled with adrenalin and dread as the penny finally began to drop. OK, Google – *Herald Media, location* . . . no; IMDB . . . no; Facebook . . . no; *shows produced by*, *website*, *career opportunities* . . . no, no, this wasn't it. Come on, there had to be something. OK, try again. Google – *Herald Media staff, Herald Media CEO* . . . Images, yes, that was what I needed, images. I scrolled through a few dozen images of logos and screen shots of TV shows I hoped never to see before I finally double-clicked on what I was looking for: a handful of photos from some low-rent awards ceremony – definitely not the Golden Globes: 'The Herald Media team toasting their success in the Most Popular Daytime Quiz Show category'. And there they were, staring up at me, champagne flutes raised and cheesy grins from here to Mars: Angela Linford, Tyler Masterson, and standing next to them, 'founder and owner of Herald Media, Callum Connor'.

I jumped up from the desk, knocking the chair over and laughing out loud like a maniac – mostly at myself. So this was what Hunter meant when he warned me there was much worse to come. And how stupid had I been not to figure out that Callum's company *was* Herald Media – or at least that there was a connection? Sure, it had seemed a little weird that GenNext got one big offer right after the other, but I had no idea Callum's company was anything like the huge corporation that Herald had turned out to be. I wasn't sure if everything suddenly made sense or if I was just losing it. I wanted to kick myself for not checking all this stuff out before the meeting – but that ship had well and truly sailed. The only thing that mattered was what I did next and how I retaliated. OK, I needed to send a return message, right? Tell them I knew who was behind the video and that I wasn't going to give in to their blackmail. Or should I ignore it? Was it just a bluff, an idle threat? I also needed to warn Ella that all this was happening, but how I was supposed to deliver *that* piece of news was completely beyond me. Oh God, somebody tell me what to do, please!

There was no time to think. Before I could make any sort of a move, AJ was hammering on the door of my room and angrily reminding me that I was supposed to have been downstairs in the lobby twenty minutes ago. I threw my laptop into my bag, grabbed my case and opened the door, heart still thumping.

The second AJ saw me, his face dropped. 'Jack, what's wrong? You look bloody awful.'

I opened my mouth to blurt out everything: Callum, the video of Ella, the blackmail, my mum, but something stopped me in my tracks. Call it instinct, call it a gut reaction, but something caused my mouth to shut like a trap.

'What is it, Jack?' AJ said again.

'It's . . . it's nothing. I'm just not feeling very well. I think I might have a bit of food poisoning,' I lied.

AJ's face softened. 'Oh, Jack, sorry to hear that. Are you going to be OK?' He put his hand on my shoulder, squeezing it firmly, and for a second I thought I might actually cry. There was just too much to think about; too much information to process, and I was trying to do it all on my own.

'Yeah, I'll be fine,' I said, attempting a smile. 'Let's go.'

As I followed AJ along the hall towards the elevator, I wondered if I could do a runner. Maybe I could just jump in an Uber and head back to Venice Beach; sit there in the gorgeous sunshine looking at the sea until I made sense of everything and could decide exactly what to do. There was no chance of that, though. Before I knew it, a porter had taken my bags off me and AJ had hurried me out of the hotel's front door. Almost immediately, a car pulled up in front of me – a blacked-out SUV, no less – and within thirty seconds I was in the back with Austin and AJ, pulling out of the hotel driveway and heading for The Four Seasons Hotel . . .

Oh . . . and I guess that's where you came in.

THE INTERVIEW (PART 2)

So there you have it. You're bang up to date with everything – right up to the minute. I'm perched on a stool next to Austin with a camera in my face and an audience of potential millions watching, and I've just announced to the world that my shoelace is undone. Nice. Austin is staring over at me, the denim-shirted host is staring at me – I don't even know his name – in fact the whole audience is staring at me, clearly waiting for something to happen. You can see now why I might be all over the place, right? This is a life-changing moment, a career highlight involving a massive pop star, yet I'm engulfed in a stinking quicksand of takeover bids, sex tapes and blackmail. Yeah, that. It's not the kind of thing a seventeen-year-old would normally be dealing with, is it? All I can think about is what the hell I'm going to do to stop everything tumbling down around my ears – and more importantly, wondering how I'm to save Ella. Any ideas?

Just as her name flashes through my mind, so do the images on the video I received five minutes ago. The video followed the threatening phone call, just as we were on our way to do the interview, which followed the mysterious text messages earlier that morning. They were all from the same, blocked number. Callum and Herald Media have a video of Ella in a compromising position with Hunter, except that he's been mostly cropped out of the video so the focus is all on her. I'm finding it hard to get my head around the idea that even an idiot like Hunter would stoop so low and do something so vile to somebody he was going out with just a few weeks back, but there's no doubt. It was Hunter's voice I heard on the phone a few moments ago, threatening to release the video – I'm sure of it. And after the incident with me at his party, I have absolutely no doubt that he's prepared to do it. It's pathetic, really. The video isn't even that bad, nothing you'd call hardcore. It's enough, though. Enough to destroy Ella and maybe ruin her chances of building a career on what she started with GenNext.

'Jack? Jack, do you need a drink of water?' Austin says, leaning sideways on the stool and shaking me out of my trance.

I've been staring down at my untied shoelace while poor Austin tries to hold it all together, chatting to the guy in the denim shirt and answering questions from the audience as best he can. When I finally look up, it's clear that all eyes in the room are on me. Most of the audience are wearing frowns and speaking in hushed tones, like 'Who's the nutter?' and 'What drugs is that dude on?'

Eventually I look over at Austin. 'No, I don't want any water. I'm cool, seriously.' Only I'm not cool. I'm not cool at all. The guy in the denim shirt, who's been doing his best to get a word out of me for the past few minutes, looks vaguely panicky and glances over at Duke for guidance. Duke, meanwhile, is waving his arms about like an out-of-control helicopter. I can't be certain but I think the essence of what he is trying to convey is let's-wrap-this-crap-the-hell-up-and-get-to-the-main-event-fast. I look back over at the red light on the camera, which is now blinking, and I'm not sure if that means that it's off or that I'm still being beamed around the world looking like a total nut-job.

Denim Shirt is talking again, only now he's really animated.

'Folks, it's finally time for the main event of the evening. Please welcome our special guest, Harriet Rushworth!'

As the room erupts in cheering and applause, I look down to find AJ right in front of the stage, looking like he's lost his mind and is about to kill someone. Actually, not some-one . . . me.

'What's wrong with you?' he hisses, but all I can do is shrug my shoulders and shake my head, wiping the sweat from my brow with the back of my hand as Harriet appears, striding regally through the parting crowd and stepping up on to the stage. Austin is looking at me like his life depends on it, but as hard as I try, I cannot for the life of me remember what I'm supposed to be asking Harriet, or what we're even doing here. I mean, this isn't what GenNext is about, is it? Sitting on stools and interviewing people like Graham Bloody Norton or Jonathan Ross. Surely we should be doing this on a roller coaster or something. That's what we do, right? My mind is wandering wildly, and I can see Denim Shirt's lips moving as Harriet sits down opposite me, but the only sound I can hear is my own heart, thumping in my ears. It occurs to me that I haven't taken a breath for several seconds, and suddenly I feel like I'm gasping for air. Is this what a panic attack feels like? Am I going to faint in front of half the world's teenagers?

Harriet gives the crowd a little wave and settles down, ready for the interview.

'It's so good to be here. Thank y'all for coming out today.'

The audience gives another cheer, and now it's over to us. Duke waves madly at me to start, and I sit up and clear my throat, trying to push the rising feeling of panic back down, but it's not working.

'Hi. Hi, I, er . . . I . . .'

Harriet clearly senses that all is not well – maybe she thinks I've got stage fright or something – and she jumps in to fill the void like the professional she is.

'So, Jack, I'm thrilled to be here with you GenNext boys.' She smiles that wonderful smile, but her eyes are flashing panic. 'I hope you're not going to ask me anything too embarrassing; I know how you boys operate.'

I stare her dead in the eye for a moment and finally I manage to speak. 'How . . . how was the ice cream?'

'I'm sorry?' Harriet looks at Austin, then at Denim Shirt and then at the audience.

'You know, when you took your dress off the other night; the Caramel Chew Chew, remember?'

Yeah, I'm totally babbling, I know, but by now my mind is sludge. It's pretty much all over for me up there. Apart from the nervous giggling from the audience, I can see the glimmer of a hundred smartphones as people try to capture the moment.

Austin jumps in with a desperate question. 'We were going to ask you about the new video, right, Jack? The video?'

The video, the video. All I can think about is the video I saw less than ten minutes ago, that horrible video of Ella, and then I think about what it will do to her, and I know I have to do something right then and there . . . I just have to . . .

Before I realise what's happening, I'm jumping off my stool and stepping down off the stage.

'I'm sorry, I have to go.' There's a squeal of feedback as I crash into a nearby microphone, knocking it flying. 'Sorry, sorry, I have to get out of here.'

AJ grabs me as I climb down off the stage, frogmarching me through the audience and into a small room off to the side. Once the door is closed behind us, he lets rip, but I can't really hear what he's yelling because I'm too busy concentrating on trying to breathe; to slow my heart rate down. We're quickly joined by Duke, who's accompanying a beetroot-faced Austin, and I can hear one of Harriet's tracks blaring out of the speakers in the main room.

'You guys just wait here,' Duke says icily. 'We're going to reset and get *our* guy to do the interview. *He's* a professional.'

I find a chair and sit down, finally managing to catch my breath.

'Can I get some water, please?'

'J, what the hell happened out there?' Austin says, waving his arms in front of my face. 'You were totally fine up in the room earlier and then you just fell apart. God, you were going on about Harriet taking her dress off, and Caramel Chew Chew, whatever the hell that is – you sounded insane. What's going on?'

'Is it the food poisoning – are you feeling ill?' AJ says, sounding more concerned than angry now.

Austin looks both furious and confused. 'What food poisoning?'

'It's not that,' I said. 'It's, it's . . . Oh, I don't know any more . . . Can you just leave me alone for a minute, please?'

I can't tell them. I just can't. This situation . . . this black-mail is something I have to deal with in my own way – that's all there is to it.

When the door to the small room opens again, Harriet stalks in looking utterly bemused.

'What the hell happened out there, boys?'

'We're really very sorry, Ms Rushworth,' AJ says. 'Jack isn't feeling too well.'

'Well I'm sorry too, but he shouldn't have gotten up there if he wasn't up to it,' Harriet says. Then she looks over at Austin and me, her eyes full of disappointment. 'You blew it, boys. I gave you a big opportunity and you totally screwed it up. We all looked like idiots up there and now I'm going to have to go fix it – thanks a bunch, GenNext.'

I want to tell her that it's OK now, that I can get back up there and do it. I want to tell her I'm all right, but that's just not the case. I feel like something very scary is happening to me and all I want to do is get to my room and crawl into bed.

The door opens again and a very stressed-out Millie pops her head around it.

'They need you back on, Harriet. We're going again in less than five – we can't afford to lose the live audience.'

Harriet takes a couple of deep breaths and looks me in the eye, her face softening.

'You're a nice kid, Jack, you're just out of your depth.'

I watch her disappear through the door, back out into the main room, and then I stand, slightly wobbly for a moment, and head back to my room. I don't look back but I assume Austin and AJ are following, silently. I guess there's really nothing more to say.

THE HOMECOMING

HOME >> NEWS >> TOPICS >>

GenNext! Is this the new cool or just amateur hour?

Harriet Rushworth left red-faced after disastrous encounter with Brit vloggers.

BREAKING NEWS

Superstar Harriet faces the GenNext boys on live TV. What happens next will leave you gasping!

The Post UK | Jen Russell

I'm awake, but my eyes are still closed, and for the first thirty seconds of consciousness I'm not entirely sure where I am. It takes a while for my brain to click into gear, and then I remember. I open my eyes and take in the familiar surroundings of my own room in Mum and Dad's house and I breathe a massive sigh of relief. Thank God. I'm not in LA any more. I'm home, and I've slept for fourteen hours. For a second, just a second, everything else – the ruined interview, the blackmail, flying home from LA in disgrace – feels like it might have happened to someone else, but that isn't the case. As I slowly wake up, it all becomes real again.

I'm barely sitting up in bed when Mum taps on the door and comes in with a cup of tea, smiling and setting it down on the bedside table.

'You OK, Jack?'

'I think so,' I say. 'What about you, Mum, are you all right?'

She sits down on the end of my bed.

'Oh, you know, I'll get there. I'm still in shock, I suppose, and I don't know what to expect with all this treatment they've got in store for me. Half the time when the doctors talk, you need a bloody interpreter, it's all so complicated.'

I nod sympathetically, taking a sip of tea.

'How are you feeling about the op on Thursday?'

'Oh, all right, I suppose,' she says, and then she pulls this goofy face, putting her hands around her throat and sticking her tongue out, which makes me laugh. I know deep down that she's frightened, but, just like Mum always does, she's trying to make me feel better about it.

'Look, I've got some egg and bacon on the go if you fancy it,' she says. 'A good old English breakfast; you could probably do with that, eh?'

'Yeah, I'm sick of pancakes and syrup,' I say, running my hands through my hair. 'I'll have a quick wash and come down.'

Mum stands up and heads for the door and I watch for any telltale signs of her illness. There aren't any – she looks as healthy and sturdy as ever. It makes what's happening – the fact that she has to have this major operation – feel even more surreal and awful than it already does.

'I'll put some of that nice coffee on that you like,' she says. 'Then we can have a proper chat, OK?'

'OK, Mum.' I try to smile, but my facial muscles don't seem to be doing what I want them to.

Once she's gone, I go to pick up my phone but then think better of it. I can't face the horror of the blackmail situation just yet. And do I really need to plough through another ten pages of vicious tweets and bitchy blogs reminding me how badly I screwed up in LA and that GenNext is probably dead in the water? I feel sick to my stomach just thinking about it. I'll have to deal with it all sooner or later, but not five minutes after I've opened my eyes, you know?

In the bathroom, while I'm cleaning my teeth, my mind traitorously flips back to the aftermath of that horrendous non-interview with Harriet Rushworth. I try to blink it away, but it's like my memory is on rewind, and flashes and moments from those final forty-eight hours in LA start speeding through my brain . . .

It wasn't pretty, the fall-out from the Harriet interview. Austin hardly spoke to me the following day, especially after it all went viral. God, there must have been forty different phone-filmed videos of me going wacko on that stage, all from different angles. Even I couldn't believe it was me up there when I watched some of them back. I looked like the biggest idiot of all time. Now I knew what 'going viral' truly meant as the videos were shared again and again all over the world.

I was so mortified, I just stayed in my room until it was time to catch the flight home. It seemed easier to stay out of everyone's way and stress over the threat from Herald – and my public meltdown – on my own.

When AJ popped up later to see how I was doing, I found that I didn't have much to say for myself.

'Have you spoken to Sai and Ava?' I asked him sheepishly.

He nodded and wrung his hands together nervously. 'They're pretty furious with you, Jack. They feel like everything was going so well with GenNext and that you've thrown it away. Even more so after they supported you over the whole Herald Media thing. They feel like all their chances have been blown in just a couple of days and that it's . . . well, they feel like it's down to you.'

'Of course,' I said. What else could I say?

I'd had a couple of texts from Ava already, the last of which left me in no doubt as to how she was feeling.

> **Why is everything always about you, Jack?**

As terrible as I felt about letting Austin, Sai and Ava down, there was still something far more urgent to deal with. As soon as AJ left my room that afternoon, I steeled myself to phone Hunter. The thought of speaking to him made my stomach turn, but I didn't see what choice I had. Since the disastrous interview, I'd had another threatening message from the blocked number. Reading it made my blood run cold. Herald still wanted us – and they were still prepared to leak the video if we said no – only since the Harriet fiasco had gone down, they'd knocked a couple of zeros off their original offer. In screwing everything up so badly, I'd put us in an even worse position; one where the price of GenNext was devalued massively.

To my surprise, Hunter picked up his mobile on the first ring. He didn't sound like his usual cocky self; more of a nervous wreck than a blackmailer.

'Penman, what took you so long?' he hissed. 'Do you know how bloody serious this is?'

'What do you think, Hunter? Of course I know,' I said through gritted teeth. 'What I can't get my head around is how you can do this to Ella. I know you hate me, but Ella? So she broke up with you . . . but a bloody *sex tape*? Really?'

'Shut *up*, Penman.'

I could hear the stress in his voice. I pushed him further, desperate to put the brakes on it all.

'Ella's *seventeen* years old, for God's sake. You've known her your whole life. You don't have to do this, Hunter. You can stop this now if you want.'

'I couldn't stop it even if I wanted to,' he spat. 'Once I gave Callum the leverage, he was going to use it no matter what. He decided he wanted GenNext right after you did the interview with The Gloves, and he'll do whatever he has to to get what he wants. So far it's always worked for him.' He paused, and then his voice turned bitter. 'Look, I know it was stupid of me to give him the video, but I was angry and I wanted revenge. Things got out of hand and now Callum won't listen to anything I say, so just do what he wants and sign the deal and that'll be the end of it for all of us. Do it, Penman.'

I scrabbled desperately for a stalling tactic.

'Look, Hunter, I can't do anything while I'm here in LA,' I said, my mind racing. 'I need time to talk the others into it because it's not just me, you know that. Tell Callum to give me a couple of days. I need to get home and convince the others face to face. Can you do that?' I hated having to beg, hated him knowing how desperate I was. 'Don't let him release the video until I've talked to the others, *please?*'

Hunter sighed, long and loud. 'Fine. I'll persuade him to give you another couple of days, but he isn't going to wait much longer, all right? Call Angela Linford and get it done the minute you've spoken to the others. Otherwise you know what'll happen.'

So that was that. Besides pleading for more time, there was nothing I could do to stop Callum other than falling in line with his demands.

'Jack! Breakfast is on the table!'

Mum's call from downstairs shakes me out of the miserable memories of the past couple of days and brings me back to the here and now. I rinse the last of the toothpaste out of my mouth, pull on a T-shirt and head downstairs to the kitchen. When I get there, Mum is sitting at the breakfast bar opposite the most magnificent fry-up, arms folded and smiling.

'That looks really good,' I grin, pulling out a stool and tucking in.

'Yes, well your dad's out doing the weekly shop on his own this morning, so Lord knows what we'll end up eating next week,' she laughs. 'Now you demolish that and then you can tell me everything that's been going on, and I don't mean the edited version or what you think might be suitable for my ears – I mean everything.'

I flick my eyes upward sheepishly, mouth full of bacon, and nod. Her face is kind but firm, so I know she's not messing.

After eating, I stand up and start pacing while Mum's eyes follow me around the kitchen. Where do I even start? What should I tell her? I know she says she wants to know everything, but I'm thinking even after I tell her she might not believe half of it.

'Jack, you know your dad and I try to follow everything you do, and believe it or not I do know how to work a computer,' she says softly. 'I've seen what's out there online but I want to hear your side of things, that's all.'

'Mum, the last thing you need is to be worrying about all this—'

'Look, Jack, my illness doesn't stop me worrying about you,' she interrupts. 'You're my son and I need to know that you're OK.'

I sit back down at the table and take a breath, and then it all comes tumbling out: the dodgy offer from Herald Media, the blackmail leading to the disastrous interview, the fact that I seem to have pissed off virtually everyone in my life, and the reason for almost all of it . . . Ella. I talk and talk, hardly stopping for breath, and Mum just sits there listening, nodding and smiling supportively in all the right places. Now that the words are out of my mouth, I feel relieved – like a great weight has been lifted off my shoulders – but I'm not done yet.

'The worst thing about it all is that I've been so scared,'

I admit. 'I've been so worried about what's going to happen to you, with the operation and the chemo, I've not been able to think straight. Now these people have backed me into a corner, and I feel like I've let it happen; like I've let everything get the better of me.'

Seeing how upset I am, Mum comes around to my side of the table and puts her arms around my neck, pressing her cheek into the top of my head while I blink back tears. 'At the end of the day, Mum, I'm no better than the kid who was bullied back at my old school. I'm the same. I've learned nothing and now I've probably ruined Ella's life as well as my own.'

Mum stands up straight and puts her hands firmly on my shoulders, spinning me around on the stool to face her.

'OK, this needs to stop,' she says firmly. 'Jack, you are one of the smartest, most savvy kids a mum could wish for. You've done such clever, wonderful things for someone your age and your dad and I are chuffed to bits for you. But that's not the only reason I'm proud of you.' She lifts my chin up so I'm looking her directly in the eye. 'I'm proud of you because you're a kind, considerate and loving person and at the end of the day that's what's most important. It's all that really matters. You're a good boy, Jack, and I wouldn't swap that for all the other stuff: fame, money, none of it.'

I do my best to smile. 'What do you mean, "boy"?'

'You're right; I suppose you're not a boy any more,' she says seriously. 'That's why you have to face this ridiculous blackmail thing head on. You've got to be honest with your friends, because however angry they are, they'll be on your side once they know the truth, and you've got to tell Ella as soon as possible because she has a right to know, however bad it makes you feel. After that, I think you should go to the police – your dad and I will go with you. You have to fight this for Ella's sake, Jack, and you have to fight for GenNext, too. You've worked so hard to build it up – all of you.'

'I know you're right, Mum, but *you're* what's most important right now,' I say. 'Maybe we should just let Herald Media take over GenNext. Then the video will go away and we can all start again, and I can focus on making sure you get better.'

Mum thinks for a moment, then shakes her head resolutely, her eyes filling with tears.

'I've already told you, Jack, you can't put your life on hold just because I have to for a while. While I'm going through this treatment, whatever happens, I want to see you living your life and getting on with things. I know you'll be there if I need you, but you have to keep on living, for me as much as anything – it can't all stop, do you understand?'

I nod slowly, and then Mum draws me into a hug that lasts a long, long time. I can feel her heart beating against me and it dawns on me that the thought of losing her is more heartbreaking and frightening than anything else I'm facing or will have to face. I'm literally blown away by how much faith my mum has in me. If she can believe in me with all she's going through, then I can believe in myself . . . right? Right.

THE DECISION

I'm in our living room, perched on the edge of Dad's favourite armchair, bright sunlight streaming through the window and warming my face. For a moment, my mind drifts back to Venice Beach and how peaceful I felt there for a few hours, despite everything. I could do with a little bit of that peace now. It's time to stop all this noise in my head, and this is a good way to start, I'm sure of it.

I glance at my phone: 1.20 p.m., so 8.20 a.m. in Canada. It's still pretty early but I can't leave it any later to call Ella; I've already had three more anonymous messages this morning – two of which I'm sure are from Hunter, one from another unknown number – warning me with escalating urgency that I have till 6 p.m. tomorrow to agree to the Herald Media deal or that's it. The video is out there.

I've been tying myself in knots for the last few hours, desperately trying to figure out what I'm going to say to her when I finally speak to her, what words I'm going to use to convey something so horrible, but in my head none of the conversations end well, so I've decided just to wing it. It's the only way.

I dial her number, hoping she's up early enough to take the call, hoping she'll even pick up when she sees it's me, especially as news of the Harriet interview will have reached her by now. She doesn't. In fact it doesn't even ring, going straight to voicemail, so I leave a message.

'Ella, it's Jack. Can you call me, please, the minute you get this? It's important, really important. I hope you're OK. Speak soon. Bye.'

I head out to the kitchen, where Mum is nibbling at a sandwich and wading through a pile of leaflets and magazines she's picked up at the hospital: 'We are Macmillan cancer support', 'Nutrition – food and weight concerns', 'Fitting treatment into your schedule'. It seems like an awful lot to take in, and she looks up at me, rolling her eyes.

'Just trying to get my head around all this,' she says as I grab my keys from the countertop. 'Are you going out?'

'I'm waiting for Ella to call me back, so I'm going to sit in the park. I need to get out of the house for a bit.'

Mum shouts after me as I open the front door.

'Good luck, Jack. Ring me and let me know what happens.'

'I will.'

The park is busy today, full of kids trying to grab as much freedom as they can during the last weeks of the summer holidays. I head to the spot where Ella and I kissed a few weeks before – yeah, I know, I'm a soppy romantic – and I sit there on the grass staring at my iPhone, as if that's going to make the bloody thing ring. I guess I'm still a bit jet-lagged because after about fifteen minutes I suddenly feel shattered, so I lie back on the grass and close my eyes . . . just for a moment . . .

'Jack?'

A voice jolts me awake and I realise I've been in the deepest sleep – but for how long?

'Jack!'

I open my eyes and there's someone standing over me, a dark shape against the sun. I rub my eyes, trying to prise them open.

'Jack, are you all right?'

'Ella?'

OK, for the first few seconds I totally think I'm dreaming. Then she kneels down on the grass next to me and pulls me into a hug and I know it's real. I'm definitely not dreaming.

'Ella, what the . . . what are you even doing here? How did you know where to find me?'

She lets go of me and I sit up, still unable to believe that she's right here in front of me. She sits down on the grass, so close that our legs touch and I can see the freckles on her nose. She looks incredible – tanned and healthy, her hair an even whiter shade of blonde after weeks in the sun.

'I literally just got back, two hours ago. I picked up your message when I charged my phone, went straight round to yours and saw your mum,' she says. 'When she said you were at the park, I sort of guessed where you might be.'

'But . . . I . . .'

'God, it was such a mistake going to Canada,' she says, on a huge outward breath. 'I suppose it was a knee-jerk reaction to everything because I felt like I needed to run away, but I'd only been gone five or six days and I just missed home so much. I missed my mates and I missed GenNext and . . . I really missed you, Jack Penman.'

'Really?' I say, still thinking that this entire conversation might just be a dream or a sun-induced hallucination. Ella, here, just when I need her the most.

'I know, what's wrong with me?' she says, screwing her face up and giggling. 'Perhaps I need some kind of medical help.' Then, quite suddenly, she stops and looks dead serious. 'I really did miss you, Jack. When I'd had time to think properly about everything that happened, you know, with us, with Hunter, it just seemed like it was something we could fix if we really tried. Nothing is unfixable, is it?'

I smile back at her nervously, my stomach churning, wondering if she might be of the same opinion in five minutes' time when I tell her what Hunter has done and what Callum plans to do.

'I'm just glad you're back,' I say, and I pull her close to me again. I wish the moment could last and we could just stay happy like this for a while longer. But we can't; I have to tell her what's going on. I take a deep breath and bite the bullet.

'Ella, there's something I've got to tell you. Actually, there's something I've got to show you,' I say, pulling my phone out of my pocket with a heavy heart. 'It's something that isn't very nice and I know it's going to hurt you, but . . .'

Ella's face falls and I feel her stiffen and pull away from me.

'Jack, you're scaring me; what are you going on about?'

I scroll through my messages and locate the video, tentatively handing her the phone.

233

'There's no way to really explain this, so I'm just going to . . .'

I watch Ella's face as she hits play, her eyes filling with angry tears as she takes in the video. I feel terrible. Every so often her gaze flicks upwards to me in disbelief, and then she looks down again, her face flushed, tears dripping down on to her trembling hand as she holds the phone.

Once it's done, she turns away from me, shaking her head as if she's simply refusing to believe any of it.

'I don't know what to say,' she says, her voice cold and flat. 'I trusted Hunter; we've known each other since we were kids. And the most ridiculous thing about this video is I didn't even . . . I mean, he and I, we didn't even . . .' She shrugs her shoulders hopelessly. 'But who cares, right? Anyone who sees this will think that we *did*, so does it even matter?' Then she looks back at me, her jaw tightening. 'Why have you got this on your phone, Jack? What's this about?'

I jump up from the grass and offer her my hand.

'Let's walk. I've got a lot to tell you.'

By the time we reach the kids' swing park, I've filled her in on the entire story. Weirdly, she hasn't said a word the whole time we've been walking, just listened with an expression of deep concentration on her face. But then again, I have been talking for a good ten minutes, barely taking a breath. By now, I'm wondering if she just blames me for everything and I might be about to lose her all over again.

At the gates of the swing park, she stops suddenly, her brow furrowed in thought.

'How long have we got before they post the video?'

I pull my phone out of my pocket and glance down.

'Just over twenty-four hours. Look, Ella, maybe we should just ring them and tell them we'll do it. I'll call the rest of the team and explain everything, and I'm pretty sure they'll see that we don't have any choice, even though they are pissed off with me. Then all this will go away and we can get on with our lives.'

Ella shakes her head and walks through the gates. She heads over to the swings, sitting down on a vacant one. I follow suit, parking myself on the swing next to her.

'I know I've let you down,' I say, staring at my feet. 'I've never been good at handling bullies, you know?'

Ella starts swinging back and forth gently, looking at me like she needs me to clarify. Suddenly I have the urge to tell her everything. I need her to understand my past, really understand it.

'I've never told you this, but the reason I left my old school and came to St Joe's in the first place is because I was bullied,' I say. The words feel strange; I've never said them out loud before. 'It got so bad that I was beaten up and ended up in hospital, and then when I got to St Joe's I assumed . . . I hoped everything would be different and better, and then I met you and the others, and it was. It was incredible, to be honest. And then everything went so crazy with GenNext . . . and now this has happened, and I don't understand how we've ended up here. It's just a different kind of bullying, from people who are old enough to know better. I feel like I tried to beat the bullies and I've failed, you know? They've just turned up in a different shape and size.'

'God, Jack, that's . . . that's horrible,' Ella says softly. I look up at her to gauge her reaction to what I've just said. Her face is a mix of anger and sympathy and I feel relieved.

Then: 'No!' she says suddenly, bringing the swing to a halt with her feet.

'No what?'

'No, we're not going to call Hunter or Callum and tell them we're going to do the deal. We're not going to give in to them, Jack.'

'Ella, if we don't, you know what's going to happen,' I say, jumping off my swing and grabbing the chains of hers, facing her dead on. Her face is determined, her eyes blazing.

'So, what, are we going to spend the rest of our lives bowing down to the bullies of this world? Is that how it's going to go?' Now she sounds really angry. 'No thanks, Jack, I've been there, done that.'

'What do you mean?' I ask.

'I've . . . I've been bullied, too. When I was fourteen.'

She looks down, and I try to hide my surprise. Ella's the last person I can imagine being bullied.

'What happened?' I say. I reach down and take her hand. She hesitates a moment and then curls her fingers around mine.

'When I was at school in Hong Kong, there was this group of American girls who took an instant dislike to me the minute I joined the class,' she says. 'I hadn't done anything wrong – God, I'd barely even spoken to them – but for some reason they were out to get me. They wrote nasty stuff about me on Facebook, cleverly disguised at first but everyone knew who they were talking about and it got quite vicious. All I could do was try to ignore it. I'd walk into class and pretend

I didn't care, but inside I was torn up. Then they stepped it up. For a while they were writing stuff every day and it was all anyone was talking about. I ended up locking myself in my room, not eating, too upset and scared to turn on my phone or my computer. It probably sounds like nothing now, but when you're fourteen and not very confident, it can really screw with your head.'

'It doesn't sound like nothing at all,' I say. 'It sounds like classic cyber-bullying, by a group of nasty girls who just wanted to feel better about themselves by giving you a hard time. What happened in the end? Did it go away?'

'Not completely,' Ella says. 'I got the messages taken down, but those girls never really had to answer for what they did. They always had one up on me, and even ages after, whenever I saw them, I'd walk past with my head down as if I was the one who'd done something wrong.'

'God, Ella, that's awful,' I say.

'You're damn right it's awful, Jack, and that's why I'm not going through it again. *We're* not going through it.' Ella stands up and puts her arms around my neck. Without even thinking, I slip my arms around her waist, so that we're standing as one. 'Look, if Callum posts the video online, it's going to be really bad for me. Everyone at school will see it, my family. I don't know how I'm going to face people; in fact I'll probably want to jump on a plane straight back to Canada. But if it comes down to it, then I'm just going to have to be brave. Yes, it'll be a hideous embarrassment and I'll feel like I have to justify myself to everyone, but I'm not letting those idiots shame me without a fight. I'll make sure everyone knows who did it, and why.' I can see from her expression that she means it, one hundred per cent, and I feel bloody proud of her. 'Plus,' she says, 'the alternative is much worse – giving up GenNext, which is what it will mean if we sign the deal, right?'

'Yeah, but after the Harriet interview, is there even much left to give up?' I say. 'I screwed up pretty badly; everyone thinks we're finished.'

'Oh come off it, Jack,' Ella says. 'Everyone has an off day, right? It'll be forgotten by tomorrow. If I can style out a sex tape, you can style this out. What we've done with GenNext is so amazing – we've got to fight for it.'

It's funny; Ella is virtually echoing what my mum said earlier that day. She's right, of course, and I'm so very happy to hear her say 'we'. Does this mean she's really back with the team? Back with GenNext? My mind is racing. I totally get what she's saying, but maybe there's still a way to stop the video going online without signing the deal. A way to defy the bullies *and* beat them. OK, so it's not going to be easy. It's not like I even have any kind of tangible proof that Hunter and Callum are behind the blackmail. They've been very careful – anything threatening has come from blocked numbers, and I'm pretty sure that if I tried to trace it back to Herald Media – or to Callum – there'd be no evidence. These guys are too smooth, too clever, not to have covered their tracks. Still, there has to be another way, doesn't there? Think, Jack. There must be something we can do – some sort of advantage we have over them, some knowledge we have that they don't . . .

Suddenly the seed of an idea pops into my head. There *is* something I can do – something I've always been good at.

It's risky, but if Callum and Herald Media are as seriously dodgy as I think they are, it might just work in our favour. Whatever happens, I now know one thing for sure: with the promise of Ella coming back to the team, holding on to GenNext is more vital to me than ever, despite the Harriet Rushworth debacle.

I give Ella a quick kiss, surprising her.

'OK. I've got an idea, but we need Austin, Ava and Sai to help,' I say secretively. 'We need our friends.'

Ella squints at me, confused but smiling, and now I'm smiling too. If we can pull this off, there just might be a tiny glimmer of light at the end of a very long tunnel.

THE REUNION

It takes a few long, convoluted phone calls and a tangled mess of explanations about what's been happening over the past few days, but that night Ella and I are standing outside Austin's house, ready to reunite with the team. I have to say, I'm feeling pretty emotionally raw. After we left the park, I told Ella everything: about my mum's diagnosis, the upcoming operation, the whole story. She was amazing about it, like I knew she would be. She even cried as I was telling her, and it was all I could do to stop myself from joining in. But it felt good to say it all out loud – a relief, to be honest. Then Ella suggested that I should tell the others about it too, assuring me that whatever had gone down, they were my mates and they'd want to help. I knew she was right. I owed them an explanation about acting like a basket case in LA, so I bit the bullet and sent a long message to the GenNext WhatsApp group telling them everything. Within minutes, Sai, Ava and Austin had all fired back messages of support, and I immediately felt like a huge weight had been lifted. Sure, telling them about Mum was hard, but I'm glad that

I've got it all out in the open. It's made me feel stronger, ready for what's to come – whatever that might be.

Miles greets us at the front door, tearing down the basement stairs and yelling, 'It's Jack and Ella – and they're holding hands!'

It's true. As brave as Ella has been, she's still pretty scared about the prospect of the video being leaked, so she's been gripping my hand tightly on the journey over to Austin's.

As soon as we head down the stairs to HQ, a sense of relief washes over me and I realise how much I've missed being in a room with these people, with Sai, Ava, Ella and Austin. It's become such a massive part of my life over the past few months, and one I'm not ready to give up or let go of. Ava is the first to rush over, hugging Ella tightly and unleashing a torrent of girly gushing about how psyched she is to have her back, before throwing her arms around me.

'I can't believe you kept all this to yourself, Jack,' she says sternly. 'You should have let us know; we could have helped, you know?'

Austin gives Ella a friendly kiss and then hugs me warmly.

'I wish you'd told me all this in LA, Jack,' he says. 'I feel like I've let you down. I feel like—'

'I know, Austin, I should have told you, but there was so much going on in my head, I just wasn't thinking straight,' I say. 'You haven't let me down, mate. We're all here now, all back together, and that's what counts.'

Austin breaks into a smile, then whacks the hell out of my arm.

'You always think you can handle everything yourself, J, that's your trouble.'

'He thinks he's Daniel bloody Craig,' Sai adds for good measure, which goes down well in the room, making them all laugh as Ava puts her arm around my neck.

'I can't believe that all this nightmare stuff has been happening – your mum being ill, the insane blackmail situation – and you've been dealing with it all by yourself.' She turns to Ella. 'And Hunter – I mean, what the hell? It's just so awful for you, Ella – how could he do that?'

'So you guys don't think badly of me about the video?' Ella says, looking at the floor.

'Are you kidding?' Ava says. 'How were you to know that bloody creep was filming you?'

'I can't get my head around the fact he actually did it,' Austin says, pulling a disgusted face.

Sai is nodding in agreement. 'You've got absolutely nothing to feel ashamed of, Ella; the whole thing is sickening. And Jack, all that stuff that happened in LA is in the past. Right now, we're behind you all the way.'

'Thanks, Sai,' I say, feeling better. 'It's good to be home.'

'So what about this idea of yours, Jack?' Ava jumps in. 'It all sounded very mysterious on the phone. What do you need us to do?'

I glance around the room, taking in the eager faces, all waiting for me to do what I should have done days ago – take the lead.

'Look, there's no way we can just hand GenNext over to Herald. We need to play them at their own game and get creative, even if that means tearing up the rule book.'

Ava looks unconvinced. 'OK, Jack, but we're talking about a multi-million-pound global corporation here. What are five teenagers – with some decent techy skills between them – realistically going to do against a company as big as that?'

I grin. 'You've hit the nail on the head, Ava. That's exactly what I've been thinking . . . that we need to go right back to basics and focus on what we're good at – what's made GenNext so successful so fast. Technology. Accessing information that's difficult to find. Finding loopholes and exploiting them, if you know what I mean.'

'OK, Jack,' says Sai, crossing his arms like an X-Factor finalist. 'What do you want us to do?'

I look at all four of them in turn. 'Right,' I say. 'Here's the plan . . .'

For the next few hours, HQ is a frenzy of activity, with Sai, Ava, Austin and Ella – and yes, even Miles – beavering away on their computers and laptops, searching for every word, every mention, every tiny morsel of Herald Media and Callum Connor they can find, anywhere on the internet. There has to be something that can help us out; give us some leverage. One thing I can be pretty certain of: this isn't the first time he's tried to screw someone over like this – it can't be. While the others continue their search, I'm on a different tack: going back to my hacking roots and hoping to God there's a way I can get into Herald Media's system. OK, it might be a long shot, but I've got to give it a go. This whole idea, this entire plan rests on me finding . . . well, finding something. Trouble is, I'm not even sure what I'm looking for.

Before any of us know it, it's after midnight and the room

is still alive with the sound of tapping. But there's nothing; in fact, there's worse than nothing. Suddenly Sai jumps up out of his chair and slap his forehead.

'Oh, you have got to be kidding me. Check this out!'

'What is it, mate?' Austin says, sliding across into Sai's chair and glaring at the screen of his laptop. 'Bloody hell.'

'Spit it out, Sherlock,' Ava sighs. 'What have you found?'

'A kids' charity,' Sai says, disbelieving. 'Herald Media are involved in this, like, foundation that funds scholarships for young people.'

'Seriously?' I say, looking up from my own laptop, which by now is a mess of links, code and open windows.

'He's right,' Austin says. 'It's called The Skyward Trust. It's been going quite a few years and it helps young people from disadvantaged backgrounds who want a career in TV or media or the arts. Not only in America, either; it's a worldwide thing.'

I'm horrified. 'So instead of finding dirt, we've actually found something that makes Callum look like a bloody knight in shining armour?'

'It looks that way,' Austin says miserably.

'Anything else?' I ask, but I'm looking at a sea of shaking heads.

'I can't find anything, and I'm really good at this,' Miles says.

'Callum doesn't have much of an online presence at all,' Ella says, frowning. 'All the stuff I've found about Herald is just about their naff TV shows, their awards and the company itself.'

'Not a lawsuit or an injunction in sight,' Ava says, getting up for another cup of coffee. 'I'm telling you, Jack, if you can't get into their files and find something we can use, it looks like we'll have to come up with a Plan B.'

'What Plan B?' I say, trying not to sound too hopeless. 'What else is there?' My brain feels tired and my eyes are starting to sting, I've been staring at the screen for so long.

'What about if we somehow secretly record the blackmail threat when you go to meet him?' Sai suggests. 'I've got these little microphones that—'

'Wear a wire, you mean, like in the American cop shows?' Ella says. 'Wouldn't Callum check that sort of thing? He's been very careful so far to cover his tracks.'

I suddenly have this moment when it dawns on me how ridiculous and unreal this all is. I mean, just think about some of the words and phrases that are being bandied around right now: blackmail, wearing a wire, hacking files. How did it even come to this?

'Callum probably would check for wires, and even if we did record him, it might not stop the video going out,' I say wearily. 'Look, it's an idea for if we get desperate, but we're not there yet.' My mind starts whirring again. Who can help us – who'll believe us? Suddenly a name pops into my brain. It'd be taking a massive risk . . . but at this stage, I don't know if we've got much to lose.

'Hang on,' I say. 'There's someone who *might* be able to help us out. I just need to make a quick call and hope they're not asleep.'

'Very mysterious!' Ava says as I grab my phone and head up the stairs. 'Good luck, Jack.'

Outside in the warm night air, I scroll for the number on

my phone and hit call. When the answer comes, the voice is chirpy and upbeat.

'Well hello! And what can I do for you at this late hour, Jack Penman?'

I swallow hard and gather my nerve. 'I need your help. I really need your help . . . Fran.'

THE SHOWDOWN

'What time is it?' Ella asks for the fourth or fifth time.

We're standing outside the gated driveway of Hunter's parents' house and I can hear her breathing rapidly. She's nervous, and I don't blame her. I wish I could be more of a comfort, but in fact I'm just as scared as she is. Can you blame us? We're about to try to pull off something so risky, so dangerous . . .

'It's two fifty-five,' I say. 'Do you feel OK?'

'Is it possible to feel ridiculously tired and wide awake all at the same time?' she asks.

I know exactly what she means; it's the middle of the afternoon and none of the team slept a wink last night. Fuelled by about ten cups of coffee each and the determination to find something concrete we could use as leverage against Callum, we just powered right through. Then at 8 a.m., hoping my gut feeling was on the money, I called Angela Linford on her private cell phone number, my heart thumping like crazy. I'd gone over and over it with the others and we all agreed this was the best way to engineer a meeting on our terms. It was midnight in LA, and Angela's distracted 'hello' told me that my call had taken her by surprise.

'Angela, it's Jack Penman from GenNext.'

Angela ramped up into her super-cool, super-phoney robot speak within seconds.

'Jack, I'm so thrilled to hear your voice. To what do I owe this pleasure?'

'I think you'll be pleased with what I have to say,' I said, sounding as amenable as I could manage without actually throwing up. 'We've decided to accept Herald Media's offer.'

'Well, well,' she said. 'I'm so pleased you came to your senses, Jack. Turning down an opportunity like this wouldn't have been such a smart move.'

'I think we both know that we don't have much choice in the matter,' I said. 'So we're agreeing to the deal on one condition: that you give us a guarantee that all traces of the video of Ella disappear, and nobody ever sees or hears about it again.'

There was silence on the line for a few seconds, and in the quiet I wondered how Angela Linford could sleep at night knowing how her boss operated; knowing that he would blackmail a bunch of teenagers and threaten a young woman's future just to get what he wanted.

When she spoke again, she feigned ignorance.

'I can't imagine which video you mean, Jack. But I really am so pleased to hear that you're accepting our offer. Of course, I'll need to touch base with Tyler and with Mr Connor, the majority shareholder of Herald, to discuss getting the paperwork signed.'

I knew she wouldn't be stupid enough to say anything

incriminating over the phone, but it still made me hate her and Herald even more.

'Well that's the thing,' I said. 'I have a few conditions over signing the paperwork, too.'

'Oh yes? And what might they be, Jack?' she said. Her use of my name at the end of every sentence was really starting to grate.

'I'd like everything to happen here in the UK, and I'd prefer to wrap it up as quickly as possible. I'd like a representative of Herald Media to meet with me and give me a written, legally binding guarantee that the video will never be shown to anyone and that everything's going to be cool once the deal goes through.'

Angela sighed loudly. 'Jack, I have absolutely no idea what video you're talking about – and this isn't how we'd normally do things. I'm not sure you're really in a position to set out the terms, are you?'

Ah, there it was. The veiled hint of a threat.

'Look, this is the only way a deal is going to happen,' I said, 'and that comes direct from Ella herself; she's with me right now.' There was silence again, and for a moment I was scared that I'd gone in too hard and Angela wasn't going to agree to our terms. I decided to switch tactics. 'Look – we're desperate, you know that, but we can't do this unless I speak to someone face to face and get a guarantee, in writing, that will protect Ella.'

There was another pause – this one seemed to go on for ever – and then . . . bingo.

'OK, Jack, I can coordinate a meeting with Callum for later today. He'll bring the requisite paperwork with him and he'll expect to leave with the contracts fully signed.' Her fake bright-and-breezy tone had been replaced with something more steely, as if there was no longer any need for pretence now that we were discussing logistics and she knew the deal was in the bag. 'I'll need a few hours before I can confirm the exact time. I'll get back to you on this number and let you know when I have something in place, OK?'

'OK.'

'You know, this partnership is going to be very interesting,' she said. 'You could go a long way if you stay smart, Jack.'

'I'll look forward to it,' I said, almost choking on the words. And that was it; it was done. We were on.

And now here we are, outside Hunter's parents' house, Ella's finger hovering over the intercom button on the wall by the gates.

'OK,' she says. 'And we're ready, right?'

I shake my head. 'Not really, no.'

'That's what I thought,' she says, nodding frantically. 'Are you sure we shouldn't have called AJ?'

'No way,' I say. 'It would have just complicated things. He might have tried to talk us out of it, and we don't need that sort of distraction. We can worry about AJ afterwards – when it's all done and dusted.'

The two of us are standing as close together as we can get as she rings the bell. When Angela called me back earlier telling me that this would be the location of the meeting with Callum, both Ella and I had to grit our teeth. Meeting Callum at the scene of Ella and Hunter's video feels like one more 'screw you' from Herald, a final twist of the knife.

Still, we've come alone, which is another one of the conditions I gave Angela. The other three wanted to come with us – safety in numbers, right? But this whole thing was my idea, and if it blows up in our faces then I'm going to hold my hands up and take the blame – I don't want the others getting into grief too. Callum's a shark, not to be trusted, so it's damage control as far as I'm concerned. Ella didn't give me a choice, however, insisting she come with me. I didn't really want her here, but there was no way she was going to stay behind and let me go it alone; then when Angela said that Callum would need a minimum of two signatures from us to seal the deal, it was decided. It's me and Ella, going in to save GenNext.

By now, the adrenalin-fuelled confidence of earlier feels dim and distant. We're tired and both pretty much nervous wrecks. I've chewed my thumbnail down to a stub. A voice over the intercom almost finishes me off; it's Hunter's voice, to my surprise, clipped and nervous.

'I'll open the gate; just come straight through.'

Ella and I glance at one another, then make our way through the gate as it slowly swings open and head down the drive towards the house. Before we reach the front door, I stop and turn to her.

'It's going to be all right,' I say softly. 'I'm going to make it all right.'

'I know you are,' she says. She takes my hand and squeezes it.

When the front door opens, Callum is behind it, his face as unruffled as his immaculate blue suit.

'How are you, Jack?'

My knees buckle under me slightly and my mouth goes desert dry.

'I'm all right,' I say, flatly.

'Well, thank you for coming. And Ella, we haven't had the pleasure.' Callum's voice is smug and mocking, his thin lips curled into a corrupt smile. 'I just happened to be back in town today; isn't that fortunate?'

He gestures for us to enter the house, where we find Hunter waiting anxiously in the hall. The minute I set eyes on him, my stomach turns over and I feel Ella freeze beside me.

'And of course you already know my nephew, Hunter,' Callum says. The nerve of this guy is off the scale.

I nod helplessly as Callum grips my shoulder like an old friend.

'Well, Jack and Ella, shall we get on with the business at hand?'

'Yeah, let's get this over and done with,' Hunter adds, fidgeting on the spot.

At that moment, Fran appears from the doorway of the lounge, smiling innocently and smoking a cigarette. Both Callum and Hunter turn to her with narrowed eyes; I can practically feel Hunter sending 'get lost' vibes her way.

'Oh hey, Ella,' she says lazily. 'Haven't seen you around here for a while.' She turns to me. 'And I know you, don't I? You work with Ella on all that Generation Next stuff.'

'This is Jack Penman,' Hunter says irritably. 'We've got some business to sort, so we're going upstairs to the private room.' He stresses the word 'private'.

'OK, cool,' Fran says, holding on to the innocent look. 'Just give me a shout if you need anything.'

'We'll be fine, I'm sure,' Callum says.

'Yeah, this won't take long,' Hunter adds coldly.

Clearly impatient, Callum turns on his heel and heads away from Fran, up the stairs.

'Leave any bags downstairs and hand your phones over to Hunter, please,' he snaps.

Hunter takes our phones and gestures for us to follow him, his eyes darting around uneasily as Ella and I tread up the stairs and along the hall towards the private room – that same room where my drinks were spiked and I made a fool of myself all those weeks ago. As soon as the doors have closed behind us, Ella steps towards Hunter like she's going to lunge at him – teeth gritted, eyes fiery.

'How dare you treat me like this, Hunter? How *dare* you?'

Hunter backs away from her. She's pretty scary, it has to be said. I grab her before she can do any damage.

'Let's get on with this. We just want to sign the papers and get out of here.'

'Very sensible, Jack, let's keep this civilised,' Callum says, sparking up a cigarette and blowing a satisfied stream of smoke into my face.

But Ella wasn't done.

'What kind of sicko are you, filming me like that? We've known one another since we were kids; what would your mum and dad think if they knew?'

Hunter shrugs, still staring at the floor, his mouth tightening as Ella takes it up a notch.

'Aren't you going to answer me, Hunter?' she demands. 'You can't even look at me, can you?'

I'm worried she's really going to lose it any second. Crap! This wasn't part of my plan at all.

'I believe we're here for a reason,' Callum says sharply, cutting Ella off and stepping between her and Hunter. 'I'm a busy man; I haven't got time for your teenage tantrums.'

By now my hands are sweating and my breathing is shallow, but I've got to keep it together, just for a short time. I've got to hold my nerve.

Callum takes a last long drag on his cigarette, blows smoke into the air and then tosses the half-smoked butt on to the carpet, crushing it under his foot. Hunter opens his mouth to say something but clearly thinks better of it and shuts up.

'Shall we?' Callum says, before dropping the small brown briefcase he's been carrying on to the desk in front of him, flipping it open and pulling out what I assume are the contracts – emailed from LA and freshly printed. 'It was smart of you to change your mind about teaming up with me, Jack. You'll be amazed at how we'll turn your little project into something global.'

'Yeah, something global that we won't own any more,' I say, my temper simmering. 'Still, we don't exactly have a choice in that, do we, Callum? We're screwed either way.'

Ella opens her mouth to lay into Hunter again, but I shoot her a stern look. We need to keep this on track or it'll all be for nothing.

'Oh come on, Jack, it's not that bad,' Callum says. 'You and your little GenNext mates are all going to make a bit of money out of this; stop being so noble, before I throw up.' He takes a pen out of his top pocket and hands me a sheet of paper, already signed. 'Now here's the *assurance* you asked for. Read that first, and then sign the contract.'

I look at the piece of paper – the 'assurance' – which, of course, doesn't specifically state what the content of the video actually is, just refers to it as 'the contentious matter under discussion'. Callum's covering his back until the very end, of course. I might not understand all the fancy legal jargon, but this document looks well dodgy to me. It's not exactly watertight. He must think we're completely stupid. He's still talking, gesturing to the contract.

'Of course, there'll be more detailed paperwork to follow, but this preliminary agreement confirms the sum of money we agreed and my controlling interest in the GenNext website, channel and brand. Is that understood?'

Ella and I nod slowly in unison and Callum hands me the pen and one of the contracts.

'So, you two are signing on behalf of the entire team for now.'

'That's right,' I say, sitting down at the desk and flicking through the contract to the spot where I'm supposed to sign my name.

'Good. Let's hurry it up then.' Callum makes a grand sweeping gesture, motioning to me to sign. I lift up the pen as if I'm about to do just that . . . But as it touches the paper, I pull away again. Then, my heart going nineteen to the dozen, I get up and throw the pen down on the desk.

Callum's eyes widen. 'Something wrong, Jack?'

'Yes, something *is* wrong,' I say, my jaw tight. 'What's wrong is you and your Herald Media lapdogs thinking that

GenNext would ever, *ever* get involved with a tragic, misguided criminal like you.'

'I . . . I beg your pardon?' Callum says, clearly unable to believe what he's hearing. 'Is this a joke?'

'Are we laughing?' Ella snaps.

Callum loosens his tie and steps forward, his mouth tight and angry.

'Jack, tell me you're not stupid enough to think you can jerk me around. You know very well what's going to happen if you don't sign this.'

'You've been told enough times,' Hunter says. 'Just sign it, Penman.'

I can hear the desperation in Hunter's voice; it's obvious to me that he doesn't want the tape going out any more than Ella does, but he's completely out of his depth. Callum, on the other hand, doesn't care who he hurts – that's very clear.

'The thing is, I don't really believe you'd actually go ahead and put a sex tape of a seventeen-year-old girl all over the internet just to make us sign a contract,' I tell Callum. 'Even you. I just don't believe it.'

'Of course he will, you freak, and then it'll be *your* fault!' Hunter sounds like he's about to explode.

Callum remains sub-zero cool. 'Trust me, Jack, the tape will find its way out there, and the best part about it is, no one will be able to trace it back to me. So go on, you just try me.' His eyes are drilling into mine. 'When it comes down to it, I don't think you're willing to risk it, are you? Not really. You're savvy enough to know when you've been beaten.'

There's a tense silence as the four of us face one another in the centre of the room. I feel dizzy with what Ella and I are about to do, but there's no going back now.

Callum steps forward again, losing his cool at last and spitting out his words.

'I'm sorry, but this is getting boring. Are we doing this, or do I put the video out? It'll only take one text message. What do you say, Ella?'

Ella paces the room, pretending to consider.

'You know,' she says thoughtfully, 'I don't think I'm going to sign after all. Jack, what about you?'

'No, I don't think I'm going to sign either, Ella,' I say, matching her tone.

'Are you two taking the piss? That's really not a good idea,' Callum says, the cool facade slipping completely. Now he sounds vicious. 'Look, if you don't want Ella's friends, her family, seeing the video, then you'd better listen to me . . .'

Ella spins around, moving towards Callum furiously.

'No, *you* listen to *me*. I don't care if you release the video, do you understand? I. Don't. Care. It won't be easy for me if it goes out, it'll be completely hideous in fact, but do you know what? It won't be anywhere near as disgusting as having to hand over our brilliant, smart, innovative, wonderful idea – an idea we've built and nurtured and loved for months – to a heartless corporation headed up by a horrible human being like you, who'll turn GenNext into mainstream mindless rubbish and ruin it. Do you understand me? I'd rather just get it all over with and then go to the police and tell them everything you've both done. So go on: do your worst.'

Hunter leans back against the desk, his eyes flicking nervously from Ella to Callum to me and back again.

'Ella, I'm sorry,' he blurts. 'I never wanted this. It's just . . . he *will* do it. I've seen him blackmail people before; hurt people even . . . he's a maniac . . .'

Callum laughs. 'You are pathetic, Hunter. Seriously, I've never thought much of you – you love to talk the talk, but when it comes down to it, you're a weakling. Now all of a sudden you've developed a conscience. I don't remember you feeling too guilty when you got dumped and were so desperate for revenge.'

Hunter opens and shuts his mouth, but says nothing. He glares at Callum, his eyes burning. If the situation wasn't so serious, I'd have a good laugh at seeing him the victim rather than the bully for once. But actually, I feel kind of sorry for him. Callum's clearly played him as much as he's tried to play us.

Callum turns on Ella again.

'And you. What a brave, inspirational speech. Bravo, really.' He claps his hands sarcastically. 'Now, are you sure you know what you're doing?'

'Ella knows exactly what she's doing,' I jump in. I screw up the contract and toss it over my shoulder. 'But I'm not sure *you* do, Callum. I mean, a video is damaging and embarrassing, but at least it doesn't show anyone doing anything illegal. Which is more than I can say for your Skyward scheme.'

Callum does his best to stay composed, but at the mere mention of the word, the corner of his mouth starts twitching like mad and his eyes narrow to slits.

'What are you talking about, Penman?' His voice is soft, dangerous.

'You know, The Skyward Trust, your charity,' I say. 'The one that's been funding the education and training of all those kids, all over the world. The one that's been building media training centres and studios in impoverished areas. That one.'

'What about it?' Callum snaps.

'Well, we thought it was such a great, charitable thing you were doing that we tried to find some of the beneficiaries of this generous grant,' Ella says. 'And when we really started digging, we found that those beneficiaries were surprisingly difficult to track down. Actually, over the last five years there hasn't been a single recipient as far as we can tell. Isn't that strange?'

Callum composes himself again, shrugging his shoulders.

'So? Skyward's something we started up and decided not to continue with. What's your point?' He smirks, clearly confident that we don't have anything concrete.

I reach into my back pocket and pull out a wad of tightly folded paper.

'Yeah, well, Herald's accounts here say different. Hundreds of thousands of dollars in grants paid out over the last few years for new media training facilities that don't seem to have been built. I don't understand all of the finer details, but I'm sure you do, so I've taken the trouble to print it all out for you. Plus there's a record of several interesting emails between you and your mate Tyler that point to the fact that you knew about all of this and were personally benefiting from it financially.'

Callum's expression changes from one of self-satisfaction to one of total fury; he rips the paper out of my hand.

'Emails? How can you possibly have got hold of my personal . . . ?'

Hunter's mouth falls open. 'That's what he does, Callum, he's a hacker. He used to be known for it.'

'The taxman's going to love you once he finds out about this,' Ella says while Callum scans the pages of the printout. I decide to press home our advantage.

'So what's going to happen now is we're going to leave and we're never going to hear from you again,' I say. 'And if there's any sign of that video anywhere on the internet, ever, we will make sure everyone knows who put it out and why – and then we'll go public with what we've learned about you and your charity scam.' I'm saying the words as calmly as I can, but my heart is banging away like it's trying to escape through the wall of my chest. 'What do you reckon all your mates in Hollywood will think about Herald Media after that?'

Callum's face is white, like a vampire's. I can almost see his mind racing, computing, putting all the pieces together to see if he has another move left in him or if it's checkmate.

'There's one more thing,' Ella says. 'As decent human beings, we don't feel like we can sit by while such a big company lines its own pockets in the name of charity. So Herald is going to start The Skyward Trust up again, and this time you're going to run it as a proper charity. Otherwise this' – she holds up another printed copy of a particularly incriminating email exchange between Callum and Tyler, waving it in Callum's face – 'is going straight to the police.'

That's the moment I see the look of resignation fall across Callum's face. The moment he registers that we've won. You can almost taste the tension as he weighs up Ella's words.

'Fine!' he spits out before he shoves past me, storming across the room and out into the hall.

We all follow him down the stairs to the front door, where Fran is waiting, looking anxious. When she clocks Callum's fury and sees the relief on my and Ella's faces, she smiles triumphantly.

'Fran?' Hunter says, confused. 'What . . . what's going on?'

'Callum is just leaving,' Fran says, swinging the front door open. 'That's what's going on. And he won't be joining us for any more family gatherings either. Right, Uncle Callum?'

Callum clenches his fists. 'Get out of my way, you stupid little girl,' he spits, and shoves past Fran, flattening her against the wall as he heads towards his car, which is sitting in the drive. The rest of us gather at the front door, watching him. Sure, we might have got one over on him for now, but he's still bloody terrifying.

A few yards down the drive, Callum turns to face us. 'If I ever find that this information has gone outside this house, I *will* make sure that your lives become a living hell. All of you, flesh and blood or not.' He looks at Ella and his lip curls. 'Exposing your sordid little video will be the tip of the iceberg, sweetheart, trust me.'

'Yeah, that works both ways,' I say, still shaking. 'You leak the video, we let everyone know what a scumbag you really are.'

Callum doesn't respond, spitting out a bitter laugh before

jumping in his car, slamming the door shut and revving the engine. The car disappears down the drive, the gates swinging open.

It's over. It's actually over.

Back inside the house, Hunter sits down on the stairs, head in hands. Ella, Fran and I watch from the front door for a while, and then Ella takes pity on him, walking over and touching his shoulder.

'Chin up, Hunter,' she says. 'It's all done now.'

'Can you forgive me?' Hunter says, looking up at her, his voice quiet. It's probably the most genuine thing that's ever come out of his mouth.

'I can,' Ella says, 'but that's about all I can do for now. I don't want to see you and I don't want to be friends, OK?'

Hunter nods sadly as I turn to Fran, who's smoking a post-action cigarette and leaning against the door.

'Are you OK?' she says, her eyes dancing.

'Just about,' I say. 'But we probably wouldn't be if it wasn't for you.'

She smiles and puffs out a ring of smoke.

'Listen, mate, no way was I going to let him get away with putting that disgusting, exploitative video out. Not on my watch. And the minute you mentioned Skyward, I knew exactly how you could stop it. It's been a running joke in the family for years that Callum's Skyward Trust was a front for him to siphon off funds without paying tax. My dad always used to go on about it, saying he'd get caught out eventually. I kind of think he wanted him to get caught, actually – they've always secretly loathed each other. Callum's basically a crook who manages to hide behind a respectable front; that part of it's a no-brainer.'

'All the same, we owe you,' I say. 'You even helped me crack his private password.'

'Yeah, that was more of a bloody good guess,' she says. 'Callum told me when he was drunk once that I was his favourite and he'd used my name for all his passwords – the creep – so I suspected it might still be Francesca with a couple of numbers on the end.'

'You're actually a pretty amazing woman, one way or another, do you know that?' I say.

Fran nods towards Ella, who's busy texting the rest of the team.

'She's lovely, your girlfriend, and a lucky girl, too. You look after her, or else.'

'I will, Fran,' I say, giving her a friendly peck on her cheek. 'I promise.'

Half an hour later, in Austin's kitchen, Ella and I are filling Sai, Austin and Ava in on everything that went down at Hunter's. We keep talking over each other, high on adrenalin, giggly and breathless as if we've been holding our breath under water for hours. We're both verging on slightly hysterical, to be honest.

Ava shakes her head in disbelief. 'I can't believe we've actually pulled it off,' she says in awe.

'You know what? I reckon they thought Ella and I were so scared about the video coming out that we wouldn't dare do something like that,' I say. 'People like Callum are so up themselves they literally think they can get away with anything.'

'Exactly,' Ella agreed. 'He would never have expected me to tell him I didn't care whether the video came out or not.'

'And would you have really stuck to that?' I ask her seriously. 'If it had come down to it and they told us they were going to release it anyway – would you still have told them to get lost?'

Ella nods. 'What did we say in the park yesterday, Jack? No more letting the bullies have their way, right?'

'That's what we said,' I agree.

A sudden bang renders us all nervous wrecks for a few moments, but it's just the front door. Austin jumps up from the floor just as his mum crashes in carrying a load of Waitrose bags.

'Oh, hello, you lot!' She looks surprised to see us all together in the kitchen; usually we're beavering away down in HQ. 'What's going on? What have I missed – anything exciting?'

We shoot knowing looks at one another across the kitchen, shrugging our shoulders innocently.

'Nah, it's all been pretty quiet, Mum,' Austin says, opening the fridge and grabbing a bottle of water. 'To be honest, I'll be glad when it's time to go back to school.'

Ava stifles a laugh and I feel Ella take my hand and squeeze it hard. I look up at her, smiling, and she winks at me and mouths, 'Thank you.'

And at that moment, I feel so happy that we did it, that we got up and fought back and didn't let the bullies win. It feels pretty amazing, you know?

THE HOMECOMING

I can hear rain on my bedroom window when I wake up, and on top of that it's the last week of the school holidays. These two things together would normally constitute a downer, but after the enormous relief of Mum's operation going well last week, I feel on top of the world. Actually, after the last couple of weeks, going back to school doesn't seem like too bad a proposition. I mean, I think a bit of structure and normality is exactly what's called for, don't you? It's been a pretty surreal summer all in all: stratospheric success, fame, being humiliated in front of the world's media, blackmail, revenge, my mum's illness. I'm kind of looking forward to school, to be honest.

Things have gone a little quiet on the GenNext front recently, too, ever since the backlash over the disastrous interview with Harriet died down. It's a relief, as you can probably imagine. After tape-gate, taking a break from online notoriety doesn't feel like such a bad thing. The site is still doing OK, and hopefully we can build it back up once we manage to salvage our reputation. Ella, Sai, Ava, Austin and

I have agreed that whatever happens, we'll concentrate on our A levels and continue to work on GenNext on the side. Ella even got in touch with Mr Allen, who agreed that our work on GenNext can double up as a major piece of course-work for our media production A level. Win. And after we finish school, if GenNext is still going strong . . . then who knows what'll happen. All I know is, I feel pretty good about the possibilities.

Meanwhile, I've got something even more important than GenNext to think about. Mum's been at the hospital this morning for her first round of chemo. Just as I'm thinking about it, I hear the front door slam shut downstairs and I jump out of bed, tearing out of the room in my boxers and a T-shirt.

'Is she home?' I shout from the landing at the top of the stairs.

'Yes, she's home, Jack; it only took a couple of hours,' Dad calls up.

'I'm coming down!'

I throw on last night's clothes and hurry down to the kitchen, where Mum is perched at the breakfast bar.

'Mum, you – you don't look too bad!' I say, going over to give her a hug.

'Charming,' is her response to the obvious surprise in my tone, but then she laughs. 'Oi, don't squeeze me too hard; my battle scars are still a bit tender.'

Her hair is pulled back and she isn't wearing any make-up, so she looks kind of young and vulnerable, but I can see that steely determination in her eyes. After everything she's been through over the past couple of weeks – a serious operation to remove the tumour in her breast and the start of chemotherapy – that determination is still there.

'So what's the score then?' I ask, sitting down opposite her just as Dad hands me a mug of coffee. 'How did it go?'

She pulls a face. 'Well, it wasn't exactly a picnic. They offered me something called a cold cap, which you wear while they give you the chemo. They said it can help to reduce hair loss; it stops the chemo affecting the hair follicles.'

'That sounds brilliant!' I say. I know how worried she's been about losing her hair. As a hairdresser, her hair is a massive source of pride for her. She's always colouring it and styling it differently, and it always looks amazing. She can't bear the thought of it falling out.

She looks down. 'Well, I tried it out, but I had to ask them to take it off halfway through,' she says, her eyes filling with tears. 'It was more painful than the bloody chemo; it's like your head's being held in icy water. I just couldn't stand it in the end.'

'Oh Mum.' I don't know how to respond; I'm gutted for her. Dad puts his hand on her shoulder, looking like he might have tears in his eyes too.

There's a pause while Mum collects herself, and when she looks back up, the expression of determination is back.

'Look, it's not the end of the world,' she says bravely. 'I'll just have to let things take their natural course, and if I lose my hair, then so be it.'

'Hair can grow back, Mum,' I say, squeezing her hand gently. 'As long as you get better, that's the main thing.'

'Of course, Jack, you're right.' She squeezes back. 'And

the doctors had a lot of positive things to say: they were so pleased by how well the op went, and how they got everything they needed to get. They're hopeful that after all the treatment they've got planned for me, the outlook will be good. No guarantees, of course; they'll do more scans after the chemo has finished to check my progress, but they're as optimistic as they can be for now.'

The relief I felt last week rushes through me again.

'That's great, Mum,' I say, holding her hand across the breakfast bar.

'We've still got a way to go, Jack,' Dad chimes in, pulling up a chair next to me. 'Chemotherapy is pretty tough, and today was very difficult for your mum. We're going to have to really look after her over the next few months.'

'Of course we are,' I say. There's a pause. 'Actually, Dad, I think Mum's got far more chance of copping it from your cooking than she has of anything else. We all have.'

My stupid joke breaks the tension and Mum starts to laugh. She momentarily winces with pain, gripping under her arm, before convulsing again. Dad and I start laughing too – it might all sound a bit manic, but it's a much-needed release from the heavy emotions and stress of the last week.

'How did we manage to raise a son with such a twisted sense of humour?' Mum asks.

'I don't know,' Dad says, deadpan. 'It must come from your side of the family.'

Mum nods and gets up from the breakfast bar, heading towards the kitchen door.

'Right,' she says. 'I'm going to have a quick wash and get changed, and then I've got a hot date with Jon Snow. I've got the whole of *Game of Thrones* season five to plough through, and I expect to be waited on hand and foot by the pair of you while I watch it.'

'Yeah, Dad can take the first shift,' I say, laughing. 'I'm diving out to the gym for an hour, if that's OK with you guys.'

Mum disappears up the stairs and I follow suit, throwing on a clean T-shirt and grabbing my gym bag. As I close the front door behind me, I breathe in the damp air and let out a huge sigh of relief. The first round of chemo is over. I know she's got a long way to go, but she's home and she's OK, and that's what matters for now.

THE GIG

As it turns out, my gym workout is much needed. Apart from being the first bit of training I've done for God knows how long, it's been a hectic few weeks and it feels good to blast away some of the stress and emotion with a good old-fashioned endorphin rush. And yes, I am struggling a little, to be honest. During the GenNext whirlwind I haven't exactly had much time to pump iron, but if I'm going to be dating the most beautiful girl in the school, I have to at least keep in shape, right?

By the time I get back to the changing rooms, I've had, like, seven missed calls from Ava. Plus she's sent me a WhatsApp containing such massive overuse of exclamation marks and emojis I just can't ignore it.

> Jack!!!! Brill news from my lovely Suki!!! 🖤 🌸 🍸 😎 💔
>
> 🎤 Cooper's track is out and gonna b massive. YouTube hits through the roof & bombing up iTunes chart. He's got a showcase gig on Thursday at the Garage in Islington – and I have an AMAZING idea!!! Call me as soon as, dude!!! Xoxo

I shower, change and drag my slightly aching body out of the gym, calling her as I head along the street to catch the bus home. Of course I'm intrigued, but by the time I reach her, she's already been on the phone to Cooper, so she's buzzing like a nutter . . . to the point where I think she's going to explode just talking to me.

'Slow down, Ava,' I yell, while she babbles at me down the line. 'You're supposed to be the cool, calm and collected one amongst us. Now tell me slowly, what's the deal?'

'The deal is that Cooper wants GenNext!' she says, calming down only marginally.

'Wants GenNext? What does that even mean, Ava?' I say, leaning back against the bus stop.

'Look, I just called to ask him for a favour. He obviously knew about the disaster with Harriet Rushworth in LA – everyone does, no offence, babe – so I was going to throw myself on his mercy and ask if we could come down to the gig and take some shots and maybe do a quick interview, you know? I told him that with him being the huge rising

271

star that he is, it would help us get a bit of kudos back and regenerate our popularity. I mean, we need something to get us back on track, right?'

'I guess.'

'Anyway, he was totally on board with it, but then he said that a few of the big online music channels were fighting over who gets to stream the gig itself . . . so why didn't he just let us do it?'

Ava finally stops talking and I can hear her panting on the end of the line.

'Are you serious?' I can hardly believe what I'm hearing.

'Deadly serious. The gig sold out in, like, four seconds, and Cooper said that he would give GenNext the exclusive on the show and the interview. His record company will insist he does some others but ours will be the first . . . and we'll be the *only* people filming the gig! That's why I've been so desperate to get hold of you. Do you think we could get something like that together, Jack? It's pretty big.'

'Of course we can,' I say, now as crazy excited as Ava. 'There's no way we can pass up an opportunity like this. AJ will be able to help us pull it together and get us whatever we need. OK, I need to go away and think, and then I need to talk to AJ and the others . . . but call Cooper straight back and tell him yes, Ava. Tell him thank you and a *massive* yes.'

After a few days of hardcore brainstorming by the GenNext team and some swift organising on the part of AJ, Cooper's gig is upon us. This is exactly what we needed – working together again, even just being together, has helped us lay the weird events of the last two weeks to rest and get back to what we're all good at.

By the night of the gig, it's gone around like wildfire that Cooper's show is being live-streamed on GenNext, and the fact that you can't get a ticket for love nor money means that for a lot of people, it's the only way they're going to get to see their brand-new musical hero doing his first major gig. AJ and the team at Metronome have pulled in a decent-sized sound and camera crew for the broadcast, and although it won't exactly be the Brits, it's a cool little set-up and more than adequate to make everything look and sound super-slick and professional.

I've never been to The Garage, but it's a pretty impressive room with a wooden floor – no seating – and a good-sized stage. By the time I walk in, there's already a cool young crowd all vying for positions close to the stage for the best view. Before the show, I run backstage to say a quick hi to Cooper, and I have to say, it feels quite weird when I poke my head around his dressing room door. Cooper just looks like the same long-haired guitar geek I watched sitting by a tree playing at Hunter's party only a few months before – same ripped jeans, *possibly* a new T-shirt – but here he is, number three on the iTunes chart, one place above the new Justin Bieber release. It's mad.

As soon as he sees me, he jumps up, bounds over and hugs me.

'Jack, it's so good to see you, man. What's happening?'

'A fair amount,' I say. 'Too much to go into right before all this glamorous stuff happens.'

'Ava tells me that you and Ella are a thing now; about bloody time,' he laughs.

I feel myself blushing slightly. I mean, I can hardly believe it myself if I'm honest.

'It's early days,' I say, 'but yeah, we're definitely a thing.'

'That's very cool, Jack,' he says, genuinely pleased.

'Look, Cooper, I know you're getting ready for the show and all that, but I just wanted to say thanks. Thanks for doing this for GenNext. It means a lot, you know?'

Cooper shakes his head, and for a moment he looks like he might cry.

'Jack, do you remember that day outside the sixth-form common room when Hunter's mates started on me? Calling me all those horrible names?'

'Yeah, of course. They smashed your bloody guitar,' I say.

'I never told you this at the time, but you were the first person who ever stood up for me when something like that happened,' he says, 'and trust me, it's happened quite a few times over the years. You probably don't realise how much that means to me, do you?'

'I haven't thought about it much since,' I say, slightly taken aback.

'I have,' Cooper smiles. 'And that's what tonight's all about. It's not just a big night for me; it's something for all of us. OK?'

I smile back at him – this is pretty cool. 'OK.'

'Cooper, you've only got ten minutes!' Suki appears from nowhere, looking stressed and holding a shirt that looks far more fitting for a rock star than the screwed-up thing Cooper is wearing. 'Oh hey, Jack, sorry, I'm in a mad rush right now, but we'll see you after the show for the interview, right?'

'You definitely will,' I say, heading out the door. 'Later, guys.'

Before I know it, I'm out in the crowd watching Sai and Ava in semi-panic mode, tearing around and making sure everything is running smoothly with the cameras and sound equipment, even though AJ totally has it all in hand. I'm happy to leave them to it and do my bit after the show. Instead, I'm standing side by side with Austin, Jess and, of course, Ella, who looks cool and beautiful in a short red dress and fire-engine-red lipstick to match. The atmosphere in the room is electric, and when Cooper walks out on to the stage to a massive roar, we all feel really proud.

The gig itself is as amazing as we all hoped and expected. Sai and Ava join us during the fifth song, yelling over the noise about how brilliantly it's all going and how many hits and new subscribers GenNext has picked up in the last fifteen minutes.

'Yes, dudes, GenNext is back in the room, and bigger than ever!' Ava shouts, shoving herself between Ella and me and draping her arms around us both.

By this time we're all well into the gig and dancing away like lunatics. It's funny, however much we took the piss out of Cooper's earnest ballads and songs of unrequited love in the past, we all knew he was super bloody talented, but with a hot band around him, his voice and his songs soar, filling the venue, and his latest, more up-tempo material literally tears the roof off.

Halfway through the gig, Cooper waits for the applause to die down and then walks toward the microphone.

'This one's for Jack and Ella!' he yells, immediately bursting into 'One Moment', the song he played while he was sitting

by that tree at Hunter's party. For a moment it seems like
that happened a hundred years ago . . . and then it seems
like it was only ten seconds ago. The music and the lyrics
swirl around us:

I felt the world turn when our eyes met,
Someone switched on the stars above our heads,
I wondered how it was that I could get so lost in a
moment.

And I got so tongue-tied when you talked to me
But your voice made everything feel good again,
I wondered how it was that I could give my heart in a
moment

Oh yeah, just one moment . . .

'Oh my God, I can't believe he did that!' Ella squeals,
looking at me with the widest smile . . . and that's when I
finally kiss her, deep and long, my hands firm against her
back, moving upwards until they're sweeping through her
hair. We kiss for ages, and when we finally break apart,
grinning at each other like lunatics, she moves her mouth
up to my ear.

'I really *really* like you, Jack Penman,' she says.

'Well, Ella Foster, I can officially confirm that I really,
really like you too.'

'That's all right then,' she says. 'In fact, it's pretty damned
perfect.'

THE ROOF

It's the last day of the school holidays, and as I step outside the house to go meet the guys, the sun comes out big time. I'm only a few yards down the street when I get a WhatsApp from Sai informing me that as it's too depressing to be in a room with no windows on the last day of the holidays, he's relocating our scheduled GenNext meeting from HQ to the roof of his flats – excellent idea.

Just as I finish reading the message and turn in the direction of Sai's, the freakiest thing happens. In fact, it's so weird I can't quite believe it.

'Are you Jack Penman? Yeah, course you are.'

A boy of about my age is standing a few feet away, smiling at me. It takes me a few seconds, and then this unnerving sense of recognition rushes through me. It's Dillon Hemingway, one of the kids who made my life a misery at my old school, Charlton Academy. You remember, the ones who kicked seven bells out of me at the back of the bus, although right now I can't for the life of me remember if he was Dim or Dimmer. Anyway, I freeze on the spot and I don't say anything, but as Dillon comes closer, I realise that he isn't looking to punch my face in – in fact he's holding out his hand.

'I thought it was you,' he says, and before I know it, I'm reaching out to shake his hand. 'You've done well, Jack. Really well. My younger sister is a massive fan of yours; she's mad about all the stuff you put up on GenNext.'

I can't get my head around the fact that he's being so friendly, so gushing, like I'm a completely different person to the kid he was so vile to at Charlton.

'Really?'

'Absolutely! Hey, do you know what would be good? If you could sign something for her – that would be amazing.' Dillon sticks his hand in the pocket of his jacket and rummages around for some paper. 'I've got a pen somewhere,' he says, like some nervous fan.

I sign the back of a receipt for him, *To Amy, all the best, love Jack Penman*, and as I walk away, it strikes me as weird that neither of us mentioned anything relating to that moment of horrible violence all those months ago. I guess I didn't mention it because it's something I don't want to, or have to, think about any more. It doesn't matter to me – *he* doesn't matter to me. When it comes down to it, Dillon's behaviour back then shows that he, like Callum, is just another sad, lonely case whose only chance of getting noticed is to flex his muscles or bully people. And do you know what? I don't hate Dillon, and I don't hate Callum either. I just pity them.

Before long, I'm up on Sai's roof with my best friends and Ella, and it feels good. This is where I belong. After the rain of the previous weekend, the abandoned sofa is too wet to sit on, so this afternoon we're perched on some old crates and two of Sai's mum's sunloungers that he's hauled up from their flat.

Ava's faded lilac hair drifts around her in the light breeze as she stands up in front of us all, clearly ready to make an announcement.

'OK, you lot, the news, as you can imagine, is pretty good. After Cooper's gig and Jack and Ella's interview in the bathroom, the amount of views we had was incredible, and this morning we officially hit four million subscribers.'

There's a massive cheer and some celebratory dancing from all of us before Ava goes on.

'So, despite Jack Penman almost killing us when he freaked out in front of one of the world's biggest pop stars the other week . . .'

'Oh, you are so hilariously funny, Ava,' I say.

'. . . despite that, I would say that this summer has been a pretty bloody amazing success and, well, basically . . . we rock!'

'Here's to the future of GenNext!' Austin shouts, breaking out the cans of full-fat Coke.

In the midst of the mayhem, AJ steps out on to the roof, looking equally pleased with himself.

'Hey, Uncle AJ, come and join us,' Sai shouts over. 'We're just talking about the future of GenNext.'

'Oh yes? And what's the plan?' AJ says, pulling up a crate.

There's a sudden silence and everyone turns to me.

'Yeah, J, what is the plan?' Austin says.

'Well, it's all very nice us being able to pat ourselves on the back and jump up and down about how well we've done, but I think we've still got a lot of work to do,' I say, standing up and taking Ava's place centre stage. 'Guys, what we've done is great, but we can make it even better.'

'You know there've been a lot of offers coming in for mergers and investment,' AJ says. 'It's going through the roof right now.'

'And that's great, AJ,' I say, 'but let's see what we can do on our own for a while, huh? Let's make GenNext the best it can be – the six of us. We're the team, right?'

'Agreed, one hundred per cent,' Ava says, saluting.

'Agreed!' Austin, Ella and Sai call out in unison.

'Agreed,' AJ smiles.

Sai hits play on his phone, and as Calvin Harris blares out of his Bluetooth speaker, there's more cheering and more dancing, during which Ella grabs my hand and pulls me in for a kiss.

'Are you happy, Jack Penman?' she says, smiling up at me.

'Yeah, I'm happy, Ella Foster,' I say.

We stay up there for another hour, laughing, dancing, reminiscing and, of course, ripping it out of one another, which is what we seem to do best. But that's good, right? That's what real friends do. You have a laugh together, you have one another's back and you *never* give in to the bullies. If I'm really honest, I have no idea what's going to happen next or where the future is going to take me or Ella or any of us. But right now, up on this roof with all my best friends . . . life feels good.

AUTHOR'S NOTE

Where do I even start? I never dreamed I'd be given the opportunity to write a book by the time I was 21. I've poured my heart and soul into it, and although it's a work of fiction there are a lot of my own experiences and real life situations in the story that are very close to my heart.

Firstly, I'd like to thank everyone reading this for supporting me and for buying *Generation Next*; you keep pushing me to create bigger and better things and you've helped me grow up – fast! The last couple of years, developing my channel and posting videos on YouTube, have been the best of my life and none of it would of been possible without you, my amazing viewers.

I would like to thank my mum and dad for always being there for me, encouraging and inspiring me to work hard to achieve my ambitions and dreams and, of course, my awesome brother James who, despite being only 13, is a lot cooler and smarter than I am.

I would like to thank my management James Grant for believing in me and signing me as one of their first Internet talents and for putting up with me for over a year now.

Emily Kitchin and the awesome team at Hodder – you guys know who you are. I couldn't have done any of this without your brilliance.

I would like to say a huge thank you to Terry Ronald, my co-writer – you absolute legend! You managed to help me get all my thoughts and visions onto paper and turn them into a terrific book.

The boys: Caspar, Joe, Josh, Mikey, Conor and Jack for inspiring me to always do better and making my job so much fun.

So yeah, that's just a few of the many people I want to thank for quite literally changing my life and helping me enjoy every step of the way. Thank you!